The Antarean Odyssey

The Antarean Odyssey

Matched

Inge Blanton

iUniverse, Inc.
Bloomington

The Antarean Odyssey
Matched

iUniverse books may be ordered through booksellers or by contacting:

iUniverse
1663 Liberty Drive
Bloomington, IN 47403
www.iuniverse.com
1-800-Authors (1-800-288-4677)

ISBN: 978-1-4620-8359-6 (sc)
ISBN: 978-1-4620-8360-2 (ebk)

Printed in the United States of America

iUniverse rev. date: 12/20/2011

The Antarean Odyssey is about the birth of a people and the fiery end of the home-world. It is a story about adventure, love, heartbreak, sorrow and of overcoming difficult and often dangerous situations.

The Antarean Odyssey
Book One
The Labors of Jonathan.

One evening Jonathan Wright overhears a conversation about a world wide cartel, and an interstellar trade agreement, and aliens called Altruscans.

The Antarean Odyssey
Book Two
The Original Four

Book two is about four girls coming from diverse cultures and backgrounds, and they are the beginning of the Antarean People.

The Antarean Odyssey
Book Three
Loss of Eden

The ending of childhood might feel like the loss of Eden. It is time for the four to meet the world. The story is about an expedition that goes terribly wrong. Sabrina races home against time and death only to find a deserted ship. The Antares is only manned by androids.

The Antarean Odyssey
Book Four
Starship Trefayne

Sabrina didn't mind leaving Acheron. But she was not too crazy about having to drop her studies and then being used as a guinea-pig, integrating a Chiron starship. If Captain Thalon aka Sargon, thought to have Sabrina safely on the Trefayne, he will soon learn otherwise.

The Antarean Odyssey
Book Five
Misalliance

Now is the time for Commander Sarah Thalon, Chief Medical Officer of the Worldship Antares to leave home to become an intern on Madras to fulfill a requirement of the Starfleet of the Planetary Alliance.

The Antarean Odyssey
Book Six
Assignment Earth

Sabrina's assignment is to see if Earth is ready to join the Planetary Alliance. She finds that Earth is still under the threat of the Altruscans with a new and a much more dangerous dimension added to it.

The Antarean Odyssey
Book Seven
Matched

Sabrina meets the love of her life, Martel Alemain. Also, since the rift between the two universes are closing, Sabot for the last time enlists Sabrina's help to round up the remaining shapeshifters.

Books still to be published are
The Antarean Odyssey
Book Eight,
I, Sargon.

Chapter 1

The garden was beautiful, and on this afternoon, it lay still and tranquil under the artificial sunlight of the Antares. Birds of all colors and sizes inhabited the trees, and the bees buzzed industriously around the flowers and jasmine bushes. White pebbled pathways wound throughout the garden and wooden benches were scattered here and there. Within the garden was a lake where willows grew along its banks. On a small portion of land jutting out into the water, stood a gazebo. This was Sabrina's retreat.

Not far off, Lanto, her gardener, sat under a shade tree, fishing. Not long after becoming part of her household, he made her garden his domain.

Over the years, she introduced many new plants. Some of the seedlings she brought back had grown into trees or bushes. Her waterfall, which in the beginning had only been a trickle, cascaded now continuously from Meghan's place. It fed the lake and as it continued on its way, formed a small rivulet flowing through a clump of fir trees, before tumbling from the edge of her cell down to Kara's place.

One a tree branch outside the gazebo, a raucous cockatoo with his crest spread wide was sounding alarm. A feline about the size of a bobcat was approaching and soon his head peeked around the corner of the gazebo. It was the black and white male, and he looked at Sabrina with baleful eyes. It was his preferred resting place in the afternoon and she was in it.

Sargon had introduced small animals, birds, fish and also some predators on the Antares. Many of the kids, coming home from different planets had brought various pets with them. One day, when Jason and Logan were still little, Sargon had given them two puppies that now were old dogs sleeping most of the time and probably dreaming of their puppy days.

The Antares, a planetoid size worldship, was honeycombed with chambers like a beehive. When Sargon had given her one of the nursery cells, Sabrina envisioned an ancient Roman Villa in it. She wanted to build it in memory of her grandfather who had been an Italian nobleman. He had been disinherited because he did not marry the heiress his family had presented him with. He married for love; he wed his Irish Lass, as he called her. Because of his family's animosity he foregone his surname and title and took his wife's last name, Hennesee. He didn't care that his name, Juliano, and his accent, sounded odd with the Irish name. He was proud of it.

Sabrina's mind returned to the present, and she chuckled at catching herself reminiscing. Sargon had ordered rest for her after she came home from a rafting trip that had turned into a disaster. But the enforced rest had only lasted until the second day. She had tied into Sargon's records and augmented his files on the Altruscans, especially the shapeshifters.

On the third day, she became even more restless pestering Medea all morning long, asking her where everyone was and what was going on, especially about Elisheba. Medea suggested that she go and reacquaint herself with the Antares and everyone else on her own time.

Sabrina stretched, then rose, thinking about Medea's advice and went to visit Ayhlean who she hoped was more forthcoming than her beloved housekeeper.

When she arrived at Ayhlean's place of work it was not the way she remembered it. A new extension had been added onto the town hall, and Ayhlean's office was now a big establishment with lots of people going in and out. To Sabrina's relief, there was a front desk with a receptionist.

"I would like to see Ayhlean Thalon," she asked. "How do I find her?"

"Do you have an appointment?"

"No," Sabrina responded slowly.

"Commander Thalon sees no one without an appointment," she was informed in a firm and officious voice.

"Oh, how hoity toity," Sabrina grumbled, incensed. Then she appropriated a piece of paper and wrote her name and rank on it. Looking at the name plate on the desk, she told the bewildered girl, "Tara, give that to Commander Thalon and tell her this is an order."

Tara, after reading the paper, gave Sabrina, who was dressed in short shorts and a short top, a dubious look, but complied. She rose from behind her desk and left.

A short while later, the door opened and Ayhlean stood in its frame.

"I'm here as ordered, Captain Hennesee," she said icily.

"Aw, cut the bunk, Ayhlean," Sabrina told her, frustrated.

A tiny smile showed on Ayhlean's face, and it grew progressively brighter as she studied Sabrina's whimsical expression. She came into the room with her arms stretched wide. "Oh boy, have I missed you," she said, hugging her.

Tara, looking perplexed by the scene, sidled in and quickly went behind her desk as if seeking refuge.

"Do you have time?"

"You got me out of a meeting."

"Could I sit in?"

"In civilian matters, I'm in command," Ayhlean told her.

"Yes, but I'm still the Captain," Sabrina said softly, pretending to finger a collar.

"Are you taking command?"

"Heaven's no. Every time I come back home, the whole damned place has changed again," she said aggrieved. "I just want to get reacquainted, that's all."

"As long as you stay out of my hair and keep your mouth shut, I guess its okay."

"Boy, aren't we masterful."

Ayhlean laughed. "I can still hope that one day I'll best you."

"I'm going to behave," Sabrina promised.

The meeting was held several doors down in a huge room with an oval table in the center.

"Sorry about the interruption," Ayhlean said. "May I introduce Sabrina Hennesee. She will be sitting in on the rest of this meeting."

Sabrina looked around. Not one familiar face. Bending toward Ayhlean, she whispered, "Where's Joran?"

"On a business trip." Ayhlean went back to her seat and sat down, letting Sabrina take care of herself.

"We have finished with old business. Now the only thing left is new business. The latest request I have here is to check the infrastructure. The sewage plant needs to be expanded, and we must find new ways to deal with the trash. We also require a bigger recycling plant. The population growth has outstripped what we have."

Ayhlean looked at everyone sitting at the table, and then her eyes fell on Sabrina. She was sitting there with a reminiscent grin on her face. I bet she remembers our first introduction into the inner working of the Antares by Android One, Ayhlean thought, and nearly lost her composure. She had to bite down hard to stifle a giggle. It took some effort to say, "Now I want several proposals on my desk by the end of this work week."

After everyone filed out, but not without giving Sabrina and her attire some curious looks, Ayhlean rose," Come let's go to my place where, hopefully, we won't be interrupted."

"I'd like a cup of tea if you still know how to make one?" Sabrina said, looking at her expectantly

Ayhlean lifted the phone. When it was answered, she said, "I'm coming home. Have tea ready."

Sabrina's finely arched eyebrows rose, and there was a glimmer of humor in her eyes as she said, "Things do change."

Ignoring Sabrina's remark, Ayhlean said, "Let's go by lift, it's a quicker way."

"But I like to get reacquainted with the Antares," Sabrina complained."

"You can do this on your own time."

"That's what everybody is telling me," Sabrina groused.

The lift stopped one level above Sabrina's area, and after entering the cell, they walked though a small park. The place still looked like she remembered it, although, Sabrina could tell that a lot of work had been done to make it feel like an old place, a place that had been lived in forever.

Talking and laughing, they crossed the vaulted wooden bridge and came up on the pagoda. Before letting Sabrina enter, Ayhlean held her back and with a flourish opened the door and pointed to the floor.

Inlaid in the tile was a red, fire-breathing Chinese dragon threateningly lifting his foot as if to bar entrance.

Sabrina stood transfixed, her breath caught. "Gorgeous," she breathed. "Ayhlean, this is awesome."

"I thought you would like my dragon." Ayhlean smiled, remembering Sabrina drawing it a long time ago. Tugging at her sleeve, "Let's go and have tea."

Sabrina followed Ayhlean toward the back of the house and for as long as she could see the dragon, her eyes were glued on it.

After entering the kitchen, Sabrina said, "Thank God, one thing hasn't changed, you're still having tea in your kitchen."

"I thought you would feel more at home here."

While Ayhlean checked the tea, her housekeeper set out the tea set and small sandwiches, then excused herself.

Sabrina just lifted her cup to her mouth when she suddenly became aware of a man standing in the doorway.

He bowed. "Lady Sabrina."

To Sabrina's questioning look, Ayhlean only said, "This is Pietry."

When nothing more was forthcoming from Ayhlean, Sabrina first scanned her and then the man.

Pietry was from Ganymede and held the same position in Ayhlean's house as Joran did while she lived on Acheron. He had attached himself to Kamila, and she brought him home to the Antares, but soon tired of him. Ayhlean, knowing of his predicament, had taken pity and added him to her household.

A quick smile quirked across Sabrina's mouth as she watched him leave, turning back to Ayhlean, "Now tell me, where's everyone?"

Ayhlean, observing Sabrina, guessed what she had done. Her eyes tucked slightly at their corners and she knew she needn't explain. "Sargon," she began, "I never know where he is. I think you have a better idea of his whereabouts. Sarah and Kamila are on Galatia. So are Davida and Soraja. Chen and Benjie are on the Explorer. Yoshi, as far as I know, is on Daugave. He's married. I haven't met his wife yet. Also Chandi and Nesrim are married and expecting. Kara and Teva are here. I surmise you know they are married and so are Meghan and George. Meghan is on a tour with Chantar right now. Your two boys, I think, are on board."

"Where's Elisheba?"

"When you're finished with your tea, I'll give you her address so you can go and visit her. I'll let her tell you her story about coming back to the Antares. I heard you had a close call."

"Yes, I was almost a goner," Sabrina said with a sour grimace, and told Ayhlean about the rafting trip. "Now to Elisheba?"

"Oh, she's okay."

It was said with such a hinting tone that Sabrina gave her a curious look. When it appeared like she was going to ask more questions, Ayhlean took the cup out of her hand and, after Sabrina rose, nudged her out the door.

*   *   *

It was already simulated dusk when Sabrina walked through the village to find Elisheba's house. She rang the doorbell, feeling a little apprehensive after Ayhlean's hinting attitude. The last time she'd seen

Elisheba was on Earth, and she had been married to an Israeli belonging to an ultra orthodox sect, and she was very unhappy.

After a while, the door was opened by a little girl about eight years old.

"Yes, Ma'am?" she was asked.

Sabrina stared at her. Then she recognized her as one of the twins. She let out a gasp when a toddler, about a year old, tried to negotiate the hallway with stumbling steps.

"Who is it?" a voice asked from the back.

Sabrina recognized it immediately as Elisheba's.

"A lady, Mom."

Elisheba came around the doorframe and when she saw Sabrina, dropped the armful of baby clothes she was carrying.

"Sabrina?" she whispered and then came running. She threw her arms around her neck, hugging her tight. "Oh, do come in. I'm a mess. I just picked Danella up from the daycare."

"You might be a mess, but I'm glad to see you; and you're looking good."

Elisheba had lost a lot of weight and was slim again and, she also looked happy.

Sabrina bent down and picked up the baby. Looking into its face, there was nothing of Elisheba, but there was something familiar to the look, but she couldn't immediately place it.

"Whose kid is this?" she asked.

Elisheba chuckled. "Guess?"

"Elisheba, that's not . . . fair," she finished slowly as the door opened and Ian was standing on the threshold. She looked at him in surprise and then at the baby. "Oooh, his kid," she said slowly.

"Well look what the devil's blown in," Ian said, as he stepped into the hallway, closing the door. "Where did you come from?"

"From Ayhlean's place."

"I don't know why I ask. Never get a straight answer from you."

"You two are not going to start sparring. Sabrina, Ian and I are married, and we have Danella."

"That's the answer I want. To the point and not your rigmarole," Sabrina told Ian, wagging her finger at him.

Grabbing the finger and kissing it, Ian said, "How about saying you're glad to see me,"

"That, I'm always." Tilting her head, "Are you miffed about something?"

Pursing his lips to hide a grin he said, "Last time we were together, you left me in a hell of a bind explaining you away. I got a lot of flack about showing off a secret military plane to my girlfriend."

"I'm surprised you weren't thrown in jail. But that fighter jet was a neat machine."

"Now, you both come in and quit that bickering," Elisheba said in a forceful voice. "There is a more comfortable place for reminiscence."

As soon as Ian stepped into the den, the other twin came running and had him bend down to be hugged.

They have grown nicely, Sabrina thought. She immediately noted the absence of the cowed and morose manner. The girls were bright-eyed and lively. "My goodness, how do you tell them apart?" Sabrina asked Ian, looking from one girl to the other.

"Oh, after you get to know them, it's easy."

"Yeah, I bet." Turing to Elisheba, "Now tell me what happened after I entrusted you to Benjie to take you safe and sound back home?"

Elisheba laughed, "Very simple, my dear, I met Ian and we fell in love."

"I can see that. Now what else happened?"

Elisheba told her about the trip back and described what it felt coming home to the Antares. The evening passed pleasurable talking about what happened here and there, remembering the past and talking about what was going on now. When they finally parted, it was late and already dark. With a nostalgic feeling, Sabrina strolled leisurely through the lamp-lit streets of the village. There was a smile on her face. The visit had left her feeling happy about Ian and Elisheba.

*   *   *

The next morning she went back to the village. It surprised her how big it had grown since her absence. Many of the establishments had expanded. There were many more houses. She had to curb her curiosity and made her first stop at the bank to update her computer chip. She had two accounts, one registering the money from her military allotment, the other, her investments from Acheron and the Antares. Most of her money was invested in the Antarean enterprises which flourished under Joran's hands.

After business was concluded, she went in search of an eating establishment and found the beergarden was still there. It looked the same as last time, only the trees had grown larger. She ordered a glass of beer and a light meal.

The newest thing she found in the village was a replica of an old drugstore from around 1960, Earth time. It had become the favorite hangout for the kids. It contained all kind of games, a jukebox and an ice cream and soda bar.

*   *   *

A week later, she conceded that her enforced rest hadn't turned out too bad. It had given her an opportunity to do the things she wanted to do. She had visited some of her friends, and there had also been time to spend with her sons. They were growing up too fast.

She was now fully recovered from spilling off the raft and nearly turning into an icicle. It had been a perfect trip until a wall of water had come down on them. Apparently, it had rained hard upstream, and the water coming down surprised them. Sabrina, being swept off the raft into the icy water, nearly drowned.

*   *   *

Sabrina sat in her study meditatively gazing out of the window when her fingers accidentally brushed over the computer keys, because suddenly, out of nowhere, Jason landed on top of her desk. Sabrina, being somewhat inured to his surprise appearances, gave him momentarily an icy stare. "See what you made me do," she chided him.

He looked at it and laughed. There were several lines of zzzz's across the screen. Diverting her displeasure, he quickly said, "I see you're writing another Pegasus story. Mom, that's great!"

Adventures of the flying horse Pegasus, with Sabrina as the heroin, had been bedtime stories her mother made up when she had been a little girl. Later on she told Pegasus stories to her sons. One day, Sargon asked her to write them into book form so other children could enjoy them, too. This was her eighth book, but the heroin's name had changed to Celesta.

"Now, first things first, would you please get off my desk, and second, explain your unauthorized presence here."

"I'm the messenger boy today. I was ordered to tell you that there is a message from Daugave, and you're supposed to report to Admiral Okada." Leaning close and staring into her green eyes, he asked, "Mom, couldn't you just tell them to take a flying leap?"

Sabrina smiled. "And why would I want to do a thing like that?"

"Because, Logan and I hate it when you're gone, and because you always get into some kind of trouble and come back a mess."

Sabrina gave her son an amused grin. Cupping his face in her hand, she looked into his green eyes and told him, "Jason, I promise to be careful." She kissed him and then pushed him off the desk and scolded, "Big boys enter a room through the door and do not land on my desk. Now, get gone," and looking at her timepiece, "school ain't out yet."

"Okay, Mom. But you promise to be careful."

"Yes, love, I promise."

"As she watched him walk away, her smile became soft and reflective. He was handsome, and he had just turned seventeen. He was slender and as tall as Logan, who began to resemble his father more the older he grew. Where Jason was quick to laugh and act, Logan was slow and deliberate in all he did.

Chapter 2

As ordered, Sabrina went to Daugave.

Almost invisible, hidden by the glare of the star, was a smaller yellow star, one of the orbiting planets was inhabitable, Daugave. The largest city, Moldavia, was the seat of the Alliance.

When she entered Admiral Okada's office, he looked pointedly at her garb; she was out of uniform, dressed Acheron fashion. He motioned her to a chair next to his desk.

"Captain Hennesee," he said, deliberately addressing her by rank. "I have a very delicate job for you, and it may call for your special abilities. It has come to my ears that key personnel on other planets have had radical personality changes just like the ones on Earth. It was noted not so much by their co-workers, but by their families. Find out what's going on. How you accomplish this job is up to your discretion."

Tilting her head to one side and after a slight downturn at the corners of her mouth, she said, "Admiral Okada, thank you for your confidence, but could you give me more particulars? Your information is somewhat scanty."

He knew he had been subtly reprimanded and pursed his mouth. "Well, rumor . . ."

"Gossip," Sabrina injected and squinted at him.

He considered her for a moment. "As you wish." Having dealt with her before, he had learned it was better to go along with her, rather than fight at every turn. She would have her fun no matter what. "Gossip has it that, especially the husbands, had a radical change in their relationships with their wives."

"Especially during pillow talk?" When Okada blushed, Sabrina dryly said,

"That's where personality changes are most notable. In an intimate relationship. Certain things can't be faked."

"Is this book knowledge or empirical knowledge?" Okada asked, tartly.

Sabrina gave him a surprised look, then, straightened her face. "Where do you want me to go?"

"That's better. We need to get down to business and leave all these conjectures. Ever been to Raglan?"

"Huh? That's right in the Orion's lair."

Okada looked at her, suppressing a grin.

"What's my script's going to be?" she asked curiously. She noted a twitch to the corners of his mouth.

"Lots of information flows into Raglan. The word is that the Altruscans have increased their activities. There are lot of innuendoes and nothing concrete. It's important to listen to the gossip. How would you like to be an exotic dancer?"

Sabrina stared at him, indignant and in disbelief. "Now, Admiral Okada, that's going a bit too far. Gossip, I can handle, but I don't know how to dance, exotic or otherwise," she protested. Naturally she knew how to dance, but exotic?

Now Okada had to laugh at Sabrina's piqued expression. "I have a teacher who will instruct you on how to move."

"Admiral Okada, Sir," she protested, still hoping he would change his mind. When she saw that he wasn't swayed in the least, she said, "But Sir, an exotic dancer? Where would a respectable person like me learn anything about a thing like that?" Not even in her wildest dreams had she ever imagined herself as a dancer, let alone an exotic one.

"Sabrina, I always enjoy your visits, but I'm very busy." There was a short pause as he looked at her. Then he handed her a slip of paper. "Here's the address. Report to me when you are ready."

She was dismissed.

Exiting headquarters, she stood for a moment on the steps in the golden light of the afternoon sun, absentmindedly watching the traffic go by. There was an imperceptible twitch to her shoulder as she descended the stairs with an irritated expression on her face. She hailed a taxi and gave the driver the address.

The drive was not long, and there was a familiarity about the scene. Cars drove by as she looked out of the window, and buses. People thronged the streets. There were shops and vendors in open stalls selling fruit or sandwiches.

The driver stopped in front of a long building with an unremarkable facade. She had to climb the stairs to the third floor. After she rang the bell, the door was opened by an older woman with untidy hair, wiping her hands on an apron.

"I'm Sabrina Hennesee," she told her.

"My mistress, Madam Imoto, is expecting you."

Sabrina hoped Okada had briefed Madam Imoto.

She conducted Sabrina through green baize doors and across the corridor into a sitting-room. It was decorated in deep pink velvet and rosewood furniture. Madam Imoto sat on a sofa. She seemed not to be very tall, her coloring was perfect with not a blemish on her skin, nor a hair out of place. She was perhaps a little too thin, her slenderness given way to angularity.

"Madam, this is Sabrina Hennesee," the woman introduced her.

"Good afternoon," Madam Imoto said briskly and dismissed the woman with a wave of her hand. She regarded Sabrina with a professional interest. "You wish to learn how to dance?" she asked with perfect diction in Galactic.

"Yes, Madam."

"Let me see your legs."

Sabrina tightened the baggy slacks around her legs.

"Not bad. It's always good to have long legs. And they appear to be shapely. Your figure is not bad either. Now let me see you move."

Sabrina was stung by her tone and by her unthinking assumption of superiority. She was not used to this, thinking, oh Okada, you will have your joke. From Madam Imoto's behavior, she deduced that Okada had not briefed her on who she was. Probably to her, she was only one of the many silly girls dreaming to make it as a dancer.

Sabrina went through some Tai Chi movements.

"You have poise and rhythm. I might be able to work with you. I charge thirty credits an hour, and we will begin tomorrow at ten o'clock. I expect you to be prompt."

Sabrina's eyebrow rose in incredulity and, amused, she realized that she had been dismissed.

*　　*　　*

Three weeks later, Sabrina reported back to Okada. After the door had closed behind her, he asked, "Are you ready to assume duty?"

"Do you want a demonstration?"

"No, Sabrina. Thank you. I know you will handle this situation with your usual aplomb. Here is an address. Ask for the owner and give him this letter from me. He owes me a favor. Introduce yourself as Sappho."

Leaving Okada's office, she almost chuckled. Martel had called her Sappho on Sarpedion. Martel, she thought wistfully. Some time ago, she had become aware of a new, but tenuous mind-echo. It had taken a while to sort it out from her boys' connection with her, or Sirtis. Finally it dawned on her, the echo was Martel. They had become bonded. She surmised it happened during or after the rafting disaster.

*   *   *

Sabrina traveled to Raglan on a third-class commercial flight. It was not the most modern liner; but as a dancer seeking employment, it would not do for her to arrive in grand style. Raglan's largest city was also its port of entry and a sprawling megalopolis. She hired an air car and when it arrived at the club, it landed on a small pad on the roof.

Sabrina rode the elevator down and exited on a long passageway. It was still early morning, and the building was quiet inside. There were very few people about as she wandered the hallway, peering at the doors. At first she received only a few stares at her and her luggage. She soon aroused enough curiosity for a young man to ask her curtly if she needed help.

"Yes. I need someone to take my suitcases backstage, and then help me to find the owner of this club."

Looking with ill-favor down at her luggage and then at her, he asked with a chill voice, "Do you have an appointment?"

"No. But I have a letter for him."

The look she received was skeptical, "Follow me," he finally said and waved to a young man. "Take these backstage," he ordered, pointing to her suitcases.

They rode the elevator up and entered a foyer. A young, very attractive receptionist rose and asked Sabrina if she could help her.

"Is Mister Melikin in?"

"Do you have an appointment?"

"No. But I would like to see him.

"No one sees Mister Melikin unless asked for."

"I understand, but I would like to see him nevertheless."

"Your name, please?"

"I am Sappho."

The receptionist called Mister Melikin's secretary and told her a lady named Sappho is asking to see him.

The receptionist listened intently, then, said, "I know. I told her. But she insists."

Sabrina put her hand on her arm to get her attention, "Tell his secretary to mention the name Okada to Mister Melikin."

After a short wait, the secretary came back on the phone.

"The secretary says it's all right," the receptionist told her and motioned to the guide to lead Sabrina down the hallway. When he asked her to take a seat, Sabrina remained standing. She went to the window at the end of the hallway and looked down, watching the traffic. After a brief wait someone behind her cleared his throat. Her guide was back. He escorted her into a spacious office.

Mister Melikin was large with heavy jowls, and his figure looked sedentary. He reclined in a high-backed chair, reading through a folder. The cover bore various code words.

Sabrina walked up to his desk and put Okada's letter in front of him. She then backed away and sat down in the chair next to his desk.

His eyes lingered appraisingly on her for a moment before he picked up the envelope. When he read it, his thick lids dropped over faded eyes, revealing nothing. He slowly folded the letter into the envelope and placed it in a notebook in front of him. Then he buzzed his secretary. When she answered, he said, "Tell Reiner to come to my office." He went back to reading his folder until the door opened. In came a small man with fussy, nervous movements. He had dark hair and a dark complexion. His smile was perfunctory.

"Reiner, this is Sappho. She gets top billing, starting tonight," he said. His mien didn't change, and the only thing that moved was his mouth.

"But, Mister Melikin," Reiner protested, "I only now booked La Lola, and you have no idea how much trouble it was for me to get her to agree to appear here."

The heavy head moved an inch, and the look from the hooded eyes was icy.

Reiner threw up his hands, "Okay, okay. I'll change the program. Turning to Sabrina, "Follow me," he said curtly.

Sabrina quickly touched his mind but all she got was cussing as he moved with swift steps down the hall to the elevator. All the way down, he never looked at her, nor spoke. In the lobby he just waved at her to follow him.

Backstage he nearly fell over her luggage. "Who in the hell put these here?" he shouted. "And whose are those?"

"They are mine. I asked someone to bring them down here," Sabrina said in her most forbearing voice.

"Bring them along before someone else falls over them." Pointing to a corner, "Put them over there, and now, let me see what you can do?"

Sabrina went to get the two feathered fans out of her case. They were large and white with black tips.

"You have some music?" she asked him.

"No. Is this your costume?" he asked, tartly, looking at her baggy trousers with the overdress.

"No. I dance in my birthday suit."

For the first time, his mouth quirked. "Then go behind there and change," he told her, pointing to a screen.

When she came out from behind the screen, her feathered fans were strategically placed, and his appraising eyes lingered on her long, slender legs.

She showed him a few of her movements, and one of her ploys was to make the audience think she was about to drop her fan. Even Reiner was taken in, and his eyes widened.

"Your act is not very original, and I have seen better. Is that all you know how to do, dance?"

"No. I also sing and play an instrument."

"What kind?"

"What kind do you have?"

Pointing to the piano, "Let me hear you play."

"What kind of music do your patrons like?"

"Anything they haven't heard yet."

After she dressed, she walked over to the piano, and sitting down, let her fingers move up and down the scales. It was excellently tuned. She played several sedate tunes and watched his face. It was bland, bored and blasé looking. Again she ran the scales, and then she grinned as she fell into a ragtime rhythm.

His bland look immediately changed into one of surprise.

"This might do," he reluctantly conceded.

"Then we could dispense with the fan dance?" She hoped it would not become necessary to appear in her birthday-suit every night. But she was quite resigned for him to insist on it. When he said no, it didn't come as a surprise.

Next on the agenda was her salary. Sabrina, reading his mind, knew he expected her to haggle for it. She started ridiculously high and he excessively low. After twenty minutes of dickering and trading insults he agreed on a price higher then he was at the beginning willing to pay.

"You haggle like a fisherman's wife."

She knew he meant it as an insult. "You're not too bad either," she told him.

They went into his office which was quite a bit smaller, less elegant and more vulgar in taste. It came across as a cheap imitation of Mister Melikin's decor.

She insisted on being paid by the week, and her contract stressed that she might join a table if so asked, but there would be no other gratuities added. When he looked at her with puzzlement, she told him point blank that she would not have sex with any of his patrons.

"But, that's where you make most of your money," he remonstrated with her. "This is where you get most of your bonuses," she retorted.

*   *   *

The name of the club was 'The Phoenix'. It was elegant and spacious, and the stage and bar covered most of the first floor. The second floor consisted of dining rooms and several smaller clubs with bars and dance floors. The third floor held the gaming rooms. The rest were rooms for various activities. The fourth floor held offices and above them were private suites. The penthouse was Mister Melikin's exclusive domain. He had furnished Sabrina with a suite in the building, and per Admiral Okada's instruction, all cameras and eavesdropping devices had been removed.

In her two weeks at the club, Sabrina attracted notice and notoriety. She had worked her fan dance, which was performed with a lone chair standing in the middle of the stage, into quite a teaser. Mostly the men cheered during her performance, trying to induce her to drop her feathers. Every once in a while when a patron was overly insistent, Sabrina would tantalize him by slightly moving the fan just enough, but not quite. It was usually received with a groan.

It was during her second week when Sabrina just happened to be in Reiner's office that La Lola walked in. She strode in as one who was used to volleys of applause wherever she appeared. She was a most striking lady, about nineteen, with enormous dark eyes, an enchanting nose, and a petulant mouth. Sabrina could see why Reiner was so taken with her.

When she found that Sabrina, now known as Sappho, had taken first billing, she walked up to her. "I am sure you know who I am, but I still like to present myself, I'm La Lola."

"No. I can't say that I do."

An austere look came into La Lola's face. "This is extraordinary. Everyone knows La Lola. Maybe you come from the outlying provinces, no?"

"Perhaps," Sabrina conceded graciously.

Turning to Reiner, and with a toss of her head, she told him, "I do not see how she can be better than I. I dance very well, and people like me. She will naturally be dismissed."

Reiner gazed at her hungrily then gave her a gloomy look. He seemed to be in a state of bottled up nerve-ridden-emotions, wringing his hands. He hated scenes, and he knew La Lola had a temper to match anything he cared to experience.

As Sabrina watched the two maneuvers around each other, she threatening and he remonstrating, Sabrina felt uncontrollable laughter bubbling up. This whole scene was just simply delicious.

La Lola did have a passion for drama, and she made a magnificent scene. She screamed insults at him. When this didn't change anything, she threw a vase.

"You don't understand," he pleaded, dabbing his handkerchief to his forehead, "It was Mister Melikin's order. I have no control over it."

Her beautiful dark eyes flashed at him. Then a look of rigidity, Sabrina had noticed earlier, possessed La Lola's face.

"I will leave for you to straighten this out," she told Reiner, haughtily. "And when you call me, I will decide if I can come back. I have a contract, but it is you who broke it. I have no trouble finding engagements." With this she sailed out of the room and the door closed with an audible slam behind her.

Reiner sighed in defeat and he gave Sabrina a tight-lipped grimace.

*   *   *

Sabrina was sipping a drink in the Phoenix lounge before her performance when a tall thick-set man took the stool next to hers. He

23

smiled at her, and Sabrina, perceiving the surfaces thoughts flitting across his mind, could see numbers clicking away inside his head. He was thinking that if he could get her to work for him, he would make a bundle of money before she was washed up, then, discarded. He had no use for women, except as merchandise.

Sabrina gave him a cold look and was about to push her drink away when she noted Mister Melikin coming in. She retrieved her drink and decided to observe.

Mister Melikin waddled up to the bar and gave her only a brief look. He greeted the thick-set man in Galactic, then immediately changed to Marathi, the Orion's language, while surreptitiously watching Sabrina from under his heavy eyelids.

Sabrina listened when he spoke Galactic, but turned away with a bored expression when he changed to Marathi.

"You heard that an Altruscan ship is coming in two weeks?"

"Yes," Mister Melikin said, looking sour.

With a smirk, he asked, "You don't like Altruscans?"

"No. They're bad for business."

"No vices?"

"Oh they have them, but not the kind that makes money."

They both laughed. Mister Melikin was still observing Sabrina to see if she understood. He seemed to be satisfied with her vapid face, and continued, "You had some information for me?"

"Triscaro resurfaced. He's on the ship. You need to tell Yafo."

When Sabrina heard the Orion's name, she almost gave herself away. To cover her near slip, she bent down as if to adjust her shoe then slipped off the stool and went backstage. Soon it was time for her to go on stage.

Yafo was the Orion captain she had shot her photon across his bow and later found he was a friend of Karsten.

She felt still ill at ease with having to go on in her bare necessities. Practicing and perfecting her dance in front of a mirror was one thing, but the stage still made her uncomfortable. She was more nervous walking on stage than on a bridge. When she walked on a bridge, at least she was fully dressed.

She checked her makeup one last time and adjusted the silver wig she wore, the hair hanging past her waist. Looking critically at the makeup, she hoped her instructress was right that not even her mother would have recognized her. Also, to cover her memorable green eyes, she wore brown contact lenses.

As her music came on, she dropped her robe behind the screen and placed the fans to cover the strategic areas. Remember, it's all in the wrist and fingers. Don't move the hands. The hand is always quicker than the eyes, Madam Imoto had assured her.

I hope she's right, Sabrina thought.

Before she stepped all the way on the stage, she provocatively peeked from behind the curtain, and then let her audience gaze on her long leg all the way up to her shoulder. Slowly she dropped the feathers over the bare areas and came out from behind the curtain. At one point during the dance, there was a pretend fumble, and the audience gasped. She tilted her head to one side and slowly let a grin grow on her face.

The applause she received was energetic.

After her dance, a magician came on. That gave her time to dress. Then it was her turn to play the piano and sing.

*   *   *

This was her third week, and time passed slowly. There was still no word about the Altruscan's ship. The information she had garnered up till now was sparse and only some of it useful. The Altruscan, she hoped, was the information Okada was after. She already had her fill with this situation.

Many of the club patrons asked through the manager if she would join their tables. Many tried to seduce her or brow beat Reiner for her to perform more than just her act. But she remained adamant and turned a deaf ear to all his entreaties.

This evening, Sabrina was dressed in a gown that covered everything and hid nothing. She moved languidly among the guests when an excited buzz about a raid on a merchant ship passed around. The pirates were said to have made quite a catch and were coming to this club tonight. The manager, rubbing his hands in anticipation, hoped they would spend a lot of their money, especially at the gambling tables.

It was surprisingly early when the pirate captain and some of his officers entered the club. They were boisterous and swaggering, bragging about their spoils for everyone to hear.

Sabrina managed to be invited close to the table where they sat. She was curious to know whom they had raided and hoped it was not one of Lahoma's ships. Lahoma Sandor was the matriarch of an interstellar merchant house where Sabrina had quite a bit of her money invested. She became entangled with the house of Sandor when she joined the Star Fleet Academy on Acheron.

When a tall individual with a nondescript expressionless face joined them, Sabrina felt a jolt. It was Martel.

He first shook hands with the captain and then introduced himself as Mendes to rest of the officers. As he sat down, the language changed from Marathi to Galactic and the conversation immediately went from bragging about the raid to a more general topic.

Soon his officers excused themselves to go to the gaming tables. After they left, Mendes changing from Galactic back to Marathi, said, "I heard you just came in."

"Docked this morning."

"By the way, there is a rumor circulating concerning M6. Did you notice anything unusual?" Martel asked, twitching an interrogative eyebrow at the captain, and languidly rearranged his frame on the chair. "Wonder what's there to find?"

"If there's something going on, it probably has to do with the Altruscans," the Captain answered with a shrug.

"Yes, you're probably right." Mendes stifled a yawn. "They are still up to making war. Not very good for business you know. Unless you're into that kind of merchandise," he mumbled with a disdainful expression and a mournful shake of his head.

"The bigger rumor is that they're going to try to disrupt an Alliance meeting. Also, they're active in the Omicron V's solar system. I've heard that there are infiltrators meddling on that planet."

Sabrina's ears perked up at the mentioning of M,6, but she had no time to listen further, and she stowed the mention of Omicron V to be looked at later. It was time for her to do her act.

After she was on stage and going through her routine, she happened to look toward the bar. Mendes leaning against it watching her with the most condescending smile on his face. Jaded fellow, Sabrina thought, and was amused at him not recognizing her. Although bonded, he didn't pick up on her presence; probably because of his iron-tight mental shield.

She was about to do the fumble with her fans when her eyes wandered back toward the bar. Her fumble almost became real and a sound of anticipation went through the crowd. Sargon, appreciatively watching the dance, stood next to Martel.

Oh boy, I'm never going to live this down, she thought.

After her performance, she changed back into her gown. She still wore her makeup and the long silver hair. When she came down to the floor, Sargon sat the pirate's table.

She smiled and bowed to the Captain and then to Sargon, who gave her only a passing glance.

Walking toward the bar, she smiled, inwardly amused. Sargon hadn't recognized her either. She ordered a non-alcoholic drink, sipping it slowly as she watched the magician's act. Midway through his performance, she left to get ready for her next number. Applause greeted her, and after she sat down she played some chords while watching Sargon. When she saw him lifting his glass to his mouth, she quickly switched to ragtime.

He sputtered and looked shocked as he put the glass down. Martel gave him a questioning look.

Singing and playing the piano was her last act and immediately after, she usually went up to her suite. This time she came down from the stage. She walked past Sargon, again sitting at the pirate's table. Sargon reached out and touched her hand.

"Would you grace our table with your presence?" he asked.

Sabrina smiled at him and noticed that he wore dark contact lenses. She gave the captain a questioning look.

"We would be honored," the captain mouthed the polite formula and very obviously wondered at his table companion's reason.

Sabrina inclined her head and sat down.

"May I introduce Captain Yano, and I'm Kyrios. We enjoyed your performance."

She inclined her head. "I'm pleased," she said.

They spoke of her performance and other trivia for a while.

Suddenly there was a hush, and Sabrina looked up. An Altruscan with two others flanking his sides stood in the entrance. Almost a physical fear went through the crowd, caused by his mere presence. He was tall and gaunt. Cold dark eyes raked over the room. He wore black from his sleek suit to his gloves. The only other she knew who could project his personality with such force was Sargon. But as soon as the Altruscan appeared at the door, Sargon literally shrank into himself. Following his action, Sabrina tightly barricaded her mind too.

The crowd parted like a wave to move away from him. As the Altruscan walked to the bar, he passed their table. Sargon leaned forward, putting his body between the Altruscan and Sabrina.

Triscaro fixed his eyes momentarily on the Captain; then on Sargon. He gave a brief glance in her direction. Sabrina, despite Sargon's shielding, became aware of a curious reaction to him.

At the bar, room was immediately made for him, and the bartender, with alacrity poured drinks for him and his men.

Even from where she sat, she could feel the menacing power of the Altruscan. He exerted an almost hypnotic pull. She half rose, but Sargon pulled her back.

Triscaro turned around. Leaning on the bar with one foot on the brass rail, he scanned the people. His information was that who aided Sabot in identifying the Mir was supposed to be working at this club. Doeros thought that she might be one of the managers, or maybe even a hostess. He knew that she was tall with light brown hair and green eyes, and that her name was Sabrina Hennesee. Doeros also said that when she was near him, he had a curious reaction to her presence.

Sabrina became more agitated as she watched the Altruscan when a blond haired man with light grey eyes bent over her, obstructing her view. Before she could react, he whispered in English, "Drop your shoes and walk in front of me."

Sabrina almost gasped as she looked up and was about to say Martel, when he forestalled her and said, "Kalmar. Now move. The back stairs."

She kicked off her shoes and slid off her chair. Before she left, with her eyes on Triscaro, she mouthed "Shapeshifter" to Sargon. Then, with Martel at her heels, she moved quickly to the back of the club. Mounting the stairs, she turned to him, "What's with your blond hair and grey eyes?" she asked tartly, and then had to grin in spite of herself.

"What's with the silver hair and brown eyes?" he shot back.

"Kalmar, Mendes, Martel, what's real?"

"Well, Sappho, now you have a choice."

They were still bickering when they entered her suite and found Sargon waiting for them. He grabbed her arm. "Sabrina, are you out of your mind?" he yelled at her.

"You're hurting me," she told him. "Dancers are not allowed to have bruises; especially when they dance in their birthday suits."

Sargon, torn between anger and laughter, asked "Where did you learn to dance like that?"

"I have talents even you don't know about," she told him, smacking a kiss at him.

"I dare say. What did you mean by shapeshifter?"

"I just put two and two together. When he walked past me, I experienced the same sensation I have when Doeros is near. Sargon, Doeros and this Triscaro are shapeshifters."

Suddenly a bright light lit up room, and to their surprise, Sabot materialized.

"Sabot!" Sabrina exclaimed.

He smiled at her, then, said, "You remember, Sabrina, when I told you that some of the shapeshifters became entrapped in the animals. The same thing happened to Doeros and Triscaro, except it was humans. You remember the recording Miri showed you of M6?"

"How can I forget? It still gives me nightmares," Sabrina retorted.

"And remember the ones we found on Earth," he continued as if she had not replied. "I found out how it is done. They first feed on human energy, then the second time they only insinuate themselves into the person. When they do this, they also absorb their memories. When they repeat this for the third time, they are familiar with the human form and their way of thinking and can, up to some degree, imitate them. I think Triscaro and Doeros have done this several times more. They can now pass as human. But as you discovered, they have no emotions and that's why you were able to detect them. Also, they have learned a new thing. individuality. The Mir, as they call themselves, have a hive consciousness. They are similar to a bee colony. The queen sends out part of herself like little droplets to gather new experiences. When she calls them back, they are reabsorbed, and she has their knowledge. I don't know how much Doeros and Triscaro will cherish their autonomy. It will be interesting to watch what will develop from that experience."

"Can you put the genie back into the bottle?" Sabrina asked, remembering the funny contraptions Sabot had which sucked the ovoids inside.

"No. Not in the same way. They're too enmeshed in flesh and cannot extricate themselves anymore. Only death will free them."

"We have to kill them?" Martel asked.

"I don't know. We will have to see."

"Will they become ovoids again?"

"I don't know that either, Sabrina. I have never encountered that stage of development before."

"What do you want us to do?" Sargon asked.

"For the time being, go on with your plans." Turning to Sabrina, "By the way, Triscaro knows about me, and he knows it was you who identified the Mir on Earth. He knows your name. He knows the name, Sabrina Hennesee."

"Does he know who you are and where you come from?"

"No, Sabrina. He only speculates, and he's way off." Turning back to Sargon, "Are you going to M6 then?"

"No."

"I think the information about Omicron V is more important," Martel told Sabot.

"Is there anything new about M,6?" Sabrina asked.

Martel looked at Sabot and told him, "Last time I went there, it was shut down. As Sabrina, Miri and Karsten found out, this is where some time ago the Altruscans stowed the ovoids. They kept them in this frozen wasteland because they become sluggish when they get cold."

"And ever since they invaded the Antares, I have been hunting down every rumor of them," Sabrina said.

What do shapeshifters and infiltrators have in common with Omicron V?" Sabot asked Sabrina.

"I'm to investigate everything about the Altruscans activities. There have been rumors that some high-placed government official had sudden personality changes which are unexplainable neither by illnesses or trauma. And this reminds me too much of what we found on Earth." Turning to Martel. "But up till now I haven't been able to uncover anything except what your pirate friend said about Omicron V. My next move was to go there as soon as I can arrange passage on a deep-space liner."

"Then you think the Altruscans are using the ovoids to infiltrate Omicron V's echelon the same way they did on Earth?" Martel asked.

"I'm not sure if it's the Altruscans or . . . last time I met Doeros, I had a feeling that he changed his itinerary."

Sargon looked thoughtfully at her and then at Martel and told Sabrina, "Meet me on Spitfire."

"You borrowed my flyer?" Sabrina said incensed.

Sargon only shrugged and waved for Martel to follow him.

When Sabrina turned back to Sabot, he was gone too.

*   *   *

Sabrina walked up to Spitfire and found it closed up; there was no one around outside. "Open Spitfire," she said, and entering the ship, "Computer, lights on." Halfway down the corridor she felt someone coming up behind her, and she knew it wasn't Sargon. She spun around to discover that it was only Martel.

"Where's Sargon?"

"He can't make it and asked me to convey his abject apologies."

"Oh, I bet he did," Sabrina told him sarcastically.

Martel shrugged and smiled apologetically. As he came closer, his look changed to one of surprise and in his best Mendes voice asked, "Where are those beautiful long silver tresses?"

"It was a wig," Sabrina told him impatiently.

"A wig?" he echoed her. Then his face took on a quixotic expression. "Oh the destructions of dreams, dreams of moonbeams reflecting off silvery tresses," he intoned in a lyric voice. Then his voice dropped a few octaves, "Reality, the destroyer of divine enchantment. You have short hair again." He said like it was a crime.

Sabrina stood speechless, then blinked. "God, you're not real," she told him and shuddered. It was uncanny how easily he could change from one personality to another.

"But Lady, it's cruel to destroy a man's dreams."

Sabrina sat down in the pilot's seat and ignored him.

"Commuter commence engine warm up."

"Commencing," the computer replied.

Spitfire came alive. When she tried to open the channel to the tower, Martel said in English, "I think I will handle communications, or we will have trouble with clearance."

"Go ahead."

Clearance came without any impediment. When Spitfire cleared Raglan and was on its way out into space, Sabrina turned to Mendes, "Did Miri teach you English too?"

"Some, but it was mostly Thalon."

"Oh. Where too?"

"I would still like to look at M6," Martel told her.

She laid in the course for M6. Turning to Martel, "You remember about Spitfire?"

"I promise I won't open my eyes."

"Okay."

When Spitfire decelerated, M6 rotated beneath them. The sensor reading showed no artificial energy output, only the background noise of the planet.

"I'll pop down," Sabrina said, "don't run off without me."

"I wouldn't do a thing like that. And how would I explain it to Thalon."

"Why don't you just call him Sargon, okay?"

"Then I will have to change Mendes to Martel, and I've just gotten used to it."

"Well, what name do you want me to use then," she asked impatiently.

"Well. I guess I'll stay with Martel."

"Okay, Martel, I'll be back in jiffy," and she popped out. Good to her promise, she was back in almost no time. "Like I said before, it's deserted. Everything has been cleared out. Now to Omicron V"

Chapter 3

Spitfire dropped into real space long before reaching Omicron V's solar system. Sabrina ordered Martel to go to sleep. After six hours she awakened him so she could get some much needed rest.

It was early in the morning, Omicron time, when her intercom chimed. "Sabrina, we're approaching destination."

"Okay, I'll be dressed in a minute."

"When she came into the cockpit, Martel's look was one of disapproval. "You can't go planet-side looking like that," he complained.

"What's wrong with the way I look?" she shot back.

"As an engineer you look fine, but as my wife . . ."

"You're what?" Sabrina exclaimed.

"I expect some refinement in the selection of your clothes," Martel finished his sentence, unruffled. "I spent all night working out a scenario while you were sleeping the hours away."

"Martel, I thought you wanted to keep some distance between you and me," she reminded him, somewhat tartly. Although bonded, still, Martel was reluctant to enter into a closer relationship.

"I know, Sabrina, but it would simplify matters, and be a legitimate reason why we're together."

"I see, only when it's absolutely necessary will you trust me."

Martel looked at her searchingly, deciding if or how much to tell her, then chose to postpone it.

Sabrina, picking up his surface thoughts, tried to probe deeper but met a stone wall.

"Sabrina, tut, tut, that's not nice," Martel said, wagging a finger at her.

"You've got one hell of a mind-shield," she complained.

Ignoring the remark, he told her, "First thing we need to do is to get you appropriate clothes. Then we will visit acquaintances of mine to see if they will put us up. And, for your information, the planet's name is Novalis, the continent we're going to is Novaya, and the city, my acquaintances live in, is called Noyes."

Sabrina only gave him a scathing look. When they approached the space station above Novalis, Martel asked permission to land on Novaya, giving an ID number. After a short waiting period, the request was granted.

The delay at the Port of Entry was brief and Martel rented a car at the Space Port. Before going into Noyes, Martel, without consulting Sabrina, had already decided that he would leave her at Port City.

"For now we better get our story straight. You are my wife," and pointing to himself, "I'm your husband. Now we need a last name."

"How about the name Sandor? Sabrina and Martel Hennesee ra Sandor."

His mouth curled into a slight smile. "Ah, I see, Acheron. I don't know if I like that arrangement. I'm more patriarchal inclined."

She knew he was laughing at her, but why did it nettle her? "Well, suit yourself, if you don't want my help."

"I guess we could go this way for the time being. Now, the people I'm going to visit are diplomats. They are from Kandura, the nearest solar system to Novalis. Both planets are part of the Alliance. Could there be a problem if they had dealings with the house of Sandor?"

"No. I'm familiar with the house history, and I can legally use the name Sandor. Let's say we are newlyweds, and I haven't been back to Acheron for some time. So you haven't met the family yet."

"That should work." Rubbing his chin, he gave her a sidelong glance, anticipating her reaction to what he was going to propose. He started with, "You know what a mall is, don't you?"

"Yes. We had them on Earth."

"I'm going to drop you off . . ."

"You're what? I thought you were going to go shopping with me since you're so fussy about what I'm going to wear."

"Well, let's put it this way. You know women, and shopping?" he asked, nodding his head.

"Martel, one of these days!"

When the building came into sight, Sabrina let out a gasp. "That's a mall?"

"Well, it's more like a self-contained city. Parking is underground. The shops are mostly on the first and second level. Above are offices and what-nots. Farther up are apartments. You do have money, don't you?"

"I have bank credits."

Martel seemed a little disappointed when Sabrina didn't buy into his jive and took his question serious. Taking a deep breath, he suppressed his grin and only said, "Okay, that's better."

Inside, the concourse thronged with people. Right beside the entrance was a nursery to drop off children. As they walked along,

Martel didn't cause much notice dressed as he was in trousers and tunic. But Sabrina, in her coveralls and soft-soled ship boots, raised some eyebrows.

"I told you to buy some clothes on Daugave," Martel reminded her.

Sabrina gave him an aggrieved look.

Martel only grinned. "Let me show you where most of the shops for buying clothes are," and later, pointing to a bakery shop, "I'll meet you there. Take your time, because I don't know when I'm going to be back."

After Martel left, Sabrina ignoring the looks people gave her and went window shopping. As she ambled along, she observed how the people dressed and wore their hair. Several hours later, loaded down with parcels, she went to the bakery shop and ordered something that looked like coffee and a fruit tart. She was almost finished with her second cup when she espied Martel and watched him scan the crowd. He looked several times in her direction and then away again. She rose from her chair and walked right by him. He looked at her short skirt and long legs, but she didn't seem to register.

Finally she walked up behind him. "What took you so long?" she whispered into his ear, in English.

Martel's jaw dropped and he held up his finger counting one, taking a deep breath, two, then taking another one. At the count of three, he expelled it very slowly. "What have you done with your hair?" he said, affecting horror.

Sabrina stifled her laughter with difficulty. "I thought you liked moonshine and silver tresses?"

"And such a short skirt! Woman, you better not bend over," he said, trying to sound severe.

"You're not real," she told him and began to laugh. Wiping her eyes, she asked, "Where are we staying?"

"At my acquaintance's house. I hope you have good table manners. They are aristocracy and very hung up on proper etiquette."

"And where do you think I come from, bushmen? I'm as aristocratic as they are, at least from my grandfather's side. Well, and if that doesn't make any inroads, tell them that I'm an alien. That should explain everything."

Martel only gave a heaving sigh.

*   *   *

The house was a small villa set in a mixture of garden and woodland. The door was opened by a butler. He took Martel's card, and after looking at them down his nose, let them enter the foyer. He told them to wait and then left.

"Do you know what he said?" Sabrina asked.

"No, I guess he asked us to wait. The en'Nuredin speaks Galactic."

"A handy language to know," Sabrina quipped.

The butler coming back, he said in a nasal, irritating tone, "The Lord and Lady en'Nuredin will receive you. Please follow me."

The room is lavish, large, but sunny, was Sabrina's immediate impression as she came through the door. The two people meeting them were statuesque and regal.

Lord en'Nuredin graciously bowed to Sabrina and to her amazement said, "Lady Sabrina, how nice to finally meet you."

"You have me at a disadvantage, my Lord," Sabrina answered him.

"You must forgive me. Kendra was our guest several years ago, and she spoke highly of you."

Sabrina's face lit up. "Kendra. Oh, how is she? I haven't seen her since I left Acheron. Have you any news about Lady Lahoma?"

"Last I heard she was well."

"Thank you, my Lord. This is welcome news. I think you know my husband, Martel?"

"Yes, we are well acquainted. May I introduce my wife, Amita."

Lady Amita was a pleasant looking woman in her late forties with a good-humored face and deep-set blue eyes.

"Lady Amita, my pleasure," Sabrina responded with a little bow.

"May I ask you to join us, we were just about to have tea," Lady Amita invited them.

Almost immediately after the introduction, the butler brought in the tea in a huge ornate silver urn and put it down with great ceremony. Two maids, one carrying the dishes for the tea, and the other, a tray with delicious looking sandwiches and small cakes, were waiting behind him.

When everything was set out and everyone was seated, the butler was dismissed with a wave of the hand. Lady Amita did the honor of pouring tea.

* * *

Later that night and up in their rooms, Martel said, "Lady Sabrina? I think I better polish my manners."

Nonchalant she waved him off with "Aw, it's not that bad. You shouldn't have any trouble with it."

Ignoring her bantering tone, he asked, "Will there be any difficulty with them knowing the Sandors?"

"No, there should be none."

"Okay then, what do married couples do when they're alone?"

"I really don't know. But I'm going to bed even if you do mind. Which side do you want?" When Martel only shrugged, Sabrina stashed her shoes under the side she was going to sleep, and then pointing to the door across the room, "I surmise that is the bathroom," she said.

When she came back into the bedroom, Martel was already sound asleep.

Chapter 4

There was a short rap on the door before it opened. A man servant brought in the morning tea, he set it next to the wall beside the door, and discretely left.

"For a moment I thought it was Tomas," Sabrina said mournfully, looking across the pillows at Martel. "Tomas is a crotchety old man with bad habits. I guess that's why I miss him."

Martel, with his chin on his arm, ignored her comment and complained, "Do you always take your half of the bed out of the middle?"

"What do you mean; me? You started out on your side and now you're next to me. You don't snuggle, do you?"

"Me? I never heard anything so insulting," Martel protested and began to laugh.

Sabrina joined in and looked under the sheet. "You sleep in the nude, too?"

"Well, it would be kind of funny if I was fully dressed and you're not," was his rejoinder.

During their sleep, unconsciously, both had moved toward each other, and been untroubled by their bodies touching. As they now lay side by side, they found that they were feeling very comfortable with each other.

Then, there was a progressively growing grin on Martel's face.

Sabrina gave him a suspicious glance and wondered what he found so amusing.

Martel pursed his lips. "You know it's kind of funny to realize that we are bonded."

She gave him a searching look, then, tried to mind touch, but found there was that impenetrable wall.

"You can't read me, can you?"

"No."

"Well, that's good."

Sabrina turned over to better look at him and asked, "Why?" A thoughtful expression came into her face as she searched his. Becoming introspective, she tested her own feelings about him and noted how much they had changed. "Do you mind?"

"No. Not a bit. It must have happened when I held you after I pulled you out of the river."

Maybe then, or earlier, she thought.

While they had been on the raft, and during camping, she came to know him better. Especially since the irritating Mendes personality had been absent. Both shown to have assertive personalities and were often outspoken. During the trip, she found that he gave orders, but also could take them. Often they had worked well together without friction or their usual banter.

"Come to think of it, that's a hell of a thing to sneak up on you." There was a shadow of a laugh in his voice. Pointing to the breakfast tray, he said, "Let's eat before it gets cold."

"Are you always this practical during a romantic encounter?" she asked, amused. She left the bed and then realized . . . "Well, I guess it's too late," she said unruffled.

"You're gorgeous. So don't worry." Then more serious, "Are you truly at ease with this situation?"

She gave him a toothy grin and said, "Well, let's say we take this predicament slowly. Give us both time to get used to it."

Arching an eyebrow at her toothy grin, he asked "Are you having misgivings?"

After a moment's hesitation, she pursed her lips. "It's funny, but I don't. It's just . . . give me time, huh?" she said, and seated herself down at the bottom of the bed, putting the tray between them.

"Okay, I think that's fair," he agreed.

"Now what's on our agenda this morning?"

That's up to our host. By the way, his name is Charn. He knows who I am, but Lady Amita doesn't."

"Then he knows more than I do. If we go the Acheron route, I better know your full name. Mine is Sabrina Mary Hennesee ra Sandor and if you're my husband it has to be Martel . . ." Sabrina raised a questioning eyebrow as she poured him a second cup of tea.

"My name really is Martel Alemain, Sabrina."

"Okay, then its Martel Alemain ra Hennesee."

"Not Sandor?" he asked.

"No. I'm only sort of adopted into the house of Sandor; not born into it. That is why I carry the name Hennesee ra Sandor. You would only inherit my name."

"Now I know what I need to do this morning. I need to get visiting cards. And you could get your hair fixed and do some more shopping," Martel told her.

"The life of leisure," Sabrina intoned with a mellifluous voice while scraping the last of her egg off the plate. "You know I like eggs. I mean real eggs," she told him and poured herself the last of the tea.

*   *   *

Coming downstairs, in the hall, they encountered the butler. This time, using Galactic, he informed them that Lady Amita was going visiting this afternoon, and would count it a pleasure if Lady Sabrina could accompany her."

"Tell Lady Amita that I accept her kind invitation. What time would be convenient for me to return?"

"Would two o'clock be acceptable? Visiting hours usually start at half-past three."

"Thank you. Tell Lady Amita I shall return by two o'clock."

Out on the street, Sabrina turned to Martel, "What am I going to do until two o'clock?"

"Go shopping. Surely there are more things you need."

"Martel, I did more shopping yesterday than I had in my whole lifetime."

"I will drop you off at the Mall and meet you there for lunch. That's the best I can do for now," he said holding the car door for her.

Sabrina gained some needed information at the mall. At the hairdresser she leafed through several fashion magazines and ascertained what ladies wore to afternoon teas. The outfit she bought was a little more on the conservative side than the pictures showed. Only her hair was done up in a more elaborate style.

She met Martel for lunch at noon.

He greeted her with, "Ah, I see, you did get more shopping done."

Sabrina looked at her parcels. "Yes, and it made me hungry. Where to?"

"There is a nice restaurant on the roof. Since it is not windy, I thought we could have lunch there. By the way, this new hairdo is very becoming."

"Do you know I distrust men with super-polished manners and charming smiles?"

Martel only gave her an aggrieved look and decided to forgo an answer.

Sitting at a table in the restaurant Martel told her, "I visited Charn at his office, and he asked me to make sure that his wife is going to visit Lady Calandra. She is the wife of the Secretary of State. Her husband, according to rumors, has undergone a substantial personality change."

*   *   *

It was not really raining, just drizzling, as Sabrina and Lady Amita left the house. They were conducted to the car by the butler holding an umbrella over their heads.

Seated in the car, Lady Amita, per instruction from her husband, briefed Sabrina on what was expected. "I know I'm presuming, but Charn insisted on it". "No, not at all. It's always good to know what to expect."

Lady Amita had judged their arrival perfectly. They were the first guests. Lady Calandra greeted Amita with genuine pleasure.

"Calandra, may I introduce Lady Sabrina Hennesee ra Sandor. She and her husband are our guests."

Calandra looked at Sabrina with interest. "I am pleased to meet you," she greeted Sabrina graciously and led them into her drawing room. "Please do sit down, and I will have tea brought in immediately."

"Oh, don't bother, we can wait for your other guests," Lady Amita told her hostess. "Tell me, how have you been? Have you heard . . . ?"

As the two ladies arraigned themselves on the sofa, they exchanged all the new gossip since they met last. Sabrina with her ability to go through people's memories, unabashed, did just that. She immediately found what she was looking for. At first, Lady Calandra had been thankful for her husband's distant behavior after the birth of their fourth child. She had given birth to four children in seven years. She felt she had been pregnant the duration of their marriage. But now she was getting anxious and suspicious. She was wondering if he had acquired a mistress. Well-bred-ladies with any sense of their dignities, and their family's survival, were expected not to notice such lapses and to continue with their life as usual. When Sabrina came to this point, her face darkened for a moment. Lady Calandra feared a scandal. People in society cared a great deal about their reputation. Lady Calandra understood that no one was high enough, that a scandal couldn't ruin. He had not only distanced himself, but also become cold. There were no feelings expressed, not with her, nor with the children. He seemed to have lost all connectedness with his family. When Sabrina reached this point in her sorting of the confused perception, more guests arrived and tea was served.

Lady Amita was her translator, since she didn't understand the language. But most of the guests only paid her cursory attention. The newest fashions for this year had come on the market last week, and there had been a big fashion show. Most of the conversation was about its merits and what everyone was going to wear. There was also gossip about mutual acquaintances and who might marry whom. When it was polite, Lady Amita excused herself on the premise that Lady Sabrina might like to rest since she only arrived yesterday.

"I hope the tea wasn't too tedious for you?" Lady Amita asked as she entered the car.

"No. It was a pleasant and somewhat a new experience for me."

"You don't go to teas?" Amita asked, astonished.

"Lady Amita, I have little time for social functions, but when I am invited, they are always enjoyable." Sabrina told her diplomatically.

"But when you are home, aren't there any social functions?"

"Yes. But most of them are very informal."

"But how would you show off a new dress?"

"Oh we have functions for that too, like a fashion show, or ball."

"I can't wait until our tour on Novalis is over and we can return to Kandura again." She said in a wistful tone. She hoped going home might improve her relationship with her husband.

Martel was waiting for Sabrina in the foyer. "Sabrina, I'm sorry, but I have to ask you to come with me. Turning to Lady Amita, "Social engagements are hectic when there isn't enough time."

After they were seated in the taxi, Sabrina asked, "Now, what's with your fired-up hurry again that I couldn't go to the bathroom," she said in English.

Martel laughed. "I'm sorry. I didn't think about that. We have thirty minutes to report to Heiko."

When they arrived inside the building, they still had ten minutes. Sabrina turning to Martel said, "You better go on by yourself and tell Heiko that I had to stop for necessary duty." She quickly walked off, leaving Martel standing by himself, shaking with mirth.

Later when she entered Heiko's office, he had an amused look on his face.

Captain Hennesee, please do sit down." When Sabrina was seated, he continued, "There will be a meeting of the Alliance Council on

Daugave. Captain Thalon has asked that you represent the Antares as her ambassador. As you know, we have intelligence that the meeting is supposed to be disrupted. Do you think you could combine your ambassadorial duty with finding out who the disrupter's supposed to be? Captain Alemain will be assisting you."

"I think we both could handle this," Martel said, glancing at Sabrina. "But our script here on Novalis is that we are newlyweds. Would that prove a difficulty on Daugave?"

"You could still pretend that you are married. According to Acheron customs, you would each use your own name. Unless you insist he uses ra Hennesee?" he asked Sabrina, with a tiny twitch to the corners of his mouth.

"Oh, there's no insistence on that," Sabrina assured him.

"Then let me brief you two on what you might expect."

The briefing lasted over three hours. When they were finally able to leave, Martel stopped Sabrina. "Karsten told me that you had a growling stomach."

"How well do you know Karsten?"

"Well enough for him to tell me all about you."

"Is this a clique or just a small universe?" Sabrina quipped.

*　　*　　*

The big embassy party was tonight.

Sabrina went in search of Lady Amita to consult her on etiquette and on what to wear for the occasion.

"Let me see what you have." After going through Sabrina's meager wardrobe, she exclaimed, "Is this all?"

Sabrina smile was apologetic. "I travel light. And there are always shops if I need to augment what I have."

"Then shopping is definitely on the agenda. There is a quaint shop where the owner designs all the gowns herself. Let's go there and see if she has something for you."

The choice was fortuitous. The couturier, as she liked to be called, after giving Sabrina's bleached silver-blond hair and sea-green eyes an appraising look, told her that she had just the gown for her. She showed her an emerald-green dress with a wide skirt, and gold lacing around a modest décolletage. When she tried the dress on, she was pleased with the décolleté, it showed just enough without being too revealing.

*   *   *

It was already late when they returned home and Lady Amita suggested a small repast before having to get dressed. Immediately afterwards, both ladies excused themselves and went upstairs to get ready.

The men naturally were long finished with their toilette and waiting for them in the foyer. Martel's complacent expression underwent a change as he watched Sabrina coming slowly down the stairs.

Lord Charn greeted her with, "Lady Sabrina, you look simply divine." This made Sabrina's chin rise just a little higher.

"Don't do that," Martel complained. "If you compliment her like that, she will be insufferable."

Lady Amita took Sabrina's hand, "Husbands," she said, pulling a small face, and waved them off as they walked out of the door.

The ride was short and as they drove up to the embassy, most people were still arriving.

Sabrina's primary objective for attending the party was to meet the Secretary of State. When they entered the room, her eyes only roamed across the men present, and she missed Lady Calandra coming toward her.

"Captain Alemain, Lady Sabrina?"

Smiling at her, "Please, call me Sabrina," she said.

"If you call me Calandra."

"Gladly."

Turning to Amita and Charn, "I will introduce Sabrina and her husband. I think someone is very eager to talk to you," she told Lord Charn, pointing to an old gentleman with a distinctive military bearing making a beeline toward them.

"Oh my goodness," Lord Charn said, and Amita sneezed to hide her giggle.

"Let's go quickly. The old gentleman is a dear, but a terrible bore," Calandra told Sabrina. Taking her arm, she introduced Sabrina and Martel to her acquaintances and friends. They came upon Calandra's husband amid a group of men. She put her hand on his arm. When he turned toward her, she said, "Sabrina, this is my husband, Lord Benlor. May I present Sabrina Hennesee ra Sandor, and her husband, Captain Alemain ra Hennesee to you?"

Sabrina noted Calandra's guarded glance as she watched her husband. "I am pleased to meet you," Sabrina said with a polite smile and an air of expectancy. Lord Benlor's demeanor remained stiff and formal. He acknowledged Sabrina and Martel with a perfunctory bow and almost rudely turned back to his group.

Sabrina glanced at Martel, and he nodded. At first she only tentatively touched his mind. When she noted no reaction to her probe, she went deeper, reading it. To her surprise, all his memories were compartmentalized from his childhood on to the present. There were no feelings, or any pleasant memories. He reminded her of Commodore Doeros whose mind was just as disciplined and all his memories were devoid of feelings and emotions. The first time, it had bothered her. Memories were mental images plus feelings. Now she had met two individuals who showed the same characteristics.

Later in the evening, Martel invited her to a very stylized dance. Touching your partner was not appropriate. Nevertheless, being in touch mind to mind, they enjoyed their bodies moving to the music in an intricate pattern. Toward the end of the evening Sabrina and Martel were asked to join the national dance. It closely resembled a minuet. Sabrina had some familiarity with it.

At the beginning, she was Martel's partner, then someone else's. During the last part of the dance, she was paired with Lord Benlor. As he danced with her, he became disconcerted, and she noticed that he was reacting to her. Something in him sensed what she carried within her, the life fluid of the Mir. He began to sweat. At first Sabrina thought little of it. But as her hand touched his again, she noticed a sticky consistency and became aware of a sweetish odor. The first time she smelled it was when she encountered the innocuous slip of a girl on the Antares. And sometimes, if she was very heated after a workout, she could smell it on herself. All of a sudden he began to tremble and almost forcefully disengaged his hand from hers.

"Lord Benlor?" she asked, alarmed.

He gave a grunt and tried to make it out of the room, but collapsed before he reached the door. Two of his aides immediately came to his side, but when Calandra tried to help, she was prevented from coming too close.

The dance broke up and the guests, uncertain of what to do, gathered against a far wall.

Sabrina went to Calandra and put her arm around her. They were standing close enough so she could get a look at the stricken man, and saw a curious dissolution of the skin.

In a short time, a stretcher was brought in by two men. Although they did not precisely look like Altruscans, Sabrina recognized them as such. They hurriedly carried Lord Benlor away.

When Lady Calandra tried to follow, she was prevented by one of the aides blocking the door. "Lady, we will take Lord Benlor to the hospital and you will be informed as soon as the doctor has determined what ails him. Please have patience."

When Lady Calandra insisted on following, Lady Amita came and placed a supporting arm around her waist. Looking at Sabrina, "I will take care of her," And to Calandra, "Please, let me take you to a chair." Turning to the guests, "Ladies and Gentlemen, I'm sorry, but could we call it a night? Lady Calandra is naturally worried and would like to be with her husband as soon as possible."

When Sabrina found that Amita and Charn would take Calandra to her home, she gave a nod to Martel before she became invisible and followed the stretcher. It was loaded into a van and put into a freezer compartment. Soon the van was en-route to the Altruscan embassy.

Inside the freezer compartment, Lord Benlor's body had totally disintegrated and the ovoid creature was the only thing left. It was grey in color and lethargic.

Suddenly, Sabrina felt a presence and identified it as Sabot. She felt more than saw him activate his curious contraption, and the ovoid was sucked into the bottle.

"Now, how will they explain the disappearance of Lord Benlor?" she thought at him.

His reply was that this was no concern of his.

*   *   *

Still invisible, Sabrina's stayed with the van until it stopped at the Altruscan embassy. In the envoy's office, the atmosphere throbbed with fear and fury. The two Altruscans who had taken care of Lord Benlor stood rigidly at attention. Fear seemed to be oozing from every pore, and the envoy, marching back and forth, stopped in front of his desk and began hitting it with the full force of his fists. "How did this happen?" he bellowed.

"We don't know. When we opened the freezer, he was gone. There was nothing there."

"Are you sure?"

"Yes, Sir. We even made Elko go inside."

"What happened at the party?"

"He was dancing and suddenly broke loose from the woman he was paired with. He tried to make it to the door, but collapsed."

"Who was the woman?"

"A Lady Sabrina ra Sandor."

"Where is she from?"

"I believe Acheron."

"Have her investigated, immediately."

"Yes, Sir."

This was all Sabrina stayed around for. She had what she needed and transported herself to Lord Benlor's villa.

"Sabrina, where have you been?" was lady Amita's first words as she walked into the salon.

"I got waylaid by several of the guests at the embassy. They wanted to know what had happened," she lied. "Has you husband been ill lately, Calandra?"

"No, Sabrina," Calandra said, somewhat puzzled. "He has always been in excellent health."

"That's what I heard from the people I talked with. Is there anything I can do for you?"

"No, but thank you. Lord Charn and your husband have gone to the hospital."

At that moment Lord Charn entered the room followed by Martel.

"Lady Calandra," Lord Charn said, taking her hand, he tried to choose his words with care. "I have the grave duty to inform you that your husband has passed away. Your husband's aide informed me that he died while en-route to the hospital. Because he had been off planet three month ago, the doctors suspected he may have brought some disease home, and ordered immediate cremation. Also, you and your children need to have thorough medical examinations as soon as possible."

She looked up, her face taunt and her eyes bright with unshed tears. "Thank you, Lord Charn," she said with dignity.

"Can we do something for you?"

"No, thank you, my Lord. I have already put a call through to my family, and they are on their way here."

*   *   *

Back at the en Nuredine mansion, Martel pulled Sabrina aside. "What did you find out?"

"Lord Benlor was not taken to a hospital, but to the Altruscan embassy. After they loaded his body into the van, it was put into a freezer compartment. The Mir devoured the body of Lord Benlor and turned back to form. When the compartment was opened, to their consternation there was nothing left. Sabot, with his contraption, had taken care of that."

"You look beat. We'll leave it for now," and he smiled apologetically at her. "That was a hell of an ending for an evening."

"What's our next move?"

"We go back to Daugave and report."

"Oh, by the way, the Altruscans want to investigate me, since I was the last person to have had contact with Lord Benlor."

"Well, don't worry. They'll get a nice report on you through Doeros, edited by me."

"When do we need to be on Daugave?"

"Oh, in about four days."

She contemplated him for a minute. "That should give us enough time," she said mysteriously, and then grinned.

"What have you got on your cotton-picking mind?" he asked suspiciously.

"A holiday on Lara's planet."

"Rafting?" he asked with raised eyebrows.

"Are you kidding? I'm thinking about Lara's bungalow, beach, ocean, and sunshine.

Chapter 5

Sabrina was diving and the feeling of being weightless was relaxing. It was a totally other world down here. Several predatory fish swam by, contemplating if she could be their dinner, but a poke from her harpoon quickly changed their minds. As she swam in toward the shore, she spotted a crustacean. She watched it for a while, considering it when she saw a second one. They were decidedly going to be dinner.

Surfacing, she spit the mouthpiece out and yelled, "Hey, Martel, what do you say to that?" holding the lobsters up, as she came out of the water.

"That should do it. I'm already boiling water. In a few minutes you can drop them in."

Martel had laid out the plates and silverware. He had made salad, and a rice dish, and was cooling a bottle of white wine.

"How did you know I was going to bring lobsters?"

"I could tell you had lobsters on your mind."

"I thought you wouldn't read my mind?"

"You can't read mine, but I always know what's on yours."

"Then read what's on mine," she challenged, and ran after him with the lobsters.

Martel dodged, and opening the lid, told her to quit and put those lobsters into the pot so they could eat.

After dinner, while Sabrina cleaned up, Martel was lying on a blanket farther up the beach under a shade tree that looked like a vast, open umbrella.

Having put the dishes into the dishwasher she came out of the house, and seeing Martel asleep, laid down beside him. She kissed him between his shoulders. He grunted, but did not move away. When her hands moved up his back, he arched it, and she could feel his pleasure at her touch. Pressing her body close against his back, she kissed his neck, and then nibbled at his ear. Martel turned slowly around and laid his mouth against hers. It went like an electric jolt through his body and to Sabrina, it was like coming home. It was as if she had always known the feel of his body. She lay warm and pliant in his arms. Subtle at first, then getting more explicit, he opened up and let his feelings merge with hers in an unfolding and exhilarating mingling of emotions and their physical need.

*   *   *

Martel was at the controls of Spitfire checking the instruments. When Sabrina entered the cockpit, he started the ignition sequence. He looked up and smiled, but when he saw her pensive face, he cocked his head at her.

"You need me to go to Daugave?" she asked.

"You want to go home?"

"Yes. I want to check up on the boys. When I try to sense them, I get some funny impressions. Logan has shut down the way he used to when he didn't want me to know what he was up to."

"I will contact you if I need you."

She looked at Martel and smiled. Bending down, she quickly kissed him, then, she was gone. Re-materializing in her living room back on the Antares, she went in search of Medea. She found her cleaning kitchen cabinets.

When Sabrina walked into the kitchen, Medea nearly dropped the dish she was holding. "Do you always have to sneak up on me?" she exploded.

"Where are the boys?"

"Didn't Sargon tell you that he took them to Earth to visit the Dehner's."

"No, he didn't, and I wish he had. Is Sargon on board?"

Before Medea could answer, Sabrina's face went blank, then it was replaced by a disquieted look, and she disappeared.

She reappeared at Sargon's place, on the terrace behind the main residence. Sargon was lying in one of the lounges. Sabrina sensed immediately that he was in distress.

"Sargon?" she asked.

"Hello, pest," he greeted her with a rueful smile. "Felt you scanning me."

"What's the matter?"

"Triscaro nearly got the better of me," he said, lifting the ice-pack he was pressing against his right side.

There was a deep gash oozing fluid not blood. Sabrina looked closely at the gash. The skin around the wound seemed to be disintegrating. When Sabrina moved to run her finger over the wound, he restrained her hand.

"Don't, Sabrina. I don't know what it is.

"Tell me, how did this happen?"

"Triscaro and I fought. I thought I had him when one of his men threw him a knife."

She looked at him. "Try to remember, was the knife clean?"

"Come to think of it, there was some kind of smear on it."

"I thought so."

Sabrina reached into one of her coverall pockets and pulled out a knife. To Sargon's astonishment she made a small incision on her little finger. But when she stared to press her finger to his wound, he started to protest then stopped.

Sabrina looked at him. "After I absorbed the life-fluid of the Mir, my body developed anti-bodies. This is primitive, but that's the best I can do with such sort notice. Now lay still."

She moved her finger over the wound, touching the skin. Then, went down into a meditative healing level, envisioning his cells healing themselves. Sargon, laying back into the chair, also went into a trance to augment her.

When she surfaced again, she immediately examined the wound. The oozing had stopped and the cut was starting to heal. She gently poked the skin around the cut and it showed a healthy gold color.

"I hope you realize that we are blood-brothers now," she told Sargon with a droll expression on her face.

He looked at her for a second, then remembered the Indian ritual and laughed. He pulled her into his arms, and to her surprise, kissed her fully on the mouth.

She pushed herself back to look into his face. "Oh," she said, "so you know."

"I knew it the minute Martel didn't mind you touching him."

Sargon, laying her head on his shoulder asked concerned, "Are you all right? Martel called and he wanted me to check on you. He was worried that you are still disturbed at seeing the disintegration of Lord Benlor."

There was a sudden retreating within herself, and Sargon felt the revulsion the memory evoked.

"I have the horrors ever since I saw the recording Miri made of the four ovoids, and the fear on the boy's face before being absorbed. Sometimes I have nightmares that I will turn into one of them." She pulled a tight face and suddenly looked tired and a little pale.

He regarded her for a moment, then, tightened his arms around her. As she lay next to him, he found the sudden feeling of familiarity pleasing. Had it not been for his bonding to Chantar, it would have been disturbing. He had forgotten how exhilarating she was, how immediate, and without pretense.

There was a sudden chuckle. Chantar, carrying an ice-pack, stood beside the lounge. A look at Sargon told her immediately that he felt better. She knew through her link with Sargon that Sabrina was here.

"If you're that good a medicine, I wish you'd stay here," she told Sabrina. "I have ordered tea. I think you both could use some refreshment." She put her hand under Sabrina's chin, lifting it. "You don't look so good. Are you all right?"

"I think a cup of tea would do the trick." Then turning to Sargon, "By the way, how could you sent the boys to the Dehner's?"

"I enrolled them at the Space Academy. When Martha found out, she wouldn't hear the boys staying in a dorm. But I prevailed. They only stay with her over the weekends. Then, both promised to behave."

"And you believed them?" Sabrina asked, incredulous.

"I also sent Sirtis along."

"She will keep Jason in line, but I don't think she's got much influence over Logan."

Where Jason had an easy going personality, Logan was more complicated. He had an air of haughtiness and disdain, and he was very deliberate in his actions. It would be his first time away from parental control and tasting a freedom not experienced before.

"I will soon be there to check on them, "Chantar told her. "I have been asked by Maria Callander to put on a concert at the United Nations on New Atlantis."

"And remember, you have a meeting on Daugave as the representative of the Antares," Sargon reminded her.

Pushing herself away from him and sitting up she asked incensed, "Why do you always do this to me?"

"To keep you busy and out of trouble. But then, trouble seems to follow you no matter how hard I try."

"Let's have something more pleasant to talk about while we have tea," and Chantar reached for the tea service.

When Sabrina saw who was carrying it, she jumped up and exclaimed, "Why, Rory!" and went to embrace him.

Rory was one of Acheron's hidden ones. He was a casualty of Acheron's atomic wars and ecological poisonings. He was Lahoma's eldest son born slightly retarded and with some deformities. He had been trained to be Joran's valet and was very attached to him.

"When Joran is gone, I stay with Chantar. You stay here?" he asked, hopefully. He loved Sabrina. She had never been condescending to him and always treated him like he was a whole person.

"No Rory. Sargon is sending me away again."

Rory looked at Sargon, "I like her to stay here. I like to go back to her house," he said, aggrieved.

Sargon gave her a hurt look. "Do you always have to make me out as the heavy?" he complained. Turning to Rory, "Sabrina has a job to do," he explained to Rory.

He seemed to understand that, because Joran also had to go to do a job.

Rory's bones had gone brittle and traveling put a stain on him. Joran, fearing for his well being, had talked him into staying with Chantar, promising him that if Sabrina came back, he could stay with her.

"When you come back, I can stay with you?"

"I promise." She hugged him and then let go. Locking at Chantar she said ruefully "I guess I need to go then."

"Do you need to pack?" Chantar asked.

"No. All my clothes are on Spitfire, and Spitfire is on Daugave."

"You're letting Martel fly your ship?" Sargon exclaimed.

"Well, he needed to report and it was good thing I came home," she told Sargon.

"For once I have to agree with you."

Ignoring Sargon she looking at Rory and told him, "I'll be back soon."

"Sabrina, now sit down so we can have tea," Chantar scolded her.

Chapter 6

Before Sabrina left the Antares she contacted Martel through their mind-link, informing him that she would pop in at the Port of Entry, and also the time to pick her up. But it was Heiko who waited for her at the terminal, accompanied by an escort.

She bowed formally, since like her, he wore civilian garb. As he was accompanied by his guard, it would not do to be overly familiar with him.

"I hope your travel has not been too strenuous?" he asked politely. Only his eyes betrayed his amusement. He naturally knew Sabrina had no need to use the conventional mode of travel.

With a serious face Sabrina replied, "It was pleasant enough, Yugiri Heiko." Using his first name she let him know that she considered herself his equal.

His mouth quirked, telling her he understood.

"I have rented a suite in the Hokeido. I hope it will meet with your approval. Most of the other diplomats will be staying there also."

"Thank you. You are very kind."

He escorted her to his limousine.

Arriving at the hotel, to Sabrina's surprise, her suitcases from Spitfire were in the lobby, but no Martel. While riding up in the elevator she wanted to ask about Martel, but decided not to.

Before Heiko let her enter her suite, his escorts made a thorough sweep through it. When she gave him a questioning look, he only shrugged. Her suite was large, on the fifth floor, and at the end of the building.

"The suite is secure," the guard reported.

"Lady Sabrina, I will see you at the council's meeting." Heiko bowed, and left.

When Sabrina entered her rooms, a young girl came timidly toward her with her hands tightly pressed to her body. "Lady Sabrina I was asked to see to your comfort," she said so low Sabrina almost didn't hear.

Sabrina inclined her head. "What's your name?"

"Zuzuki," came a shy answer.

"Okay Zuzuki. Let's unpack and put my things away."

"Lady, Lord Heiko asked me to direct your attention immediately to the packet he had delivered," Zuzuki said, pointing a shaking finger to a thick envelope lying on the table.

"Thank you, Zuzuki." When Sabrina turned, she caught a weary look on the girls face. A slight mind touch told her that the girl was inordinately frightened of Heiko, and terrified of a nameless awesome something. Maybe a God? She wondered, but stowed it for later consideration.

She went to the table and opened the envelope. It had a sealed folder with a groove. Using her ID, she slipped its edge into the groove to open it. She was about to release the catch when she saw Zuzuki coming from the bedroom with her eyes cast down, but Sabrina had the impression that she was trying to get a glimpse at the content of the folder.

She came close to the table and asked, "Lady, would you like me to order tea?"

"Yes, Zuzuki, that would be very nice, but I will take it downstairs."

After Zuzuki left, Sabrina closed the folder again and left the suite carrying it under her arm. She went into the dining room and selected a table at a far wall. With her chin cupped in her hands, she sat at the table, musing over Zuzuki's extraordinary fear. It puzzled her who or what could inspire such terror. As far as she knew about Daugave, there was no social unrest, and religion was a private matter. So what could instill such a fear? There was a down turn of her mouth when her mind turned to religion. God, maybe? She remembered at first having some difficulty with Benjie. He had been raised Moslem. And since he was living on the Antares, it made it somewhat difficult to know which direction to kneel to pray. But there had been no fear of god in him. Also there was a time when she had been curious about god and her mother told her to think of god as love. Her father, who was of a more practical persuasion, told her that the only thing she need to be afraid of were humans. He didn't think that god needed or desired to be feared. When Sargon was asked by Regina, on of Kamila's little sisters, about god, his explanation was that people always envision their god as something they can identify with. But that had not been enough for Regina. Recently, she'd seen a movie about a religious service, and been impressed by it. She thought to start something like that on the Antares. She also wanted to know how she could serve god. Sargon told her curtly that she should learn to respect people with the respect that she thought she deserved. If she wanted to serve, become a doctor or nurse. If you care about children, learn about their needs. After that he had stalked out and left it for the rest of them to take care of Regina's ruffled feathers.

Sabrina shuddered and thought what in the world made me think of that. Then there was Zuzuki's interest in the folder.

A waiter came and tried to get her attention at first with a gentle cough, which became somewhat louder the second time. When she became aware of his presence, he asked if she would take her tea here.

Finally, she opened the folder. It contained the layout of the building where the meeting was to be held. Also, a complete coverage of the agenda plus a personnel roster. Listed were all the diplomats, giving a short dossier of each. She saw that Elkatma and Thalia would be present and smiled. There was another sealed folder. When she opened it, inside was a letter.

Sabrina, we have intelligence that this meeting will be disrupted. The Altruscans are suspected. But there is no conclusive evidence.

The Orion Hegemony is trying to dissolve their alliance with the Altruscan Empire. Their venture with the Altruscans has been too costly for them in investments and in lives. They rue the constant warfare. They found that war is very bad for business.

There is turmoil within the Altruscans Empire. The subjugated planets are in revolt, and this is naturally abetted by us.

We have a new name, Triscaro. He has escaped, and is hiding deep within the empire. We will be tracking him.

I will give you a more detailed briefing.

Heiko

She put the papers back into the folder, but kept the letter, putting it into one of the manifold pockets of her Acheron attire.

Why all the clandestine rigmarole with something so obvious, Sabrina thought as she sipped at her tea. This was nothing new. She was meant to get the answer, but not from the folder. Okada! Yes, I think I will give him a visit. She called Headquarters, and made an appointment.

*   *   *

Sabrina decided to walk after she left the Hokeido. Do all space ports look alike, she thought. There were plenty of curio shops, clothing stores, restaurants and clubs. There was little difference between the ones on Madras or Acheron.

She strolled across the broad sunny plaza to the Alliance Fleet Headquarters. Pausing at the door to look back and smiled. The plaza thronged with people from all the Alliance planets.

Walking briskly toward the central lift she was about to insert her ID card when she saw Yoshi.

"Commander Hireyoshi," she called out.

"Sabrina?" He strode toward her and embraced her enthusiastically, holding her tightly to him for a time. "It's so good to see you. I have missed you, woman," he said, kissing her. "You're never home when I'm there. What have you been up too?"

"Oh. A little adventure here and there," she said light heartedly.

Holding her at arms lengths he said, "You know you're out of uniform?"

"No, no, no," she said, wagging her finger at him. "I'm Antares' ambassador to attend the council meeting. What do you say to that?"

Yoshi grinned. "You are the most un-diplomatic individual I know. You think Sargon's slipping?"

They both laughed.

Looking at her timepiece, she said, "I'm sorry but I have an appointment. Can I see you later?" Sabrina asked.

Yoshi took a note book from his shirt pocket and tore out a leaf. "This is my address," he said, writing it down and handed it to her. "Best time to come is after six. I should be home by then."

Sabrina looked at the writing, "Cherry-Blossom Street? Okay. I'll be there about seven." She gave him a slap on the arm then inserted her ID in the door.

Yoshi caught the movement out of the corner of his eye and half turned. "What's with the ID?"

"Top secret," she told him, dead pan.

But when the elevator came, Sabrina stepped back to let the people off and made no move to enter. Yoshi surmised she wasn't teasing. As the doors closed, he looked at Sabrina who only shrugged. Immediately another car came, and after she held her ID to a scanner, the door opened.

"See you tonight," she told him before the door closed.

The special elevator took her to the sub-basement of the building. Sabrina guessed it was many levels below the street. The temperature was of a comfortable seventy degrees, and the hallway was brightly lit.

There was an ensign on duty at the front desk. She nodded curtly at him. "I'm to see Admiral Okada," she informed him.

"Yes, Ma'am. If you will follow me, please."

He went to another set of lifts and with a key opened the door for her. A few minutes later, she stepped through a door four hundred feet underground. Few people were privileged to know of its existence.

The huge subterranean complex was deserted. She read the numbers off, and when she came to sixteen, she rapped sharply at the door.

"Come in."

When she entered, Okada was sitting absorb at a computer console, giving her little heed.

Sabrina walked up behind him and leaned over his shoulder to look at the screen.

"Nosey," Okada said.

"Of course. How do you think I get any information?"

"That's what I thought," he said with a tight smile and turned the screen off. "What brought you down here?"

"Non-information," and gave him Heiko's letter.

He scanned it and handed it back. "What do you want from me?"

"A briefing," she told him.

He arched an eyebrow at her. "Why do you think I should give you a briefing?"

"Because, I'm the Captain of the Antares and an Alliance member. Also, I represent the Antares as a delegate to the Council, and I am a member of the Security Council."

Okada only gave her a bland look.

The Antares was a member of long standing, and as her representative, she had a right to ask, even if the ship was only sparsely populated. But what no one outside herself and Sargon knew was, that the Antares floating so peacefully in space was also a devastatingly powerful weapon. If ever threatened, she could move a planet out of its path by switching polarity. Also any energy weapon fired at her would return tenfold, refracting off her smooth hull, just like Miri's Peregrine. If Sabrina seemed a little arrogant, she had the muscles to back it up.

"Would you like some cold tea," he asked. He had watched her and she exhibited the same self-confidence as Sargon, and there was knowledge, a power, he had yet to fathomed.

"Yes, thank you."

"You know, it was Sargon who showed me how to make iced-tea."

He went to a small refrigerator and took out a pitcher, and then got two glasses. While he poured, he said, "I have some information. I will condense it," when he saw a movement of her hand, he quickly said, "It will be complete."

He gave her the glass and walked to an alcove containing two easy-chairs and a small table. "Sit down and be comfortable."

When she was seated, and after she took her first sip, he asked. "Are you interested in Triscaro?"

"Not really. I like to get to the source of the Mir. I know from Sabot that they have a hive-consciousness. Up till now we have only been dealing with singular portions. They are not entities in the sense we use that word. There has to be a central coordinator of some sort. Triscaro is only dangerous because he is an Altruscan. Ergo, ruthless."

"Then, what you want to do is to find whatever you want to call it," Okada told her.

"Why not Queen Bee?"

Okada shrugged. "As you wish!"

"Will you consider it?"

"Who do you want to accompany you in that venture?"

"The only ones I want to know about this is Martel Alemain, and Serenity."

"How about Sabot?"

"He will be there if I need him. Now, for something more mundane. What do you wear on Daugave when you're invited to dinner?"

"Anything, except your coveralls."

Sabrina grimaced at him as she rose. She made a short bow and left, hearing Okada chuckle as she closed the door.

*   *   *

The ride was far too short; Sabrina would have liked to have seen more of the city. The taxi deposited her precisely at seven o'clock at Cherry Blossom Street. The house looked the same as its neighbor on either side. It consisted of four stories and a wide, sweeping entrance leading up to the door. She stood for a moment reading the name on the door, The House of Tranquility. Her finger was just making contact with the button when the door opened by a liveried young boy.

"I'm Sabrina Hennesee to see Commander Omi Hireyoshi."

"Ma'am," he said flustered. He had no idea how to pronounce her name and was embarrassed to ask if she would repeat it.

"Sabrina! Come on in." Yoshi came from the back of the house. "I made it early so we can have time to talk before everyone else comes."

After the door closed, Yoshi embraced her, kissing her on the cheek. Then, held her at arms length, "You're as beautiful as ever," he said in English.

Sabrina was dressed Acheron style. She thought it wise to be appropriately dressed, and modestly covered. Her slacks this time were not her baggy ones, but tight fitting, of a solid jade green, and the overdress was of a lighter shade, with a red and yellow floral print.

"I thought it would be an intimate dinner, just the two of us," Sabrina teased.

He looked at her levelly, ignoring the teasing tone and said, "I want you to meet my wife."

"Yes, I think Heiko said something about your being married."

They crossed the hall and he opened the door. The room was decorated largely in faint yellow with a bright floral design and the rug a deep red. There were several vases filled with flowers, and a large window overlooking a small garden.

The single occupant of the room was a slender woman in her thirties. She had an oval face and her lips were beautifully shaped. The look of the dark oriental eyes was steady and direct.

"Sabrina, may I introduce my wife, Kiritsubo."

73

"Lady Kiritsubo," Sabrina said, and bowed.

"Lady Sabrina, welcome to my home. Yoshi told me so much about you. It made me so excited to finally meet you."

"I hope what he told you were only nice things," she said, and gave Yoshi a sharp look.

"He told me that only Sargon or you could make him mind."

"Kiri, you're not supposed to tell her that," Yoshi gently reproved her. "How can I ever bluff my way out of a tight spot if she knows about it?" He turned to Sabrina smiling, with all his teeth showing. "Now tell me, what have you been up to?"

Sabrina looked at him faintly amused. Used too, her being up to something, always meant excitement in the old days. Sabrina was the one who most of the time landed herself in trouble, and the only one who at times dared to defy Sargon.

After they were seated and served tea, she told him about Elisheba who had been his first love. Everyone had been sure the two would marry, except for an incident that tore them apart. Sabrina began her story after Elisheba had left the Antares and what prompted her flight from Sarah's home.

Yoshi grimaced. "She must have had a hell of a time."

"Yes. She did. She thought she had let Sargon down by letting herself get captured, and then raped. Then Ras al Khazim telling her that Sarah consented for her to be his concubine during her confinement, really topped it. She fled Sarah's apartment and wandered from one ship to another until she met Yussuf, an ultra orthodox Jew. She thought if she made it right with god by becoming a Jewess, her life would be better. Well, it didn't work out. She was unhappy. When I first saw her she was very obese . . ."

"Elisheba?" Yoshi interrupted. The Elisheba he remembered was slender and willowy.

"And she had two of the cutest little girls, twins," Sabrina finished.

There was a knock on the door and the butler came in. "Sir, the guests are gathered in the reception room."

"Thank you, Zataki." Yoshi rose, and shaking out his clothes, looked at Sabrina and asked, "Is my face straight?"

"The inscrutable Yoshi," she said. Kiri had watched the performance with a smile.

The room they entered was very large and formal. Her attention was immediately absorbed by the people who were staring at her. Sabrina almost found it unnerving until she saw Heiko. She jabbed Yoshi in the back, discreetly pointing at him.

"Kiritsubo's father," Yoshi whispered, amused at Sabrina's surprise. "He has been minding the store while we were visiting."

Two dowagers were the first to come forward and bowed. One of the dowagers said something to Kiritsubo. When Kiri answered, they looked at Yoshi and then Sabrina. They bowed to Sabrina, and she returned the courtesy. The two left with a perplexed look on their faces.

"I introduced you as Yoshi's elder sister," Kiritsubo enlightened her.

"Oh," Sabrina said, "That should confuse them for a while."

Naturally Sabrina with her sea-green eyes and honey-colored hair looked nothing like Yoshi, who was Japanese.

Kiritsubo introduced Sabrina to the other guests, smiling politely and bowing.

Sabrina would very much have liked to talk to Heiko, and was just about to ask Kiritsubo to present her when the door suddenly opened and two guards stationed themselves at each side. Okada walked through, and as he entered the room, he came face to face with Sabrina.

Okada inclined his head and Sabrina's bow was only a fraction lower. Okada's face remained expressionless. Heiko gave the traditional bow to a superior. Everyone else bowed from the waist.

Although everyone had their eyes averted, they saw and were curious. She had greeted Okada as an equal in rank.

Yoshi took Sabrina by the elbow which gave a considerable rise to her eyebrows, and eased her a little aside while Kiritsubo greeted Okada.

"Sabrina, you were rude," he told her, concerned, scanning for Okada's reaction. He was hoping no offence was taken, since Sabrina was his guest. "They're touchy about precedence."

"Yoshi, Love. Who do you think I am? I am the representative of the Antares. Ergo I'm a head of state. The Antareans are a unique and cherished alliance member. Don't you ever forget that," she added low, in a terse tone of voice.

Yoshi gave her a startled look.

Heiko came up to Sabrina. "Zataki informed me that dinner is served. Let us go in." He offered Sabrina his arm. Okada led Kiritsubo into the dining room.

It was a state dinner. A liveried attendant stood behind each guest. There were ten courses. It was expected for everyone to eat from each dish. Sabrina took only tiny bits from each course offered.

Heiko turned to her during the dinner, and to her surprise used Kreala, the language of Acheron, and said, "You have drawn attention to yourself. That's not like you."

"But Okada expected it." When Heiko looked at her with a frown, she said, "Why do you think you were asked to invite me?"

Heiko colored. She had been perceptive enough to deduce it.

After they were finished with dinner, everyone was invited back to the reception room.

Kiritsubo came over to Sabrina, who standing off to one side, looked at a painting. Her fan fluttered and she seemed to be nervous. "Lady Sabrina, will you excuse me if I see to my other guests?"

"Of course Kiritsubo, I will be fine."

She knew she wasn't here just to enjoy the party. Okada had a certain scheme in his mind. If she only knew what it was? She turned away from the painting to look at the guests and to observe.

Sabrina noticed an elderly dowager, languidly fanning herself, who was watching her covertly; then, she leaned over to say something to the dowager standing beside her.

Sabrina, being curious because of the condescending manner, tentatively skimmed through their surface thoughts. She was surprised, they thought of her not only as an off-worlder, but a barbarian. Someone of no worth, nor culture; the two were repelled by her golden hair, and pretended to shudder at her green eyes. But what they said and what they thought were two different things. They were envious of her golden hair, and amazed at her green eyes. But it wouldn't do to admit anything not of Daugave. There was danger, and there were changes ahead.

The first dowager said, "Soon our world will be free of them."

"Yes, soon the Shining One will reign over Daugave, and life will be back the way it used to be, and all the foreigners will have left. They will not pollute our ways anymore," the second dowager assented.

"Have you heard the Prophet's speech last week?"

"My sons did. They said he was very inspiring. He moved their hearts with fire and patriotism."

"Yes, our prophet has done his work well," the first dowager said.

"Like yeast in the bread. You add a little and it works itself through the whole loaf."

Another woman joined them. "You should not be talking about things like that," she reproved, having heard the last sentence.

"She doesn't speak our language. I heard her speak that foul speech they call Galactic," the first dowager said.

"But I heard her talk in another language to the Lord Heiko," the new comer warned. "Maybe she is just pretending not to understand.

"Let's go outside into the garden," the first dowager suggested.

Sabrina's mind followed them and they talked about last week's meeting where the Prophet promised that the Shining One would soon appear and overthrow the present government. The picture she gleaned of the Prophet was that of a grim looking old man in his seventies.

"Sabrina, are you woolgathering?" Yoshi asked, coming up beside her. "You have been standing here like you're rooted to the spot."

"Who are those two old biddies out there?" Sabrina asked, pointing to the two dowagers.

Yoshi grunted. "Those two are the old glory days. They always talk about the good old days like it was Daugave's golden age. Their fathers had been prominent men in the government then."

"I see. Where's Okada?"

"Last I saw him, he was in the library."

But when they entered the room, it was empty.

At least three sides of the room were covered with books. In the center were several divans with side tables and deep comfortable chairs.

But against the fourth wall, in a glass case, lay a Japanese guitar, a Samisen.

Sabrina walked to the case and opened it. Turning to Yoshi, she asked, "May I play it?"

"Yes. You're the only one I will entrust my treasure to."

She carefully took it out, and sitting down on one of the divans, she gently strummed the plectrum across the strings.

"You play, or just keep it tuned?"

"I play, sometimes."

Sabrina bent over the Samisen and began playing a children's tune she had learned as a little girl while living in Japan.

Heiko walked by the window, stopped and looked into the room.

"Don't put it up. Let me get Lord Okada."

Sabrina, lifting her head from the instrument, only smiled at him.

In a short while Heiko was back with Okada.

"Now you can play. Yoshi, what's the song Kiri likes?"

"Cherry Blossoms, Sir." Looking at Sabrina, "Can you play it?"

"Yes. It was one my mother's favorites."

She played and then sang and soon drew an audience.

The two dowagers came in too, and sat against the far side of the room. They listened politely. With Okada being in the room, and obviously enjoying the music, prevented them from saying anything uncomplimentary.

After she finished the song, Sabrina put the Samisen back into its case.

"Lady Sabrina," Okada said, "I thank you for gracing this evening. As a return I would like to show you a special flower which only blooms in the night when the moon is full. I would be honored if you accompanied me out into the garden."

Sabrina laid her hand lightly on Okada's offered arm, and let him lead her through the archway into the garden.

The garden was beautiful in the moonlight. She could see Yoshi's hand in it. A path meandered beside a tiny pool. Ornamental trees were laden with green and yellow fruits. A fountain tinkled sweetly and mingled with the sleepy sound of a bird. Insects hummed. As they crossed over the pool on a small, vaulted bridge, Sabrina stopped with a long drawn out "Oh. A Japanese Teahouse," she whispered, awed. Then she inhaled deeply. The night breeze carried the scent of the flower's intoxicating fragrance.

"Come," Okada said gently, and smiled at her. She had lifted her face to the moon and even in the moonlight he could see the dimple deepening. She was smiling. Ah, if I could just tell her how much I like her. How much she awes me. But he knew it wouldn't do. He led her to a miniature tree. It contained only one white flower. "It only blooms every seventh year and only for one night," Okada informed her. To honor the occasion, Heiko is giving this party to share this miracle."

"Thank you for sharing it with me. It was a precious moment." Sabrina said, her voice husky.

He looked at her and hated to break the moment.

"What have you gleaned? I hope you have listened to some of the conversations?"

"Oh, Okada," she said, disgusted. "This was so beautiful, and you had to break the spell. Did you have to bring up business?"

"Yes, Sabrina. I had to. Now report."

"The glory day dowagers," Sabrina said, glancing at Okada who gave her a surprised look.

"Yes, we know them," he told her.

"They'd like for the old days to return and the off-worlders to disappear. There's a prophet who is promising just that. He is talking of the Shining One who will rise, and everything will be back the way it used to be.

"They're talking about the overthrow of the present government," Okada said grimly. "It began very insidiously, with a murmur here and there, disaffections and slight innuendoes; a change back to the old way of dressing and the revival of an old religion."

"Do you know who the prophet is?"

"No. We can never get hold of him. He is very elusive. We don't even know what he looks like."

"I can help you there. He is an old man in his seventies. I can draw you a likeness."

"That is what we need. Now we can at least find him. Someone is bound to know him."

"I will have it on your desk tomorrow. But who is the Shining One?"

"A myth."

"Sabrina!" It was Yoshi coming over the bridge.

"We're here, Yoshi," Sabrina called back.

Okada took Sabrina's hand and to her utter amazement, kissed it. "Thank you for sharing this enchanted moment with me. I have to go back. There's always more work than I have hours in the day." He turned to leave, but Yoshi's hand stayed him by touching his sleeve.

"Lord Okada, Sir. I would be honored if you could come to a Tea Ceremony tomorrow evening."

"A Cha-No-Yu?" Sabrina asked.

"Hai," Yoshi replied.

*　　*　　*

Yoshi took great care to prepare for the ceremony. First he scrubbed the floor and dusted the walls to make sure the Tea House was spotless. Then he placed five cushions at equal distance around a low table. In the center of the table was a crystal bowl containing only one Tea-Rose for simplicity. Then he placed several candles, seemingly at random, in different places. The effect was a play on shadow and light. He also prepared appetizers arranged in a pleasing pattern. When everything was ready, he went into the house to bathe.

Yoshi had always been foremost Japanese, even if he grew up on the Antares. His parents instilled the Japanese culture deeply in him. Especially, during the Earth's upheavals when they had been forced to live in the crowded conditions of a spaceship. His parents descended from an ancient line of Samurai. His grandfather had been a general.

Yoshi was ten years old when he came on the Antares and selected Ayhlean, who was Chinese, as his big sister. She had encouraged Yoshi to learn about Japan. Ayhlean in many of her ways was very Chinese, and proud of her ancient heritage.

Before deciding on a tea ceremony Joshi had talked it over with Kiritsubo and explained that the occasion was to honor Heiko and Okada, but especially Sabrina who he knew would understand the meaning of the gesture.

Shortly before his guests arrived, Yoshi lit the charcoals he arranged in a pyramid and went back to the house.

When his guests arrived, he conducted Okada and Heiko to the Tea House, and as they seated themselves on the cushions, Kiritsubo entered with Sabrina.

Joshi rose and greeted Sabrina with a deep bow. "I'm honored by your presence, Sabrina Mary Hennesee."

"Sabrina bowed to Joshi, but not quite as low, and then to Heiko and Okada before she seated herself on the cushion.

While the water boiled in a small kettle over the charcoal fire, Joshi explained the meaning of the tea ceremony, the Cha-No-Yu. Then he took five porcelain cups out of a bamboo basket. Using the traditional bamboo spoon he measured the right amount of tea, stirring the powder and water until it blended perfectly. Then he deftly poured the tea into the cups and replaced the kettle on its tripod. He added a spoonful of cold water to each cup, and with a bow, handed the tea to his guests. After everyone finished their cup, they handed them back. Yoshi repeated the ritual three times, and, after carefully washing the cups, he put them back into the basket.

After a gentle cough, Sabrina asked Heiko, "Has Joshi ever talked to you about the history and culture of his country?"

"No," Heiko said astonished. "We assumed he's from the same world as Captain Thalon."

Sabrina chuckled. "Let me assure you the Antareans are a people. But at the very beginning we all came from different corners of our world. And I say this for your ears only." She looked pointedly at Heiko, and then at Okada. "This is also for the Lady Kiritsubo. I noticed the prejudice shown toward Joshi because he is an off-worlder, so I will tell you something of his background.

Joshi comes from an ancient lineage. His people are not much different then the people here. For a long time his country was closed territory because they did not like their ancient culture polluted. And they thought themselves quite civilized. And so they were. Just like the people of Daugave. When you married Joshi," Sabrina said, turning to

Kiritsubo, "you did not marry beneath your station. Joshi comes from an old and illustrious family. I've seen the lineage of his ancestry. It is impressive."

"Sabrina, I married Joshi because I fell in love with him," Kiritsubo said.

"I know. But I just wanted your father to know," Sabrina said, looking at Heiko.

Heiko's eyes smoldered at her. "I arranged the marriage between Omi Hirejoshi and my daughter. I talked to Sargon, and I did ascertain Yoshi's ancestry."

Not daunted by Heiko's stare, Sabrina said, "Then you understand when I say that Joshi is Samurai?"

Joshi gave a short cough, then bowing to Heiko and Okada he said, "Sabrina is also Samurai."

Sabrina gave a low, warning grunt, and Joshi broke up laughing. "You don't have to take it that far," he told her.

"The joke is between the two of you?" Okada asked Yoshi.

"Yes Sir. I think we better leave it at that," Yoshi said.

"Has Sabrina told you that there is a conspiracy to disrupt the meeting of the Alliance Council? The Altruscans were suspected, and our investigation went that way. But thanks to Sabrina's information, we know now that it is a domestic affair," Okada told him.

"No, she had not had time to inform me. But then, she never does," Joshi added aggrieved.

"Little brother, I'll let you know when you need to know," was Sabrina's rejoinder.

Chapter 7

Sabrina was on duty on the Antares, and before her shift was over, Soraja handed her a note telling her to meet Martel on Acheron.

"It came through channels," Soraja told her.

"Okay, as soon as Chandi comes, I guess I'll pack and leave."

"You know what this is about?"

"No, I don't."

"Who's Martel?"

Sabrina's eyes crinkled as she looked at Soraja. "A friend of mine."

"What kind of friend?" The crinkling about the eyes had not escaped Soraja.

"I will introduce him to you, someday. Maybe."

The doors to the lift opened and Chandi came on the bridge.

"Hey, Chandi, Sabrina's going on an assignation," Soraja told him.

"Does Sargon know about this?" Chandi asked.

"Chandi lay off," Sabrina told him. "Lieutenant, you have the bridge."

"Aye, Captain, I have the bridge. She's not going to tell us who he is," he told Soraja.

"I think there's something mysterious going on, "Soraja whispered sotto voce back.

By now the whole bridge was listening in.

"All right, you two have your fun," Sabrina told them and left, using Spitfire to fly to Acheron.

*   *   *

Sabrina met Martel at Acheron's Port of Entry. When she saw him walking toward her, her whole face lit up with a bright smile.

"Martel!"

"Hi, Sabrina," he said in English. As they interlaced their fingers, their barriers came down. He reached out for the familiar presence that was her, and she tightened her fingers on his hand. The touch, the meeting of their eyes, made Sabrina feel as warm and comforted as if she'd lain in his arms.

"It's been some time. I missed you," she told him.

"I'm glad. I love you too."

Reluctantly she disengaged and pulled her feelings back. "What's all this about?"

"You don't know?"

"I only got a note telling me to meet you on Acheron."

"We're going on a mission. I'll fill you in later. What kind of formality do I have to go through?"

"Lady Thalia has in all probability taken care of everything."

Sabrina knew Martel had never been on Acheron proper, so, suppressing a grin, she led him out of the building. There were throngs of people milling about the huge plaza.

Martel looked around and suddenly let out a gasp. He pointed to a carriage drawn by two horses standing at the foot of the steps. "My goodness, what's that?"

"What are you talking about?" Sabrina inquired, innocently

"That contraption," he said, still pointing.

"Oh, that. It's our conveyance into the city."

"You must be kidding." He looked at her and perceived her suppressed mirth.

"You get conveyed inside of this?" Sabrina told him.

"Having fun at the expense of your old man?" Martel asked, suspiciously.

"Hardly," Sabrina said rather too quickly, trying to stifle the chuckle rising in her throat.

When Martel entered the ancestral home of the Sandors, he looked around. "Wow, that's a house," he said in English. Turning to Sabrina, "How do you fit in here?"

"As I told you before, I sort of got adopted," she told him. When he gave her a questioning look, she amended, "The Lady Lahoma thought to do a little exploiting for the good of her house. In many ways it backfired on her. But she still enjoys my company whenever I can come here. Joran is her son," Sabrina added.

"Meaning what?"

"There is regard for Joran, but not the love he had hoped for. He belongs to my house."

A side door opened. Startled, Sabrina took a step back. She had not expected to ever see Machir Aram again. Since he could not retreat, he stood, holding a submissive posture.

"Sabrina, sometimes it is expected to be forgiven," Lady Lahoma said. She had entered the house through another door, coming from the courtyard.

Sabrina turned to look at her. "Lady Lahoma, something's may be forgiven, but never forgotten. Tell your grandson to go about his business."

Sabrina turned her back as he passed with his face averted. Only when the door closed behind him, did she turn back to Lahoma.

"You came early, I did not expect you for another week," Lahoma said, inquisitively staring at Martel.

"Seems I have gotten orders, I only came to tell you that I can't stay and to say goodbye. Until next time, take care of yourself." She went to Lahoma, taking her hand as it was her right, and kissed the inside of her palm.

"If you are loath to introduce your companion, at least stay so I don't have to eat by myself," she said, aggrieved.

"You mind?" Sabrina asked, looking at Martel.

"Nope, I'd like to share your table," he told Lahoma, offering her his arm.

"I think the more I see of him, the more I'm going to like him," she commented, amused, looking back at Sabrina following behind.

"That's just old age. It has a mellowing influence," she told Lahoma tartly.

"You haven't lost your bite, yet."

*   *   *

Leaving Port City they hired an air-car and flew out to the Space Port. Martel informed her that he had taken the liberty of including Spitfire into his scenario. "We might need its special effect,"

"I see. Now what's our script?"

"You're suppose to be my slave, and I'm the master," he teased her.

"Fat chance!"

"Not entirely my idea, but that's the script."

"You better explain."

"There's a mole in the Alliance. Too many secrets were leaked. Sometime ago Heiko and Commander Melkan screened everyone by supplying partially wrong information. It has gotten to whoever is paying for the information. Guess who the mole is?"

"Doeros," Sabrina replied instantly, and without surprise.

"So they said you told them. Now we need to find the other end of this trail. We will backtrack from Sheitan. Lots of information can be gathered there."

"And, what's my role?" Sabrina asked with some insistence. She hoped the master, slave thing was a joke.

"You're going to be my woman."

Her tart reply to this was, "Not a very original script."

"I know, but it always works. You think you can play it?"

"I can, but don't like it."

"Also, when I take on a role, I never fall out of it, not even in private. Unbeknown, you can be under surveillance. So remember, the role will be played until the end, no deviation, not even in bed."

She looked at him and said icily, "Oh, the master requires bed-time stories?"

"Would be out of character if I didn't."

"What's your character supposed to be?"

"All around bad guy, thief, murderer, etcetera."

"And me?"

"Someone I'm keeping alive to pay back a slight. Maybe you spit in my face. Also your face has to be altered, especially your green eyes. I have drops that will diffuse your eye color. And some drug that will make your hair fall out. Let's see what else I can do to you."

"Martel!" the alarm she felt registered in her voice.

Before he could answer, the air-car angled down beside Spitfire. Noting Sabrina's absentmindedness, he pointed out of the window. "We have arrived," he told her.

Her mind again tried to scan him to see if her senses would register some impression. She was halfway out of the car when it registered. Holding on to the door, she turned to stare at him from across the car's roof. Now she knew what the little prod in the back of her mind had tried to tell her. She saw that Martel had guessed her revelation.

"You are a Chamaeleon," she accused him. It wasn't that they change color, but their personality, and sometimes their appearance. They were excellent actors, whatever the role, they became the character.

"Only in part; like you, I'm a mutant. I only guessed what I am very recently. What else I am, I don't know."

Sabrina quickly came around the car and taking him by his shoulders looked searchingly into his face. "I have met Chamaeleons, Chantar sometimes employs them. I should have recognized it. Before we go on this mission, I want to see the real Martel otherwise it's a no go."

"Sabrina, you have seen me. This is who I am. I told you that I love you, that's real; although, you might forget it. I want you to remember whatever happens, I love you. Then, I don't want to give an account to your sons, or even Sargon." As he looked at her, his mouth broke into a lopsided grin.

"As your so-called slave, do I have to do favors for someone else?"

"Sabrina, that's something I would never ask of you. That's the only time I will allow you your disappearing trick. Use your PSI ability carefully; someone else might be scanning you. Also, no breaking into my mind even if the house is on fire. You understand?"

"This script is a stacked deck, and you know it."

Chapter 8

When they approached Sheitan, Sabrina's beautiful green eyes were now only dark opaque smudges, and she didn't have a hair on her body. She walked cowed in a stoop, with a malicious expression on her face when she thought no one was watching. He called her Lepra. Martel's behavior had also changed. He wasn't physically cruel to her, but his behavior had become harsh and derisive.

When contacting the Space Port, he called himself Mendes, and the ship Boots. He was told to circle in a holding pattern until instructed otherwise. After half an hour, instructions to land were given. When they exited the port, a man was waiting outside for them.

"Hey, Brog," Mendes called to him. "Are you the welcoming committee?"

"The boss wants to see you, and fast."

"All right, hold on to your shirt."

"What's with the broad?"

Martel reached back, grabbing Sabrina by the ear," This thing here, she goes where I go. You understand? I like to keep her around, you know."

"Ransom?"

91

"More than that; revenge." He said the last word with relish, and with a very repulsive grin.

Sabrina was roughly shoved into the transport, and with Brog in the driver's seat, they sped off.

The boss was a nabob of Sheitan, and living a very opulent life style. His villa was huge and elaborately built. Tasteless junk, Sabrina thought, as they mounted the steps to an ornate front door. After Martel was shown into a reception room, his posture became even more swaggering. They approached an enormously fat man, sitting on a raised dais on a huge overstuffed couch and surrounded by bodyguards.

"I see you're back. What brings you here this time?" he asked, grimacing until his eyes were almost hidden in the fat folds of his face.

"Carr, as always you're oozing charm. I came because I'd like to do a little business. And I know you like exquisite and rare things."

As his greedy eyes raked over Sabrina, Martel said, "Uh, uh, wrong. Not this one."

"Then what do you have?" he asked, trying to hide his avarice.

Martel slowly reached into the pocket of his tight trouser and carefully pulled out something wrapped in cloth. He prolonged the unfolding, tantalizing the fat man. When the cloth was removed, there were four perfect emeralds lying in his hand.

There was a sharp intake of breath, "What you want for them?" he asked, barely able to hold his hands in check

Martel had a perfidious smile on his face. "Depends on what you have to offer. Right now, I'm buying information?"

"What kind of information?"

"Information that is wanted in high places."

"What do you mean?"

"There's someone buying important information. I only want know who it is. If you can get me that, the four emeralds are yours."

"Mendes, you're treading on dangerous ground. What you want can cost you more that you're willing to pay."

"That would be my problem." Martel stepped backward, and stumbled over Sabrina, who had remained silent, cowering at his feet. "Stupid bitch," he said, kicking her butt.

When he turned to leave, "Carr said, "Why don't you stay. I'm having a party tonight."

Martel knew the reason he was invited was because Carr didn't want to loose sight of the emeralds. This played very well into his hands, because he wanted Sabrina to have time to go through Carr's computer files.

One of Carr's bodyguards summoned a servant. "His Excellency would like for you to prepare a room for his guest," the servant was told.

Martel was assessed, and Sabrina dismissed. "Follow me," the servant said haughtily.

Martel was turning to do just that, when he noticed Sabrina still sitting on the floor, playing with her fingers. "Lepra, I'll kick hell out of you if you don't come along."

She rose dispirited, and still cowering, slowly followed him.

Unobtrusively, Martel checked the servant's fingers. Sabrina was right, he was an Altruscan, and maybe not the servant Carr imagined. It might do well to keep on eye on him. He made a mental note to check it later.

The room offered them was poorly furnished, Sabrina couldn't forgo a grin after she entered, but said nothing.

Martel showered and cleaned up. She had to stay with him, even when he engaged in a more private activity. When she wrinkled her nose, he threw a brush at her, barely missing her head. After that he laid down to rest.

Sabrina went into meditation. Letting herself drift, she carefully probed, but her mind picked up no one with any PSI ability. Her probing became more direct. She picked up the diverse thoughts emanating throughout the house. The thoughts were not happy ones. Most had to do with greed and violence. Carr was ruminating on how to get the emeralds away from Martel, without having to exert himself, was also contemplating a business deal that had to do with Anshar. She also found out that he conducted most of his imported business from his villa.

Going to the party, Martel left Sabrina locked in her room. When she sensed no one in the area of Carr's office, she appeared there. Having gathered the access number from Carr's mind, she engaged the computer. According to his files, his business dealt in import-export and from precious gems to drugs to slaves, also weapons; especially weapons outlawed by the Alliance. An anagram kept popping up throughout his major business transactions. Carr was exceedingly wealthy. She down loaded all his files onto the computer on Spitfire.

Sabrina had just returned when Martel came back, followed by one of Carr's servant. "Go with him," he commanded.

The servant led her to the more lavish section of the house, and to Carr's bedroom. Sabrina kept her face bland, and when Carr entered, she stood with her eyes averted. A woman came in. "Clean her up," she was told curtly.

Oh, that's where the wind's blowing from, Sabrina thought.

She let the woman lead her into the bath, and thoroughly enjoyed her ministrations. She was bathed, and had oil massaged into her body. When she reentered the bedroom, Carr was already in the bed, and motioned for her to come.

Obediently she lay down beside him. Without preamble he began very ineptly to paw her body. Gritting her teeth she was barely able to tolerate it. When she noticed his arousal being quite well in progress, she began reaching into his mind, leading him into a hypnotic sleep. From there, she let him spin his own sexual fantasy.

Slowly she rose from the bed and looking down at him, shuddered. Quickly she visualized the interior of Spitfire and disappeared.

She slept through the night. For most of the next day she remained in the craft, part-time working on the anagram, and also, the business deals she had gathered from Carr's files. Later on, using what little shapeshifters ability she had, she forced the hair on her head to grow. What she got was only a little fuzz. But it was enough. She colored it black. Then she began to alter her facial features, making them appear a little rougher. She examined her face, and then her breasts. After rearranging them, it was difficult to tell which sex she belonged to. And, she still didn't have any eyebrows or lashes.

Changing from the bathrobe she wore into a black, tightly fitting outfit, she left Spitfire to go into town to look for Martel. It was the fourth place she entered when she saw him sitting dejected at the bar. Sidling up the next stool, she watched him for a while as he glumly sipped at his drink.

"You look like you lost something," she finally said to him in Galactic.

He growled and turned away.

"Not very friendly, are you?"

Slowly he turned around. She had her head resting in her hand, her faces was unreadable as she looked at him.

Recognition dawn when he noted the absence of eyebrows and lashes, S . . ."

"Seb," she injected quickly

"Hello Seb, I thought I lost you."

"Proverbial bad penny," she told him. "What happened?"

"I accused Carr of kidnapping you. I nearly tore his house apart looking for you."

"What did he say?"

Martel's dark face became even darker, and he scowled. "He wanted you back as much as I did," he told me. Then anger flashed in his dark eyes, making them hard, glaring like obsidian. "You hellcat," he hissed, then grabbed her by the collar and pulled her toward him, "I told you, you could use your disappearing trick if he asks you to go to bed with him."

Sabrina gave him an uncomprehending stare.

"He gave me a blow by blow description of what he did to you and what you did to him."

Suddenly comprehension dawned and she began to laugh. "I'm not responsible for his imagination."

He stopped in mid motion, releasing her collar, "You didn't?"

"Of course not."

"It was all his imagination?"

"Mendes, you ass. What makes you think I would stay around with that tub of lard."

Martel laughed, his relief clearly audible. "I tortured myself, thinking of you in his bed . . ."

"You have a lot to learn about me," she interrupted him, and nailed him with an icy stare. "This script will never ever be resurrected," she said firmly.

"You don't like to play second banana," Martel said in English, teasingly grabbing her chin.

"My dear Mendes, they," giving the people in the room a meaningful look, "will suspect you of . . ." She let the last word hang in the air and walked off with an decidedly masculine stride.

Martel tossed a bill on the bar, and chuckling deep in his throat, followed her. Back on Spitfire, he asked, "Did you have time enough to riffle though his computer?" When she nodded assent, "What did you glean from Carr's files?"

"Carr is very rich and deals in anything saleable from flesh to weapons, to drugs. You name it. His business is far flung, but the thread always leads back to Voltar and Anshar. There was an anagram, I finally deciphered it. Does the name Armedes mean anything to you?"

Martel whistled through his teeth. "You're sure?"

"Yep".

"They are a large, powerful family in interstellar trait. But up to now we have considered them kosher."

"Well they might not be. What's Merca?"

"It's an airless moon, orbiting Raglan, a planet in the Orion's belt."

"The Orion Hegemony?"

"Could be. Let's have Melkan in on it."

"Why Melkan?"

"He works for Heiko, and coordinates all the information about the Orions and Altruscans."

Chapter 9

Sabrina keyed in the coordinates to Daugave, using Aldebaran as a navigational point before she engaged Spitfire's special effect.

Martel called Headquarters before landing, and both were met by a staff car. After arriving at the Alliance's Headquarters, they were intercepted by Melkan's secretary and immediately ushered into his office

Melkan rose. "You have solved the case already?" he asked, his eyes crinkling.

"No," Sabrina said, pursing her lips, "but we have an idea we would like to share with you."

"Please, do sit down," Melkan said, pointing to the seats in front of his desk. "Now, what have you discovered?"

"How familiar are you with the Armedes?" Sabrina asked.

"Humm. All we know about them is that they are very powerful. Very private. Not many outsiders can get in or even close. Most of the business transactions we could discover are legit. But that doesn't say much."

"No, it doesn't. One of the links I discovered lead from Sheitan back to Voltar. Carr is the key element linking the Armedes family with his trade. They are dealing in contraband, which are not only slaves and drugs, but illegal weapons.

"You have proof, or only suspect?"

"I have some prove," Sabrina said, handing him the computer chip with the information she had gleaned from Carr's computer.

"You know this is only a drop in the bucket?"

"Well, to do more we could use more information." Martel said, joining in for the first time.

There's a moon in the Orion we are interested in. We have noted some activities around it. Its star is in the outer belt; the planet's name is Raglan. Sometimes people with certain qualifications disappear there. We don't have enough evidence if their disappearance is tied in with the Orion Hegemony.

Sabrina and I are familiar with Raglan. We could go and see."

"No Martel, Miri and you. I will team up with Lara," Sabrina told him.

He looked at her. "Still mad about the slave girl script?"

"Nope. I think you'll be safer with Miri. We could work in two teams. Melkan, what's the story about Doeros?

"We have known for a long time that he is a mole. He has been useful to us." "What's Doeros goal anyway?" Martel asked.

"To break up the Alliance," Melkan told them.

"Then he is still diligently working for the Altruscans?"

"I don't think diligent is the word for it," Sabrina interrupted. "Last time I saw him; there was something else on his mind. He is contemplating changing his agenda."

"Are you sure?" Melkan asked.

"No. It's only an impression I got."

"Could you call Commander Miranda Vindilicii and Lara Ensor in, and we'll see about Raglan?" Martel asked Melkan.

"They are already here. I called them in case we had to rescue both of you."

"Martel, isn't it nice to be worried about?"

"We take good care of our best agents. Then we don't want to get cross with Captain Thalon," Melkan told her.

Sabrina laughed. "Let Martel and I work out something with Miri and Lara. After that, we'll get in contact with you."

"You have a suite in the hotel adjacent to here. I'll call Vindilicii and Ensor and they should meet you in the lobby."

*   *   *

The hotel lobby was crowed with people milling around, or standing by their luggage, but no Miri, no Lara. Sabrina and Martel walked up to the desk and asked for their key.

The rooms were spacious and luxurious. Sabrina looking around had a premonition that she was not going to have time to enjoy all this luxury. She found a note propped up on the desk saying, when you get in, call us, we're at this number.

Martel, looking over her shoulder, dialed, when Miri answered, he said "We just got in. Give us some time."

Sabrina looked questioningly at him.

"Well, there is a whirlpool in there. I decided we deserve to have some fun before meeting with the others. Don't you agree?"

Sabrina heartily agreed. Two hours later, Miri and Lara joined them. When the door opened, Sabrina's eyes were immediately drawn to the third in the party. He was not as tall as Martel, but more powerfully built. Also, he was of an undetermined species.

"Hello Tinian," Sabrina said surprised, greeting Miri's mate.

Tinian and Martel clasped hands and went off talking with each other while Miri went to the phone to order lunch.

"The two look like long lost brothers," Sabrina remarked to Lara.

She only got a cursory look, as Lara joined the men. Soon they were deep in a discussion. Miri, after having placed the order, sat sideways on the arm of Tinian's chair, listened intently.

When lunch came, instead of breaking up, they continued their exchange of ideas. Martel was filling them in on what he and Sabrina had discovered. Sabrina was more on the sideline, listening while eating. When the conversation came to a more personal interchange, she went to a small table strewn with brochures and began lazily leafing through them.

Suddenly she sat up. She had the beginning of an idea. There was a pleasure cruise leaving for Raglan, and it was today. Melkan had said that people with certain abilities had disappeared after embarking to Raglan. Idea and action were quickly coalescing. Unobtrusively she left the room and went back to the Headquarters building.

She asked to see Melkan, and was ushered into his office.

"Melkan," she said without a preliminary, "there's a pleasure cruise leaving for Raglan in an hour. I want to be on it. Can you get me a reservation?"

"What about Martel?"

"He will go with Miri and Tinian," she told him.

*   *   *

She would later explain things to Martel. Right now, it was important to her to follow her hunch. Only for a second did she consider that Martel might be mad, but she passed it off. She was a little disconcerted by Melkan's perceptive glance.

Some time ago Sargon explained to him that Sabrina's seemingly erratic behaviors were based on hunches, and that they had always paid off in the end. Sargon had asked that Sabrina be given a free hand in all she asked. So he was not surprised when she deviated from the planned course.

"You will have the boarding pass when you get there. Under what name do you want me to make the reservation?"

"My own, without the rank."

She left his office, humming to herself, her mind swirling around with ideas. Using her special account, she went shopping since the only clothes she had right now was her leather outfit. The rest was on Spitfire. And she knew she needed something much more fashionable for a pleasure cruise than she had in her meager wardrobe.

With only ten minutes to spare, she made the Space Liner. The stateroom was nice, it suited her well. She went to lay out her toiletry, and put away the new wardrobe she had acquired in such a hurry. She decided to dress in simple white slacks, pink blouse, and a short white jacket.

When Sabrina entered the dayroom, she paused until the steward could attend to her. The room was dotted with small, individual tables. She took a table toward the wall, and ordered a drink. Most of the passengers seemed to be well to do. There were a few whom she considered dandies living off women, or gambling. They were either good looking, or could be considered exotic. Several observed her, apparently assessing her availability or status.

She tried not to appear too eager for company. There was a band playing, and she sat back and listened to the music. Afterward, she went to the casino. She lost some, but won back slightly more than she had come on board with.

Next day, just to fit the character of a tourist, she asked about Raglan, its location, and a description of its tourist attractions. Later she struck up a conversation with a junior officer, letting it drop that she was an engineer on a holiday.

Two days later the Liner went in orbit around Raglan. Shuttles ferried the passengers down to the planet. At the Port of Entry, Sabrina was met by two men.

"Miss Hennesee?"

Sabrina turned. "Yes?"

"Would you please follow us?"

"Is something wrong?"

"No. Just a formality! We like to get it processed quickly so you can enjoy our tourist attractions."

"I hope it won't take too long," Sabrina said affably, and meekly followed them to an office.

Once there, someone from behind, put a cloth soaked in a narcotic over her mouth and nose. The last thing she felt was being carried off on a stretcher.

When she awakened, she was inside a ship's hold. There were rows on rows of berths with other beings lying shackled to them. Slavers, was Sabrina's first thought. I only hope it won't take too long. It stank; some had relieved themselves where they were lying. Many, especially women, were crying. Thank god, there were no infants. When the ship was underway, air ducks came on, and the air became a little more breathable.

The narcotic hadn't worn off all the way and Sabrina fell into a stupor, but she knew she was not on the ship anymore. When she came to again, she was roughly pulled from the berth, and prodded with a rod to follow the others. Cattle prod, Sabrina thought, when she was shocked with it. Before they entered a huge area with showers, their clothes was literally cut off of them. After the shower they were given coveralls, with a number in front and back. Then they were herded into a mess hall, and made to fall into a chow line. In the eating area were rows on rows of benches and tables. Sabrina sat down with her bowl full and ate every drop of it. The food was simple and not bad tasting.

Through all this, on a hunch, Sabrina had kept her mental shields up tight. She let only normal surface thoughts leak. Suddenly she felt a probing, it was clumsy, and she controlled what was gleamed from her. All the prober obtained was that she was appalled and frightened.

Later they formed a line and were being processed. When it was her turn, she was asked her name and occupation. She said that she was an engineer, and that she had received her diploma on Acheron. She was then separated from the others, and two guards took her to an office.

A man behind the desk gave her a cursory look. "You know how to take care of turbines and generators?"

"Yes, sir, I can. Any engine. Also environmental controls."

"Good, put her in engineering," he told the two guards.

After they arrived at the worksite, on old man came up to her and asked, "You the new engineer?"

"Apparently."

"The last one made a mistake and they took him outside."

"What do you mean?"

"Girly, there's no air and it's hot outside and you just boil away in a second. So don't make any mistakes. Then, looking at her closely, he said, "Around here's best to keep your thoughts to yourself."

"Yes Sir."

"I like your manners," he said. "My name's Asa."

"Thank you, Asa. What do you want me to do?"

Asa, being an old man, liked company. He took her under his wing, pointing out the overseers. "Don't want to mess with them. They're mostly murderers and cutthroats. Most of them come from Sheitan. They're not very nice to women. Better do as they ask, even if you don't like it. See that fat woman over there? She's a snitch. Don't tell her anything. It always goes back upstairs. She comes on nice and friendly like, fools some of them around here. Don't trust her. The others, they're just like me, trying to stay alive. We do the best we can. Anything else, they shove you outside."

"Where's this place?"

"Don't you know?"

"I was drugged."

"This is Merca, one of the moons around Raglan."

"And this place is dug into the rock," Sabrina asked.

"Shhh, we have company," he whispered.

A female approached them. As she came closer Sabrina noticed the small ridge on top of her head. Reptilian, she thought, and turning toward her, she waited silently, with a dull expression to her face.

The woman's face was flat, her nose coming to a triangular point with two openings which could be closed by a loose membrane. Her eyes were two contracted slits. Her hands ended in long sharp claws.

"Your name?"

"Hennesee."

"Come with me."

A manufacturing plant, Sabrina thought, as she entered a huge area. People from all corners of the Galaxy were working here; some were of a species she had never seen before. She kept her face expressionless as she walked past the work benches. One of the generators had quit.

"Fix it," she was told, curtly.

"Tools," Sabrina said.

"Tar, give her Geno's tool-set."

She was handed the tool box, and went to work, never giving the others another look. Within thirty minutes it was working again.

Throughout her shift there were minor breakdowns. The machinery was old and outdated. Unobtrusively, she looked around. The goods manufactured here were parts for engines or space crafts and weaponry. Some of the parts they should not have had access to. Looking down toward the far side, she noticed a large bay door standing open, and she saw the hull of a space craft.

At the end of her shift, Asa came by to show her to her sleeping cubicle. "Only because you are more valuable, you're given this privilege of a private room. I have to sleep with thirty others in one dormitory. Men and women all stacked together. Another thing, you'll get to eat again tomorrow morning."

"Only once a day?"

Asa nodded, and left.

When she opened the door, there was a cot, a table and a chair. Before she could close the door, one of the overseers, his foot in the door, prevented her from closing it.

"If I have time, I'll be coming tonight," he said.

Sabrina only looked at him, and after he removed his foot, closed the door, then jammed the chair under the doorknob. During the night she heard him try to open the door.

After the end of her next shift, when she came back, her table and chair were gone. So, before she went to sleep, she pulled the cot against the door. Next time she came back, her cot was gone, and the mattress was lying on the floor. She slept on the floor against the door. When he tried to remove her door, the reptilian woman, Sabrina had learned that her name was Nera, told him to put it back. Looking into the now empty room, she ordered him to bring the cot back. Sabrina standing inside the door, straightened up as Nera walked past her. She looked at Sabrina, her face stony and expressionless. Sabrina didn't move a muscle in her face, knowing that any acknowledgment would have been a mistake. She only gave back the same stare.

*   *   *

A week passed, and no opportunity presented itself yet to get at the computers. Sabrina planned that once she had accessed the Armedes operation, to send the information to Spitfire, Spitfire was set up to receive the data on a certain frequency.

Into the third week, there was a break down in the environmental control. It involved computers. Sabrina was in business. When she crept up the small space of the crawl-way, she found the trouble. Sabotage! She hid the tell-tale signs.

After she came back out, "What did you find?" the supervisor asked.

"An electrical short. The conduit was worn. I'll fix it."

She had watched the men standing around and noticed a slight relaxing of tensions. So, they were sabotaging the installation.

Nera was asked to watch over her and she ordered wires from supply. While waiting for the wires, Sabrina checked the computer console, bringing up a schematic layout of the computer communication lines. Then she did a little sabotaging herself. Suddenly the screens went wild. The overseer came back, red faced and blustering, accusing Sabrina of messing with things she didn't understand.

"She didn't do any of these things," Nera defended her. "I was watching her the whole time."

So, Nera was on her side for what ever reason. Out of the corner of her eyes she saw Nera standing in the way so the overseer couldn't see what she was doing. Nera looked somewhat wane. Mottled, Sabrina thought, a little drawn around the mouth, and she wondered.

No one could fix the computer; the screens were still going wild. The wires came, and Sabrina climbed back up the crawlspace. Looking down, and when she saw that no one could see her, she went on until she found a room with a computer. She tied into the main computer. Using her skill, she broke into the stored data, and sorted out what she needed and sent it to the receiver on Spitfire. Then she did the same after she connected with the Armedes main computer on Voltar. After that she inserted an empty disk and recorded the whole layout of the station on it. Then she programmed that on her signal, the electronic screen protecting the facility would come down, also a complete environmental failure. She had just finished when someone walked in. She quickly hid the disk, and then hit the key sequence to restore computer functions throughout the complex.

"What are you doing here?"

"I was told to fix the break in the conduit, and I needed a schematic of the layout so I wouldn't connect the wrong wires."

"I thought the computers were not functioning."

"Oh, I fixed that, too. Somebody probably hit the wrong key," Sabrina said.

He went to the computer and entered the number on her coveralls. "You're an engineer. It doesn't show here that you're a Computer Service Engineer."

"Every engineer has to have computer experience. I thought you knew that."

"Don't get impertinent. Who's the guard assigned to watch what you're doing?"

"Nera."

He went to the intercom and told Nera to come.

When Nera entered, there was a small twitch to her eyes when she saw Sabrina.

"You watch her," she was told. "I'll get the overseer to see where she was supposed to be."

When he left, Nera said, "You screwed up for both of us."

"It's going be all right," Sabrina assured her.

"Well, it doesn't matter to me anyhow."

"What you mean?"

"In nine days, I'm going to be history."

"Why is that?"

"If I don't get back to my people, I'm not going to survive."

"Has that to do with how you look? Your skin seems to be mottled."

"Yes. I'll die if I don't mate, and I can't, nor would I do it here."

"Nine days you said? Don't give up hope, no matter what the situation looks like. You understand?"

"Yes, I hear you, but you're talking out the other side of your mouth."

The man came back with the overseer of Sabrina's work shift.

"You had no authorization to be here. And you're quite some way from where you suppose to be. What have you been doing?"

"Like I told you," Sabrina explained patiently," I needed to see a schematic to fix the break. And I also followed the crawl space to check on the other wiring. I found several worn spots."

Suddenly the door burst open and Sabrina's nostrils flared. It took all her discipline to keep her face from giving herself away.

"Ah, I see you found her. Hello, Sabrina."

"Hello, Garth," Sabrina said. They had met before, but not under very happy circumstances for Sabrina. She had never felt so humiliated and been so degraded as during her experience with him. Miri had finally located and rescued her.

"I see you haven't forgotten about our encounter."

"No. It was memorable enough," Sabrina conceded.

"This time, my dear, you won't get away." He said it almost pleasantly.

"What do you have in mind?"

"You'll see."

The intercom sounded and Garth went to answer it. "Have you found her yet?" a female voice asked.

"Yes."

"I want to see her."

"I don't think so," Garth told her. "I'm going to take her outside right away. She's full of tricks. I won't let her get away this time." Turning to Sabrina, "I would like to prolong this rendezvous, but I have learned not to trust you."

He prodded Sabrina through the door and into an elevator. When they exited, Sabrina recognized it as the receiving area where she had first entered.

Several individuals were waiting in front of a gigantic metal door. One was a woman; probably the voice on the intercom.

"The least you could do is telling me what you have planned for me?" Sabrina asked Garth.

"I guess I could," he conceded. "You see, this is a moon; no atmosphere. It gets very hot during the day and very cold during the night. I didn't think you'd like to freeze to death, so I thought to let you out during the day." Outwardly his face remained composed, but his mind was seething. She had cost him dearly. He had been demoted, and his rivals had used it to reduce his family's standing within the clan.

"You know what you can do with your mother," she told Garth, vehemently.

As an answer, he shoved her through the door. She looked back and gave him a nasty sign. He watched as she walked slowly down the rock-hewn passage. At the end it made a turn, and glaring sunlight blinded her. The last thing she heard was the slamming of the door. Quickly, before her air ran out, she visualized the interior of Spitfire.

Materializing, the first thing she did was to draw a deep breath. Then she realized Spitfire was still sitting on the tarmac on Daugave. She went to the computer and played back the data. She smiled. She had precisely what she needed.

After she had all the information sorted out, she contacted Melkan and asked him to send a staff car.

"Sabrina, you gave us a scare," he scolded her as soon as she came through his door.

"I have what you need to close down the Armedes operation. They are building a space ship, with several attack vessels, like my Spitfire. Also, someone used the computer to write out a plan to disrupt the Alliance. I think it will make interesting reading. Also, the Altruscans think I'm dead. So, Doeros better not find out that I'm still alive and alert them that my demise was erroneous."

"I see. What are you going to do now?"

"Hummm." Sabrina hummed, scratching the top of her head. Then she let a strand of hair glide through her fingers. It has grown back nicely, she thought. Looking straight at Melkan, "I'm going to see my boys. No," she amended. "I have to keep a promise first."

"What's that?"

"I promised Nera I would help her. When are you going to have the people lifted off Merca?"

"As soon as I contact the Minoan. She's in the vicinity."

"Well, could you do it now?"

"Sabrina, you're a pest."

"I know. But Nera has only seven days. If I don't get her home, she'll die."

"Who's Nera?"

"Oh, I haven't explained. Nera, well she's reptilian, and she's molting right now. If she' not able to mate, she'll die. She's the only one of her species still alive at the compound on Merca. The others, not wanting to bear their young into slavery, opted to die. By the way do you have any idea where she comes from?

"She didn't tell you?"

"We didn't have much time for conversations. She didn't inform on me. And in her way, she protected me. So you see, I feel obligated to help her."

Melkan looked thoughtfully at Sabrina. Before he had granted Sabrina's enlistment into the Special Forces, he had a lengthy conversation with Thalon. Her tantrum on the Trefayne had not endeared her to the Space Command of the Planetary Alliance.

Melkan's impression of Thalon was that of a cat purring when he spoke of her, as if he enjoyed her immensely. Now he knew why. She was unconventional, with a spontaneity that was startling at times. But for all her idiosyncrasies, she was thorough and very competent in all she did. Thalon's advice had been to give her all the leeway she needed. He reached for his console and brought up the solar system. "They're still pastoral with few industries. They're pre-flight. We have had only initial contact. I think it was Doeros' meddling that brought them to the Orion's attention."

Sabrina looked at the configuration on screen. "Taking it from Earth, they would be in the southern hemisphere. I know," she suddenly said, "the Southern Cross. I have been in that sector."

It was close to Lara's hideaway. She remembered seeing the yellow dwarf with eight planets, but never found the time to investigate. But she didn't tell Melkan this.

While Sabrina was talking, Melkan contacted the Minoan, and ascertained their position. He told their Captain to expect Sabrina, while handing her the coordinates. "Now you're going to pop out again," he said in mock exasperation. "Some day I hope you'll stay long enough to have a conversation."

Sabrina's eyes crinkled as she looked at him. "Someday, I promise, we'll have a date." She rose, waved goodbye to him, then she whirled and sped out of the door.

* * *

Spitfire took her to the Minoan in no time. The ship's commanding officer, whom she had never met before, introduced himself as Captain Brolan. She noted that he was somewhat reluctant to have her on board, because whatever the situation, she outranked him. She immediately assured him that she was not here to take his command; she was only on a rescue mission.

On the bridge, she asked him to bring up Merca on screen.

"Magnify," she directed. "See this dark spot," she said to the Captain, pointing. "This is the entrance to the dock. When we get closer, I will create a disturbance. Their screens will come down, and they will be very busy with a lot of malfunctions to their environmental controls. It should give you the opportunity to storm the installation." She inserted a disc into the console. "This is the layout of the place. I brought it along so you can plan your attack."

"Are you sure I'm handling the situation, or, are you taking over?" he asked her.

Sabrina gave him a surprised look, then, broke into a grin. "I know, I'm terrible that way. It's your ship, it's your command," she assured him. "I have been there and I know the layout. I'm only looking for two people, an old man and a reptilian looking female. Then I'm going to be out of your hair."

Before the Minoan showed up on Merca's screen, Sabrina sent a signal toward it. Suddenly the defenses came down and as the Minoan approached, there was no resistance.

At Brolan's questioning look, "They're busy trying to breathe," she explained, pulling her shoulders up to her ears.

The Minoan's assault team went in. They met with little resistance. Soon all the managerial team was separated from the slaves. When Sabrina spotted Nera and Asa on the screen, she pointed to the old man. "Captain, I want him and the woman next to him brought onto the bridge. I can't run the risk of someone seeing me. I'm supposed to be dead, and I'd like to stay that way."

Amazed, Captain Brolan looked at her. "Any other orders Ma'am?" he asked.

"I'm addressed as Sir, Captain," she informed him, deadpan. But the corners of her mouth twitched.

Brolan chuckled. "I'm glad I don't have to deal with you very often. You said you were leaving as soon as you have those two people?"

"Yes Sir. I'll be off your ship in a jiffy."

He looked at her sideways, but forestalled to ask what a jiffy was. He gave the order for Asa and Nera to be brought to the bridge.

Nera walked in first. When her eyes fell on Sabrina she looked startled.

"I told you to trust me," Sabrina said.

"I thought you were dead," she replied.

"Well, look again." Then, turns to Asa, "Where do you want to go?" she asked.

"Nowhere," he said his eyes dull and dispirited. "I was twelve when they brought me to Merca. There's no place for me to go to."

"If you like, I have a home. I could make a place for you."

For the first time, his eyes showed a spark of life. "You're not kidding?"

"Nope. Where you're going won't be a planet. My home is on a Worldship. Would that make a difference?"

"I don't care where, as long as it is home," he said, a broad smile breaking the sullenness of his face.

"Okay. Captain Brolan, he belongs to the Antares." Reaching into her shirt-pocket, she pulled out a small notebook, and wrote in English: This is Asa. He belongs to me. Sabrina. Turning to Asa, "You can give that to anybody on the Antares, and they'll know where to take you," she told him, then, turning to Nera, "I think we'd better leave. You only have seven days left."

"By then it will be too late," Nera said.

"Didn't I tell you to trust me?" To Captain Brolan, "The ship is yours." She saluted and left the bridge with Nera.

Down in the hangar deck, and after entering Spitfire, she turned to Nera, directing her to sit behind the pilot-seat. "You sit back there and strap in. Now listen carefully to what I tell you. When we leave this ship, and are well away from it, there will be a bell you'll hear. Close your eyes tightly. Whatever happens, don't open them. When you hear two chimes, you can look again, but not before. You understand? When Nera tried to say something, Sabrina interrupted, "You have to do as I say. You'll be all right." Then turning back to her seat, she opened a drawer, "I think I better put this on you, just to be safe," and pulled a blindfold out. "Now don't be frightened," she assured Nera. "I won't harm you. I'll only take you home."

"Why are you doing all this for me?"

"Because you didn't squeal on me, and I know you protected me several times from unwanted attention." She smiled at Nera, and for the first time touched her. Her skin was dry and raspy. It felt hot. "Are you always this hot?"

"No. This is because I'm getting ready for mating. If I don't, the fever will cause death."

"You're very interesting. I'm glad I don't have that kind of a problem," Sabrina grinned, leaning toward Nera, she put the blindfold on her.

Spitfire accelerated, to Mach 2, and the computer took over. The bell sounded once. Sabrina closed her eyes tightly. Once, out of curiosity, she had peeked, and never forgotten it since. What met her was nothingness, no familiar reference point to anchor her mind. Her whole world had gone out of focus.

"Were those two bells?" asked a meek voice from the back.

"Yes, you can take the blindfold off."

"I hate when I can't see," Nera explained.

"Look through the window. You see that planet below? That's your world. Now we have to find where to set you down."

Nera looked through the window. "Oh, how beautiful! But it looks like a ball."

Astonished, Sabrina turned to look back. "You've never seen . . . damn, that's right. Your people haven't developed flight yet. Well Nera, that's how your world looks from outer space." Then another thought occurred to her. "Nera, do you know where you are?"

"Yes. I understand now. But my people don't. They think only birds can fly," she said, and there was a rumble deep within her chest.

"I think you're laughing," Sabrina interjected.

"I thought I would never laugh again."

"Nera, watch the monitor, I'll bring up pictures of your world. Let me know if you see something that's familiar to you. Which continent, Nera?"

"I don't know," Nera said bewildered from the back. "I was very young when they took me from my people."

"What would you recognize?"

"My home."

"That's going to make it Jim Dandy. Let's see. Did you grow up in a city?"

"We don't have cities."

"What do you have?"

"Clusters."

"How can you tell one cluster from another?"

"The houses look different," Nera said suddenly, remembering. "All clusters have different geometric configuration. My cluster has round domes."

"That's something to go for." Sabrina fine-tuned the magnification of the sensors until she could see the individual houses. A cluster was probably a clan, Sabrina deduced. Clusters were interconnected houses of the same geometric designs. She could see squares, crosses, octagons, hexagons, but no round domes.

"Any landmarks around your cluster, like a mountain or a lake?"

"No. It's only flat. We have a lot of woods around though."

Sabrina flew down the small continent from North to South, frame by frame.

She was about to give up when Nera snorted, "Those woods," she pointed, "I recognize them. I forgot that they were planted in a round pattern to match our domes. That's my home, Sabrina. I just know it."

It was a large complex, surrounded by a high wall.

Sabrina had never known a lizard could be so exuberant, since her usual demeanor had been sad or taciturn. She looked back and smiled. "You're sure?" she asked.

"Yes. Yes. I'm sure."

"Okay. Now see this platform?" Nera nodded her head. "Stand in the center of it."

Nera walked over, stepping gingerly onto it. "Do I have to close my eyes?" she asked

"No. This time you can keep them wide open," Sabrina told her. "Goodbye Nera, I wish you happiness," Sabrina said and engaged the transporter. She watched Nera materialize on a grassy knoll and heard her shout. Soon she was surrounded by what Sabrina hoped were members of her family. She was embraced, so Sabrina knew she was safe. She laid in the co-ordinates for the Antares, and re-engaged Spitfire's special effect.

Chapter 10

As always she was touched and just slightly awed by the majestic view of the Worldship hanging in space in all its immensity. If she was truly honest, the sight always took her breath away. Contacting the bridge, she requested the opening of the antechamber to the smaller hangar deck where Spitfire was usually parked. Shutting the engine down, she glided easily into the antechamber, and after pressurization, the door to the hangar deck opened. After securing the ship, she barely cleared Spitfire's door, when someone jerked her off the steps and down to the floor by grabbing the front of her shirt.

Her arms immediately swung up to break the grip.

"Damn you," Martel shouted, enraged, and glared furiously into her face. "If you disappear on me like that again, I'm going to thrash the life out of you."

"If you ever grab me like that again, you're going to be dead," Sabrina retorted.

"Martel," Sargon said softly, "may I talk to you?" Turning to Sabrina, "You're dismissed," he told her.

She walked away sulky, looking back several times. She still hated Sargon's peremptory manners. Not wanting to disturb the household routine, she went to the cafeteria to grab a bite to eat. At this time of day it was usually empty, the noon break being over for most of the youngsters. After selecting her food, she sat down in her corner to eat. She liked to look at the fresco on the wall. A long time ago, she and Elisheba had painted it, trying to make the cafeteria look less cold and functional. Later, during one of her absences, some of the younger kids had changed it by adding some of their own touches.

A while later Martel walked in. After getting a cup of coffee, he came and sat down, beside her.

Sabrina made a face at him. "What did he talk to you about?" she asked, her eyes bright with a mixture of anticipation and laughter.

"He explained you to me," he said surly, cupping the drink in his hands.

Sabrina laughed out loud. "Good gracious me, are you any wiser now?"

"He has you pegged," he said, his humor surfacing in his eyes.

"After all these years, he should have learned something."

"I guess."

"Are you still mad at me?

"Would it make a difference?"

"No. I would still love you."

Martel chuckled.

"Where did you finally wind up?"

He knew what she meant. "I took an apartment," he told her.

"Why not my place?"

"Because, it is your place."

Sabrina looked at him. "I usually like to know how I stand. So a straight answer. Is there only a, you, or is there an, us?"

Suddenly his mouth widened into a toothy grin. "Are you proposing?" She looked at him, not sure if he was joking. She took a deep breath. "Are you sure? I don't want to second guess."

He reached across and took her hand. Kissing the inside of her palm, he looked deeply into her green eyes. "Are you sure you want me? I'm not Sargon."

"Sargon was a young girl's dream."

"Is there any formality, or do I just move in with you?"

Her smile was wide and illuminated her whole face with happiness. "There's only a computer entry. But if you like, we could have Sargon perform a ceremony."

Martel laughed. "No, I don't think so. Let's put the entry into the computer, then, I'll follow you home."

"I don't think you want to finish that coffee," Sabrina said pointing to his cup.

Martel looked at his cup. The coffee had gotten cold. It had only been a pretense. After they rose, he intertwined his fingers with hers. Together they walked from the cafeteria to Ayhlean's office.

When they entered, Ayhlean gave him a perfunctory glance, but rose when she saw Sabrina. "I heard you were back," she said as an opener.

"Martel, this is Ayhlean. Don't let her grouchy demeanor discourage you. That is only a professional mask she wears."

"And whoever told you to explain me?" Ayhlean said.

"I don't know. Sargon just explained me to Martel."

"Then what do I have to do with you?" was Ayhlean's comeback, her hands on her hips.

Sabrina walked over, and cupping her face with her hands, kissed her on the mouth. "Hello, Love, it's nice to see you again."

Ayhlean laughed. "Sabrina, you haven't changed. You're still incorrigible as always. Where have you been? I haven't seen you for a while."

"I was on a mission. Ayhlean, this is Martel Alemain. I want you to enter him as a member of my House.

Ayhlean looked at Martel with her eyes crinkling. "You didn't?" she asked, but looked at Sabrina.

Martel shrugged. "What was I to do? She proposed to me."

Ayhlean broke into a peal of laughter as she turned toward the computer and brought up Sabrina's family tree. "I guess you couldn't refuse." She grinned up at Martel. Turning to Sabrina, "Okay, where does he go?" she asked, pointing to Sabrina's name.

"Next to mine."

Martel looked at the screen. Knut and Sigrid Jensen were listed as Sabrina's maternal grandparents. Juliano Roncali and Kathleen Anna Theresa Hennesee as Sabrina's paternal grandparents. Anna Noel Jensen and Brook Hennesee as her parents. Logan was shown as a descendant of Sabrina and Sargon. Jason was entered as direct descendant of Sabrina. There was a special line that listed Joran Sandor ra Hennesee. Marlo and her daughter Margali were unrelated members of her house.

*   *   *

As Martel and Sabrina walked into the entrance hall his admiration of Pegasus was interrupted by a shouting match coming from the back of the house. Both stopped and looked at each other.

"Boy, you have a noisy household."

Sabrina shrugged and Martel followed her through the living-room and out into the rose-garden. But the shouting came from farther back, from behind the separating hedge. When they walked around it, Lanto and Asa were standing by the kitchen-garden yelling at each other, unaware of having an audience.

Sabrina clapped her hands and was met with a startled look.

"I'm glad you're back," Lanto said furiously. "This, this . . . individual, he is causing more trouble than I have ever experienced in my whole life."

"Okay, now what have you to say?" Sabrina turned toward Asa.

"I'm just trying to be helpful. But this ingrate doesn't understand that. I need something to do. He always shoos me out of his way," was Asa angry response.

"I see," she said turning back to Lantos who asked, "Who is he anyway, and why is he here?"

"I promised him he would have a home here, Lantos," Sabrina said simply.

There was a pause, and then a long "Ooohhh."

"You have a place you stay, Asa?"

"Yes, Medea gave me a room," and when he saw Sabrina's raised eyebrow he quickly added, "It's really nice."

"Then you are comfortable here?"

"Yes. Thank you. All I need is to have something to do."

"There are hobby shops on the Antares, or if you want to start a business, I could help."

"No Sabrina. I only want to be here. I only want to be home."

"Since the day he came, he just hangs around here. He never goes anywhere," Lantos complained.

Sabrina gave Asa a puzzled look. "Explain?"

"I only want to be home," Asa replied, looking obdurately at Lantos.

"I guess I understand." She remembered Asa telling her about being on Merca since he was twelve years old. And, that there was nowhere for him to go. Turning to Lantos, "Give him something to do, let him help you. Also, I think there's plenty to do in the house. I will talk to Medea. Sorry, family crisis," she said, turning to Martel.

"Don't mind. Quite interesting! Do you always pick up strays?"

Sabrina gave him a surprised look, then, broke up laughing. "I don't try to," she told him, after regaining her breath. "I sure hope you don't consider yourself just a pickup? Come, let's find a place for you." Then she gave him a mischievous look and broke up laughing again. "I didn't mean it the way it sounded," she apologized.

*   *   *

The next day with Sargon's help he selected furniture for himself. Martel had chosen the rooms over the entrance hall since it was connected by a private stairway to Sabrina's apartment. There was a slight look of amusement on his face when Sabrina made no comment on his choice. He was not prepared to share everything with her; not yet.

When she gave him a questioning look, he said, "Sabrina, I don't know much about families. I never had one. Your sons might not appreciate me assuming a position I don't have in their life. Then I don't want to cramp your style, and I don't want you to cramp mine."

She looked slightly taken aback, then, collected herself with a tiny smile. "I see. I never really thought about it. I just took it for granted that we would be together, you know, same bed and all."

"Did I stick my foot in it?"

"Well, like I said, I never really thought about it," she said a little too quickly. "I guess I can adjust." She gave him a shrug and walked away.

Martel instinctively started forward, then caught himself and bit his lip. This hasn't come off to well, he thought, but was not prepared to back down. Being a touch-empath, he needed privacy, a place to be alone.

In his leisurely fashion Martel mounted the stairs and slowly looked around. This would do. He walked around the place touching every thing in it and thought maybe home at last.

There was a knock on his door.

"Come."

Tomar entered, but before he could say something, hand clapping came over the intership's system.

"What it that?" Martel asked, astonished.

"Martel!" came Sabrina's voice from the bottom of the stairs, "do you want to come?"

"What's going on?"

"I don't know. The clapping is a call to assemble."

"All right!" Martel came down the stairs and followed Sabrina.

"Mostly when this happens there's a civil dispute and it can only be settled by vote, then the whole ship is called to the Queen's chamber. We are a close-knit community, and when this happens everyone comes, because they are nosy."

Kamila suddenly came around a corner. "Hey Sabrina," she said, then looking Martel, "Nice seeing you again."

"Oh, that's right I did introduce you to this the little pest I grew up with."

"That's a nice introduction. What's he going to think of me, humm?"

"I wouldn't worry about it," Martel told her. "I only take half of what Sabrina says serious."

"You do. You're smarter than most of us."

"Kamila, cut out the nonsense. What's going on?"

"I dunno. I came along, same as you."

"Well, let's go then."

"Boy, I just got to see you after all this time, and you want to get rid of me already. You know, I'm deeply hurt." Kamila pouted, looking put out.

"If that's a delaying tactic, it won't work. Let's go."

"Sabrina, I hope Martel can show you some manners. You're insufferable. But if you wish, you can go, I'll see you later."

Martel and Sabrina were the last to enter the Queens chamber, and they were barely through the door when a band started the wedding march.

Sabrina was startled and her hand flew to her mouth. Sargon suddenly appeared at her side and took her by the arm, Chantar pulled Martel's arm through hers. They were led to the middle of the chamber to a large table containing a wedding cake.

Sargon rang a bell. There was instant silence.

"Ladies and Gentlemen, I finally have the honor of giving Sabrina away," he intoned like a master of ceremony. "I have waited a long time for this moment and I'd like to savor it. Martel, I give Sabrina into your hands. Martel, this female, she is yours."

Sargon was paying her back for the time she had used the formula of relinquishing him to Chantar.

Chantar was barely able to hide her amusement. She whispered into Martel's ears, "Your response is supposed to be, Sargon, this female, she is mine."

"I don't know if I want her," Martel said in his best Mendes manner into the silence of the room.

There was a momentary look of shock on Sargon's face, but the crowd roared at Martel's reply.

Looking at Sargon, "Well that comes from getting too precipitous," Sabrina told him dead pan.

"Well, anyway, welcome back home," Sargon said, trying to regain his composure. "We all missed you. Let's have a party."

Sabrina turned to Martel barely able to contain her laughter, and after Sargon had walked away, she told him, "Thanks for not repeating the formula. You see, I used it to relinquish him to Chantar after Logan was born. He didn't like it."

She swaggered as she walked away seeking Sarah and Ayhlean. There was a wide grin on her face. His intended revenge had fallen flat.

First she met up with a giggling Kamila, who embraced her, hugging her tight. "I have never seen him so nonplussed," she whispered into Sabrina's ear. Their eyes were bright with amusement as they followed Sargon moving through the crowd.

Sargon, with his lower lip pushed out, thoughtfully watched Sarah and Ayhlean converging with the other two. Suddenly his irritation evaporated as he turned toward the band and asked for the drummer to begin the rhythm to the snake dance. He began clapping his hands as a signal for everyone to join in. He wanted to prevent the four from enjoying themselves on his account.

As soon as the drums started, the kids let out a whoop and formed the line for the dance, cheering at the adults for still standing on the sideline.

Walking up to Sargon, "What's going on?" Martel asked curious.

"The snake dance," Sargon said, his voice devoid of expression, dismissing the subject with a wave of his hand.

But Martel wasn't going to be side tracked. "Seems to mean something since everyone is joining in."

Sargon's smile widened into a grin. "Really, it doesn't mean anything. Sabrina and Sarah, to release tensions, started the bunny hop, as it was called then. But later with more people, it metamorphosed into the snake dance. It's a silly thing to do, but somehow forms a cohesion for this far-flung family, and the kids enjoy it."

The snake dance started slowly; the stomping feet matching the rhythm of the drum, becoming faster and faster in tempo as it went on. At Sargon's signal the drum stopped and the music for a dance much like the Virginia reel began.

The briefest of smiles flickered across Martel's face as he watched Sargon's delight in seeing Chantar enjoy herself with abandon. When he searched for Sabrina and found her reacting with the same joy. Chantar went to were Sargon was standing and grabbed him to join in the dance. The music was catching and Martel discovered his foot tapping to the rhythm.

When the reel ended, Sabrina joined Martel.

"Love," she told him. "If you care to make it here, you need to loosen up. If you want too, I'll teach you."

"You do all this exercise just to have fun?" Martel asked, feigning incredulity.

Sabrina laughed and flipped her finger at his nose. "Try it, you may like it. Let's go and see what they have for edibles." She grabbed his hand, and pulled him along.

Later on the band played an English waltz and a tango. Sargon and Chantar were the only ones on the dance floor. Sabrina explained to Martel that they were Sargon's favorite dances.

"Wonder what Sarah's up to," Sabrina mumbled. She saw her talking to the band. The Tango faded out and started up with a somewhat livelier tune.

Sarah walked up to Sargon and told him "Let's boogey." The jitterbug was still alive and well on the Antares.

Martel's eyebrows went up as he watched. "I would have thought Sargon to be more dignified," he whispered into Sabrina's ears.

"What, and miss having fun?" Sabrina said and her eyes sparkled as she looked at Martel. "It was Sargon who taught us to jitterbug. But I think it was my mother who taught him. One night my parents and Sargon were coming home, laughing, well, they were downright boisterous as I remember. Naturally I was curious and came down the stairs to see what was going on. Sargon, then known as Jim Thalon, told me that my mother had taught him an old dance she had learned from my grandmother . . . Wonder what Kamila's up to?" she interrupted herself.

Now it was Kamila who was talking to the band. Suddenly she knew. The music was insinuatingly slow and rhythmic. Sabrina giggled, the music came from Galatia. Kamila and one of her husbands, it was Jamil, were out on the dance floor, both gyrating their bodies in a belly dance. Kamila's second husband Rama was beckoning Sabrina to dance with him.

She looked at Martel, then weaving her body and arms with the music; she slowly moved away from him and joined Rama. As the beat increased, she gathered her long flowing skirt, and her movements became suggestively lewd, as her eyes fastened on Martel.

To his consternation, and to Sabrina's amusement, he felt the heat rising on his face and he knew he was blushing.

Suddenly Chandi's voice came over the intercom. "Sabrina, if you don't relieve me so I can have some fun, I'm going to beat the stuffing out of you."

"Keep your pants on little brother, I'm on my way," Sabrina replied. Shrugging her shoulder at Martel, "I have bridge duty," she told him, and with a wave of her hand she said, "I'll see you tomorrow."

After Sabrina left, Martel joined Chantar. "May I have this dance?" he asked her.

"I thought you didn't dance?" Sargon said.

"What, and miss all the fun?"

The party lasted well into the night. After Sargon and Chantar left, the band members changed, and so did the party-goers. Some went home, as others, coming of duty, joined.

It was late when Martel realized he needed someone to lead him though the maze to Sabrina's home.

Kamila was just walking toward the door when he had the presence of mind to hail her. "Kamila", he called out," wait a minute! I need a guide through that confounding labyrinth. Care to help?"

* * *

Next morning, Martel looked in on Sabrina. She was still sound asleep. After breakfast, he decided on a walk through the Antares. But as it turned out this was easier thought than done. The walkways meandered and turned and twisted and went up and down through three levels of nursery cells, until his usually acute directional sense was completely confounded. At unexpected turns there were small parks with splashing fountains and benches for sitting down, and children's playgrounds.

He hadn't met a soul yet; either the Antareans slept late, or it was he who was dilatory, he thought amused. He was about to give up when the walkway he was coming down, led into a long vaulted passage.

Curiosity made him decide to see what lay beyond before picking up a phone to call for directional assistance. To his utter amazement, he stepped into a village, with a central park. The vaulted passage was part of a huge building. When he looked up, he saw writing above the second story, proclaiming it to be the Town Hall. Encircling the park were many small shops. Most had second stories with curtained windows. Martel surmised that the owner's apartments were probably over the shops. As he walked on, he passed a boutique, selling small items such as jewelry, ties, hats, and handbags. Next to it was a shop selling fruit and vegetables. There was a book store, and across from it a bank. Shingles, hanging over several doors, announced offices of lawyers, dentists, and so on. When he walked into a side street, the smell of freshly backed bread greeted him. He was almost past a barbershop when he was hailed by Joran who was getting a hair cut.

Martel grinned at Joran, "How do you pay for a haircut here?" he asked, running his hand thought his shaggy hair.

"With credits."

"What do you do if you don't have any credits?"

"You charge it to Sabrina."

"Can I do that?"

"I could sign a voucher."

After being ministered to, Martel looked at his reflection. "That looks and feels much better."

"Yeah, nothing like a haircut to make you feel better," Joran replied.

"Is there a way I could transfer credits to the Antares?"

"Sure, through the bank. Let's go in and I'll show you how that's done. The bank is tied into the Alliance's banking system. So you can transfer funds to wherever you need to send them. Most of Sabrina's money is invested in a shipping business on Acheron, also on the

Antares. She is funding much of the trade the Antares has with other planets. I take care of her investments."

Martel gave Joran a curious look. "From what I gathered what little she told me of her life, you are part of her extended family."

"Yes. According to the laws of Acheron I asked to be accepted as a part of her family."

"What's your status on the Antares?"

"I'm a lawyer. You see, I studied interplanetary trade laws. Mostly I'm heading the financial system here. That's the capacity I'm employed on the Antares."

"You have also been Sabrina's lover," Martel said bluntly.

Joran was startled for a second. "Yes, that's true." He made the reply a statement. "Are you bothered?"

"No, just curious."

"Long story. Someday, if you're still interested, I'll tell you about it."

They had arrived at the bank, and Martel transferred some of his credits to the Antares. Joran watched over the transaction and explained the banks proceedings, then asked, "Would you like me to manage your credits?"

"There's not much to be managed. My only income is my soldier's pay I receive from the Alliance." This was said with a depreciating grin.

"I could multiply it for you, if you want me to. Let's go to the restaurant and have a beer. It's good, its home brewed. Someone, thank heavens, started a brewery here. He doesn't have the resources to expand, so he wants to talk credits with me. Also, if you want to know the newest gossip, it the best place to gather it."

"Whose idea?" Martel asked making a sweeping gesture. They had traversed several narrow picturesque streets with houses, gardens, and interspersing shops. Some sold merchandise, others were repair shops.

"I don't rightly know. I came back one day, and there it was."

They walked on in silence until they came to a Beergarden.

"Hey, Joran," he was hailed, "you're late. You can't break traditions you know. Who's that fellow with you?"

"This is Martel Alemain, "Joran introduced him. "Martel, this is Lenno, the loan director of the bank. Next to him is Abgar, the lawyer in this transaction, and this is the fine fellow who wants to brew the beer. We are here to discuss, and then draw up the loan contract."

The beer was brought by a young boy. From his looks, he was the Brewers son. Martel took a deep drink. After wiping the foam of his mouth, "It's good, I'll grant you that," he said to Joran.

"You live here?" Abgar suddenly asked.

"No, I'm just visiting," Martel replied, with a flat expression on his face.

"What's happening on the other worlds? We all like gossip," Lenno told him.

"I spend most of my time on ships. It's a closed world with not much going on," Martel replied, noncommittal.

After that they talked about what was new on the Antares. Sabrina was mentioned several times, and Martel, watching Joran unobtrusively from under his lashes, noticed his insipid expression. So, he didn't let it be known that he was from Sabrina's house.

Suddenly everyone became silent, looking over Martel's shoulder. When he turned, he saw an orange-skinned woman with black hair, swaying her skirts as she walked toward them.

"Hello Tangerine," Abgar greeted her. "We would be delighted if you join us," he said, rising, then, pulled a chair out for her to sit down.

"Good morning," she said courteously.

Martel moved a little, turning halfway toward the newcomer so he didn't have to crane his neck. There was a tangy fragrance coming from her as she passed by him.

When Martel was introduced, she was intrigued. Her look toward him was inquisitive. He aroused her excitement by the unfathomable aura he gave off. He seemed more than he was; tall, lithe, with his black eyes.

Her smile was brilliant, as she greeted him. "I haven't seen you before. You must come to one of my parties. I'm giving one tonight in honor of the Ambassador Najoth from Ramatha."

"I don't know"

"Didn't you say that Sabrina will be there also," Joran asked Tangerine, interrupting Martel.

"Yes, she said that she would come." Her mouth puckered suddenly like she had bitten into a lemon.

"You see, Martel is Sabrina's guest," Joran informed her. "So I surmise that he will accompany her."

"Oh, of course." Her demeanor cooled several degrees toward Martel after that.

"Joran, you have a telephone call," the brewer's son informed him.

"You need to excuse me for a moment," Joran said, and looked surprised when Martel rose also. Out of earshot, "You needn't have left," Joran told him.

"I'm not a piece to be manipulated," he told Joran amused. "Who is she?"

"Tangerine? She plays hostess on the Antares, and if she likes you, and you intrigue her enough, there's no telling how an evening will end."

"You mean she's a courtesan?"

"That's very nicely put."

"She doesn't like Sabrina."

"No. The dislike is entirely on her side. Sabrina could give a penny less about what she's doing. Sabrina is not very impressed by her. I think Tangerine feels overlooked."

"Where did she get the name Tangerine from?"

"Sabrina gave it to her, and it stuck. She said she looked and smelled like a Tangerine. No one here knows what a Tangerine is. So she's not too sure how the name was intended."

"Does Sargon know about her activities?"

Joran laughed, "There is very little that goes on Sargon doesn't know about, and for that matter, Sabrina. By the way, where are you going?"

"Just taking a walk," Martel informed him.

"Oh. Well, if you follow this road, it will lead you out into the country," Joran told him amused.

"Country?"

"Oh, the Antares has country. But don't wander into the wilderness, you'll get lost."

"I think you're amusing yourself on my account."

"No, just warning you. There's more to this world than meets the eye." Joran's eyes twinkled. "See you this evening."

Martel turned and followed the road Joran had pointed out. It wound around several houses and gardens, then, led through an opening into farmland. As he followed the road, he came to a village, arriving at its center, he encountered an altercation. Ayhlean was standing in the middle of a group of men engaged in a heated dispute. As Martel edged in closer, he heard Ayhlean arguing.

"It was all explained to you in the beginning," she asserted, facing a very angry, red-faced individual. "The law of inheritance of land and house on the Antares is from the mother to the first-born daughter. Men do not inherit property. When your wife died, and you gave your daughter in marriage to another man, you forfeited what your wife owned. Since there is no other daughter, you are allowed to take the furniture and the other possessions, except farm equipments. For these you might seek compensation."

"We have never heard such nonsense," the priest said. "God's law says that women are subordinate to men. How can a woman inherit land? She doesn't have the brains to manage it," he said derisively.

"I'm not disputing anatomy here, only the law of the Antares which says men cannot inherit property, such as land and houses."

Martel eased himself forward until he faced Ayhlean. "You mean Sabrina's sons cannot inherit her house?"

"Precisely, if Sabrina dies without female progeny, her house goes to her daughter by adoption, which in this case is Joran's daughter Margali. Her father's name is Joran Sandor ra Hennesee, the ra means of the house of Hennesee. Neither Logan nor Jason can inherit her house. The same is with Sargon; his descendants are reckoned through Chantar to Sirtis. His other daughter inheritance is through their mothers. Sargon does not possess a house." Ayhlean suddenly stared at him, "Why do you ask?"

"Out of interest. Also, I'm asking questions someone else might like to ask, and doesn't know how. If women own all the property, what of the husband?"

"If she's happy with him, I guess she'll keep him. If not, she can return him to his mother's house. All she had to say is, this male, he is your offspring, he is yours."

Martel chuckled. "It's that easy. What if the older daughter inherits the house and land? Where does her father stand?"

"If she has acknowledged him, and if he nurtured a relationship with her which is happy, she will share her house with him. If not, all she has to do is call an assembly of elder women, and say to them, this male, he is no blood of my blood, he is not a member of my house."

There was a stifled sob from the cloaked group of women. Slowly a shrouded figure moved timidly toward Ayhlean.

I'm Dina," she said, looking pleadingly up at Ayhlean. "Is it true what you have said?"

"What do you mean?"

"Lady, my father treats me very badly; especially after my mother died."

Ayhlean tried to reach out, to touch her; but Nina recoiled and shrank away.

"Are you injured?"

When Dina tried to bare her arm, her father moved in, trying to prevent her from doing so. "You shameless girl! You are ugly, no man will ever look at you. You are deformed, you're nothing. You should be grateful that I'm taking care of you. What are you trying to do? Do you want to shame your family?" he shouted, raising his hand to slap her.

Ayhlean intercepted his hand, and bending it back, made him wince with pain. Her face took on a forbidding look. "You will not interfere with anything I do. Do you understand? I am the law here."

Ayhlean carefully pulled back the sleeve and gasped. Dina's arm and shoulder were covered with black and blue bruises. She reached into the satchel she carried over her shoulder and pulled out a communicator. "This is Ayhlean, who's on the bridge?"

"Sabrina."

"Sabrina, I need you with the N'ai."

"Give me a second, Soraja you have the bridge."

"I hope she doesn't pop in out of thin air and scare these people to death," Ayhlean remarked to Martel.

"I heard what you said." Coming toward them with her free swinging stride, her eyes swept over the crowd, "What do you need?"

There was a movement, and a sound of astonishment from the N'ai men, as they stared at Sabrina, striding toward them. Dressed in her Antarean uniform, she looked tall and slender, an imposing figure. Her honey-colored hair had grown out, touching her cheeks

"This is Dina. I want you to look at her," Ayhlean said.

Sabrina turned toward the girl, giving her a reassuring smile. She had already read her mind and picked up on her emotions and the pain. She unclasped the top of her dress and gently pulled it away from her body. Even being prepared, she still gasped.

"Ayhlean, give me your communicator." She activated Sargon's telephone line, and when he answered, she said, "Sargon, this is Sabrina. Come to the N'ai area. Please."

While they were waiting for Sargon's arrival, Sabrina turned toward the huddled women. "I gathered none of you were aware of the Laws of the Antares."

An older woman came forward. "No, Lady. We live here as we always lived. The men tell us what we need to know. We do God's will; we are his chosen people."

"I see. Did the men really tell you all you needed to know? Were they not amiss in not informing you about the Laws of the Antares? Why do you think this was so?"

"I don't know, Lady. We are only ignorant women."

"And why do you think you are ignorant?"

"We are given to men so they take care of us."

"What's your name?"

"My name is Gana."

"Tell me Gana, who gives birth to men?"

Gana chuckled." We do, of course," she said with a shrug of her shoulder.

"And if you would not give birth to men, what would happen?"

"There would be no men." Gana chuckled again, her face crinkled with amusement

"But you haven't thought that through, have you? It is you who gives birth to the men, and you nurture them. Because of you, they live."

"But they make babies. Without them, we would have no babies."

"No, Gana, they make it possible for you to have babies. Without you, there would be no babies. It is the other way around. Don't you think God knows that? Why do you think the men lied and turned the whole story around?"

Gana's old face crunched with consternation. Turning to the other women. "Did all of you hear that? We have to come together, and we need to think about these things. We have much talking to do. Will you come someday and talk to us?" she asked Sabrina.

Before Sabrina could answer, Sargon arrived on what looked like a motorcycle without wheels. It rode on an air cushion and made very little noise.

There was a gasp from the women; their eyes stared with amazement at him. Most of the N'ai men were slender, and of medium height. Sargon was a golden skinned giant who stood well over six feet, with broad and massive shoulders. In comparison, he dwarfed the N'ai.

"You said, please," he said to Sabrina. "So it must be urgent."

"Sargon, I want you to examine this girl. Her name is Dina. Gana," she pointed to the old woman, "will you show him to your house. But first, scan."

Sargon scanned Dina and received the same miasma of pain and degradation. With a motion of his hand, he asked Gana to go ahead and lead the way to her house.

When he returned, his face was grave, and he was alone. "Ayhlean," he said, reaching for her communicator. He motioned for Sabrina to turn the translator off. "Security, I want two men to come to the N'ai area. Who's on the Bridge?" he asked Sabrina.

"Soraja."

"Soraja. This is Sargon. Is the ore freighter still there?"

"Yes. But the Captain has already asked to unfasten."

"Tell him to hold, and then switch him down to me."

"Okay, will do."

"Captain Thalon, is there a problem?" the Captain of the ore freighter asked."

"No problem. I need a favor."

"Name it."

"Do you still need a stoker?"

"I thought you didn't hold with such things."

"I changed my mind. I have a man here I think could fill the position. Will you hold until then?"

Sabrina, Martel, and Ayhlean looked at him askance. The life of a stoker was usually very short, given the onerous job. It meant to be down below, amidst the machinery, the smell, and the noise, with no chance for any other assignment. No one ever opted for the job of a stoker.

When the security guards came, Sargon switched the translator on again. He turned to the man. "What's your name?"

"I'm Bara," he said. He had hoped when Sargon came on the scene, he being a man, he would take his side. But now he was not too sure. It showed in his face.

"Bara, I am a physician, and I have examined your daughter. She has been severely beaten, and you have also raped her. She is torn inside and needs to be taken to the hospital were she will be cared for. Also, her disfigurement is a minor problem and can be easily taken care of. On this world it is unlawful to rape any woman. It is also unlawful to abuse your privilege of being a parent. I, being the highest authority on this world sentence you for the rest of your life to work on an ore freighter as a stoker."

Bara collapsed when he heard the verdict. Sinking to his knees he begged not to be sent away.

"How often has your daughter begged you to have mercy on her?" Sargon asked instead. "My ears are as deaf as yours." Turning toward the Security men he said "Take him away."

The silence was heavy as it was tangible.

"I will have your report," Sargon said to Ayhlean, then turned and walked toward his motorbike.

"And I need to be back on the bridge. I feel like slinking away. That was terrible. Martel, what are you doing here?"

"I was taking a walk through the Antares. An interesting place you have here. Full of surprises," he said. Intrigued, his glance took in the group of N'ais still standing around.

"The planet the N'ai came from was a member of the Alliance. Its sun went Nova. The N'ai here is a religious group which held on to old and outdated practices within their own society. We took them in because nobody wanted them. Most of them are farmers, and craftsmen, skills needed on the Antares. They are not a very likable people with their religion. They think they are the chosen of God. Their life style is their own, we seldom interfere. But here, religion is a private matter, and it is not publicly acknowledged. They know the laws of the Antares, and have sworn to abide by them. I guess they forgot to tell their women. Will I see you at Tangerines party tonight?" When Martel shrugged, she said, "Don't get lost in the wilderness."

"That's the second warning today."

"Heed it," Sabrina said, and abruptly disappeared as soon as she was sure no one was watching.

"Can you do any of that funny stuff?" Martel asked Ayhlean.

"No. I'm just all-around normal. Are you going to continue with your walking?"

"Might as well. It's been interesting so far."

"Follow that road, and stay on it. It should lead you to the next village," Ayhlean said with a peculiar smile.

Martel walked away, not too sure how to take that smile. He turned back to give her a curious look and a raised eyebrow.

She only shrugged and motioned for him to go on.

The road wound among fields and meadows. When he came to a forest, he thought he might have entered the wilderness everyone had warned him about. But after a mile or so, he came to another entrance that led into another countryside of fields and meadows. After a while he came to a bridge and crossed a small stream. Now, there were orchards. Soon he became aware of roofs peeking through the trees. As he walked toward the houses, he was suddenly surrounded by a group of children. They were small, well fed, and had round, happy faces. Soon the adults, attracted by the noise, came out of their doors. It was noon. Most of them were about to sit down to their midday meal. To Martel's surprise, all the adults coming toward him seem to be less than five feet, and he felt very conspicuous.

"Hello," he said, after turning the translator on.

"We speak English. Who are you? We have never seen you before. I'm the mayor of the town. My name is Sam."

"Hi Sam, I'm Martel. I'm on a walking tour."

"Walking makes for a hungry stomach. Can I invite you to share our table?"

"You're right, walking makes you hungry. I would be happy to accept your invitation."

He joined the mayor, his wife and five children of all ages at their table. It was a happy occasion; there was a lot of talk, teasing, and laughter. The food was simple, but excellent. They were loath for Martel to leave. He had to promise to come back.

As he left, Martel reflected on the contrast between the two villages. The other was bleak, and this one was all light and laughter. They, too, had warned him not to get lost in the wilderness. Taking their advice he followed the road around their village to get back without getting lost. The wilderness could wait for another time.

When he arrived home, he found Sabrina in the back of her garden. She was standing very still underneath a tree. Martel walked slowly up to her, leaning his cheek against her honey-colored hair.

Peering over her shoulder, he saw what she was watching. There were two birds, a fledgling, the other probably its mother. Every time she found a worm, the young one would eagerly scurry up to her. Letting out a squawk, it opened its beak wide, expecting her to stuff the worm into its mouth. When she didn't do it, it became agitated, fluttering its wings and complained. Soon the mother gave in, and began feeding it. Later, after her offspring was sated, she tried to coax it back up to the nest.

When the fledgling was safely up the tree, Sabrina reached back and entwined her hand in his. She led him farther back into the garden up a small incline to a clump of conifer interspersed with leaved trees. There was a bench underneath the trees and they sat down. The air was soft and fragrant, and the water was gurgling over rocks. Soon the light dimmed, simulating dusk, and not too far off an owl hooted. Sabrina had programmed the holo for a full moon with stars. They sat for a long while in companionable silence, just enjoying each other's nearness.

After a while, there was a sidelong glance from Martel. "You are not going to Tangerine's party?" he asked.

"No. I'd rather stay here and be with you."

*   *   *

It was mid-morning when Tomar entered Sabrina's study and handed her a note from Kamila. At first she turned it over in her hands before opening it. It was very rare for them to write notes. They usually called each other, or just walked in.

When she opened it, Sabrina's eyebrows rose. It was a request to come, and that it was urgent.

She arrived at Kamila's apartment with alacrity, and when she entered, she found she was not the only one. Sargon, Ayhlean and Sarah had preceded her. Everyone seemed uncomfortable as they were standing around. Inquiringly she looked from one to the other, but everyone just shrugged. The exception was Sargon, whose face seemed unusual serious.

When Kamila entered the room, she was accompanied by her children and two warrior women from Galatia.

"I see you're all here," Kamila said, her face drawn. She was fidgety, her hands constantly clasping and unclasping. "I have already talked to

Sargon," she continued, "so I will shorten the suspense. I'm going to leave the Antares to live on Galatia."

Everyone was thunderstruck. Then a quivering sigh escaped Ayhlean. The two of them had always been close, Ayhlean being the big sister when they had been young. "But Kamila," she said, her voice chocking, her hand reaching toward her.

"I'm sorry Ayhlean. Really, I am. But you see I never fitted in here. The Antares has always been a strange world to me. You all have found a place in it," she said, looking at Sabrina, Ayhlean and Sarah, "but I have always felt the alien. On Galatia, I have found a home I can identify with. I have family there, and a world I can understand."

"But, Kamila"

"She is right," Sabrina said sharply, interrupting Ayhlean. "Here she has always been like a fish out of water. She should go where she is happy."

Kamila looked surprised. She had expected the most resistance to come from Sabrina, and had been worried about a confrontation. "Thank you," she said, looking relieved. "I was worried what you would do. I love you all, but I need somewhere to belong. Soraja will stay with her father, but my other children are more accustomed to the lifestyle of Galatia." Then putting her arm around one of the Galatian women, "This is Morrigan, my sister-love. She has come to take me home."

Sabrina frowned, then, she recognized Morrigan as the girl who had visited the Antares before. Their closeness had always intrigued her. Then a tiny smile appeared as she remembered what sister love meant.

Kamila went to embrace Ayhlean, then Sarah. When she came to Sabrina she said, "You were always a hard-ass." As she said it, she smiled sweetly. "No offence, but you gave me a heck of a time. Thanks for not making this difficult. I do love you, and whenever you come to Galatia, look me up. Okay."

"Will do, Kamila. Good luck and much happiness. I love you too."

Then Kamila went over to Sargon. "Thank you for all you have done for me. I'm glad there are no hard feelings between us. I would like to be your friend, always. It's been nice knowing you, even in the biblical sense, she added quickly with a broad grin.

At first, Sargon looked nonplused. Then he chortled. "Yes, that was very nice," he said, and then he let her feel how much it had meant to him.

Kamila chuckled, and Sabrina, picking up on the exchange, guffawed. Sargon gave Sabrina a blistering look, then, turned back to Kamila. "I will still look in on you, if it is all right with you?"

"You will always be welcome, you know that."

"Well, I don't know about you all, "Sarah said with a drawl, "but I thought we were the Original Four. You know, Sargon and the four of us. I don't like breaking up a team. It means a lot to me. What are we going to be now?"

"We'll rewrite mythology," Sabrina said, letting the words drop slowly.

Sargon looked at her and then in disgust turned and walked out.

"What did you do now?" Sarah asked surprised.

"We need to rewrite the myth about the golden god and his four consorts."

"Sabrina you're a damned ass," Ayhlean exploded. "Why do you always have to do things like that?" Then suddenly she broke into peals of laughter.

"What is she talking about?" Kamila asked Ayhlean. "I don't understand a single thing she's saying." When the three howled with laughter, Kamila looked as confounded and hurt as she had done a long time ago. She had never understood Sabrina's skewed sense of humor, then and now.

"It's all right, Kamila. It's just one of Sabrina's silly jokes," Ayhlean reassured her, as she said it she caught a glimpse of Morrigan who had a hard time keeping a straight face.

"Morrigan, you will take care of her?" Ayhlean asked her mien serious again. "We all love Kamila, and don't really want her to go. She's one of us. She always will be a sister. You understand that?"

"Yes. I understand, and I will see that nothing bad ever happens to her. I will protect her as you have." Looking straight at Sabrina, "Even you," she said. "I know and understand you." Then walking up to Sabrina, she reached out with her arm, and smiled as Sabrina firmly clasped hers. "You and I are warriors, but we are also women."

Sabrina turned, and walked swiftly from the room. She was too agitated to return to her home, so she went up to the bridge.

Chandi was on duty and grinned as she walked in. "Hi Sis, I was paging you. There's a communication for you from the Alliances Headquarters," he informed her while handing her a printout.

Sabrina first just scanned it, then, began reading it more thoroughly. "Damn," she cursed, and left the bridge without giving Chandi another look.

She went immediately in search of Sargon, only to find out later that she missed him by a floor. As she exited the lift, Sargon was waiting for the lift on the floor below. Had she only stayed on the bridge, she need not have gone searching for him. Getting nowhere, she finally sent out a mind call for him.

"I'm on the bridge," he answered her, having already been informed by Chandi of her orders.

When she returned to the bridge, he was waiting for her by the door. "I already had plans to accompany Chantar to Acheron, and for you to take over the Antares."

"I can take over the Antares," Chandi assured Sargon.

"When you have command rank, I might consider it," Sargon replied icily. Chandi was thirty-eight, and Sargon knew he was quite capable of commanding the Antares. But in his eyes Chandi was still a youngster.

Undaunted Chandi replied," If I don't get the chance to command, how are you to know if I am capable?"

"He's got a point there," Sabrina told him, needling.

"You stay out of it," Sargon ordered, curtly.

Sabrina's "Sargon!" came in a warning tone.

Just then the lift doors opened, and Martel came on the bridge. "Am I walking into something?" he asked suspiciously, already back stepping.

"Not really," Sabrina said, "but I'm glad you came. I'm ordered to report to the Alliances Headquarters," she told him, handing him the printout. "Sargon had thought to leave the Antares, but now he can't."

"But I am perfectly capable running the Antares," Chandi injected again. "If I have failed you in any way, tell me. But don't shove me off like an incompetent." Chandi was now angry, and with his five-feet-two was standing up to Sargon.

There was a twitch of a smile on Sargon's mouth as he looked down at Chandi. "I know your capabilities. You haven't failed me. I just don't like leaving the Antares for a long time to anyone, unless it's Sabrina, or maybe Joshi," Sargon said with a depreciating smile. He disliked appearing sentimental, and maybe just a little paternal, being afraid of letting the child take over.

Sabrina was rocking back and forth on the balls of her heels, taking in the scene, understanding Sargon's reluctance. She was enjoying herself.

"I could keep an eye on the situation here, if it would make you feel better," Martel said, trying to save Sargon's feelings.

"That's right; you do have command rank, Captain." Sabrina suddenly said.

"You rifled through my files?" Martel said in mock outrage.

"I thought you couldn't read him?" Sargon asked.

"Oh, I can't, but I checked him out at the Alliances Headquarters when we first met."

"Oh, isn't she a trusting soul."

"Same as you," Sabrina replied, grimacing at Martel.

"You wouldn't mind staying here? Just to keep an eye on Chandi," Sargon asked, with a note of relief in his voice.

"I'll mind the store," Martel assured him.

"I hate to disappoint Chantar. She has worked to hard assembling a troupe from several different planets to put on a show on Earth."

"That sounds great," Sabrina said. "I wish I could come.

Chapter 11

At the Alliance headquarters, Sabrina was led immediately to the briefing room. Okada rose. "Captain Hennesee, I'm glad you could make it," he told her. Sabrina knew it to be civility for him to say so. It had been an order for her to come. Melkan acknowledgment was an almost imperceptible nod.

Sabrina smiled at Miri and Lara, then, sat down.

"I reviewed the tape you gave Melkan," Admiral Okada told Sabrina," and we found it very interesting. We would like to develop a plan to break the Orion Hegemony, and so the power behind the Altruscans. There are three more families besides the Armedes with almost unlimited funds."

"If you have such a plan, I'm all ears," Sabrina remarked eagerly. Her remark was met with silence, and at her raised eyebrow at Okada, she only received a shrug, then suddenly there was a giggle from Miri.

"I almost verbatim said the same thing with the same results," Miri informed her.

"Oh," Sabrina said as enlightenment dawned. "Let me rephrase. I'm very interested."

When she received only a bland stare from Okada, she said, "Please, feel free to continue."

Okada's eyebrows went up, and this time he chuckled.

"Melkan, you will have to make allowances for those three," he said, making a sweeping gesture with his chin. "They are invaluable to the Alliance and so have been allowed to be more individualistic than most."

A pucker formed between Melkan's brows as he met Okada's eyes. "I'm well aware of everyone's leniency toward their behavior," Melkan said softly. "So, I will propose that we use their talents and let them work out a plan on how to uncover and disrupt the workings of the Orion Hegemony all on their own."

"Excellent, Melkan." Okada beamed his enthusiasm around the table. His zeal was met with rather mixed feelings by the three."

Lara kept her temper and said as quietly as it was possible for her. "But we couldn't do without your valuable input."

"No?" Stroking his chin, Melkan said, "I think the three of you are very capable in devising such a strategy. If I'm not mistaken, your talents lie in that direction.

Amused by the turn of events, Sabrina, molding her face into a severe mien, shook her finger at Okada, "Have you been telling tales out of school?" she asked him.

"No my dear, Melkan is rather quick to catch on," Okada told her.

"Before you leave, I would like the tapes I gave you back. Did you have them deciphered?"

"Yes. And the tapes are on a special computer," and pointing to the consoles, "those three consoles are tied into it."

"The password?"

"M.I.V.R."

"Okeydoke," Miri said to Sabrina's amusement after Okada and Melkan left.

"Let's get the tapes on screen." Lara was all business as she typed the pass word in.

Sabrina watched for a while passively as the ledgers came on screen. "Wait a minute," she suddenly said, "What was that reflection?"

"I didn't see anything," Lara said.

"What did you see?"

"Miri, I'm not dreaming, but there was the reflection of a woman's figure very briefly on the screen. It's not on the tape. Nor is there anyone in the room."

"You're seeing ghosts?"

"Maybe Lara. Wait a minute, there's something missing. There are some dots missing, or periods, or commas, whatever you want to call them." She grabbed for the phone and dialed for Okada. When he answered, "Okada, those tapes have been tampered with," she told him, "and you're having ghost walkers in this building."

"I'll be down in a second."

When he entered the room, he carried several discs in his hands.

"Those are my discs," Sabrina stated, pointing to them.

"Yes. I had other discs made, and I will keep yours in a safe. Now let's see what you mean by being tampered with."

When he ran the discs on a console, and compared what was on screen of the other console, it became immediately obvious that there were several omissions.

"Those periods meant something," Sabrina said more to herself than to anyone else. "Let's magnify those periods."

The dots showed an intricate lacy design.

"Okada, who deciphered the discs?

"I don't know if he's still here. He requested a transfer, stating family problems. Let me see if he's still assign here." Okada made several phone calls. "I got him."

"I want to see him without him being able to see us," Sabrina told him.

"Okay, I have him brought up on some pretext. You can see him in another room through a two way mirror."

All three moved to the other room to have a look at the translator. Sabrina rifled his files.

Suddenly Lara said, "He's an Orion. He's a mix, that's why his face isn't round. See his scanty hair growth?"

"Yes, you're right. Now we have the houses of the Armedes, Amri, Javan, and Hesran. That was what the dots meant. He has deleted them to see if he can sell his knowledge."

When Okada came back, he asked, "You have what you need?"

"Sabrina has," Miri said.

"And now about the ghost walker? What did you mean by that?"

"Your friend here," pointing to the translator still sitting in the chair, "has installed a very curious device that walks. He has given it the ghostly shape of a woman. It's really a holo that moves about. It records everything that goes on in this building."

"Oh, that. We already discovered it. What's walking around now is an edited edition. Now it only records what we want it to see."

After Okada left the room Lara said, "Oh, then Sabrina wasn't losing her mind when she said she saw a ghost. I'm glad to know that. Very reassuring."

Sabrina only gave her a scathing look as she walked ahead toward the conference room.

"Now, how are we going to plan our mischief?" Miri asked, delighted.

Her remark was met with a pointed silence.

"I have an idea," Sabrina suddenly said. "If I can get Morrigan to play along."

"Who is Morrigan?"

"Kamila's sister love."

"Kamila's what," Lara looked suspiciously at Sabrina. "What are you talking about?"

"Morrigan is a Galatian warrior. If I can only interest her in playing a part." Looking at Miri," I think we can begin and get this ball rolling."

"What do you want her to do?"

"Oh, just plan a little insurrection."

"Oh, buying weapons, maybe."

"No. No, only ordering weapons. How would you like to play on the stock market?" Stroking her chin, she added, "Joran can play a hand in this game, me thinks."

"There goes her Irish. You better watch her now" Miri quipped to Lara.

"I know. I already got her drift. If there's money to be made, I know of a few players. If I get my contacts on Sheitan, I think . . . I think I know what I can do."

"Carr?"

"I forgot you met him. Filthy creature, huh? And he's greedy."

"I'll hit Raglan," Miri mused, playing with her bottom lip, "and . . . no I think I will visit Orcus first, and gamble my money away. I have some contacts there." Then holding up her hand, she said, "but foremost, I'm hungry."

"My sentiments exactly. Let's have a bite to eat. I never have been to the restaurant on the roof. Let's see what they have, and hobnob a little with the elite," Sabrina agreed.

"Just elite, doesn't make it with me," Lara growled.

"Okay, then we go for the food, but I must eat," Miri conceded.

On top, the restaurant was full of elegant people conversing in subdued chatter. Sabrina looking at her two companions. "I think we're a little under dressed," she commented.

"We can always pretend we are modeling new fashions," Miri giggled. She was looking at Lara's tight flight suit, and Sabrina's baggy pants and loose blouse.

"Be glad I don't wear my usual attire," was Lara sotto voce commentary.

"We would be arrested," Sabrina remarked.

"My, my, my," Miri suddenly said, "look over there." She was pointing toward the back of the restaurant.

"Oh how hoyty toity can you get?" Sabrina said, the tone was light, but there was also a little envy in her voice. Sargon and Chantar were dining with Heiko and Okada. "Bet we're not going to be invited."

"Let's go, before I bite someone," Miri remarked quickly before Lara could go and invite herself. She had heard the undertone in Sabrina's voice. She had also seen Thalon snub her openly whenever he felt she invaded his privacy. But it was too late. The hostess had arrived asking them if they would like to be shown to a table.

The table was not far from Sargon's and he noticed them immediately as they were seated. He gave them a scanning look, especially Sabrina, then turned back and continued his conversation with Heiko.

"Let's ignore him completely," Miri said loud enough for him to hear.

When the waiter came, they quietly ordered. The food was excellent, and at the end of their meal, when the bill was presented, Lara took it up and began reading it.

"My goodness!" she exclaimed, passing the bill to Miri. "You didn't say that it was that expensive!"

"Miri gave the bill to Sabrina, dithering like an old lady, "Oh dear, dear, dear!" she clucked.

Sabrina clicked her tongue, and shaking her head, said, "Oh. Oh dear, who's going to pay that?"

The waiter was completely confounded, not knowing what to make of the situation since the bill was quite substantial.

"I know," Miri said, raising her fingers as if she just had discovered a brilliant solution. "We ought to give it to Thalon for snubbing us."

"Yes, serves him right." Lara crooked her finger at the waiter to bend down. "We want to play a trick on a friend of ours," she told him. "See the gentleman with the curious eyes," she asked, pointing to Sargon. "Give him the bill. We only want to see his reaction."

"I'm sorry but I would rather have management take care of this. Would you ladies please wait?"

"Of course," Lara told him. When the waiter left, she asked Sabrina, "Where are we going first?"

"I'd like to go back to the Antares and pick up Joran." Sabrina said Joran's name lout enough to carry to the intended table. As she had expected Chantar turned at the familiar name. "Sabrina!" she said surprised, and walked over to her table. "I didn't know you were here."

"Sargon intended it that way," Sabrina told her.

She looked amused at Sabrina. "Another snub?" she asked.

"Yes, and he is paying for it," Miri told her, pointing to the manager just approaching Sargon's table with diffident manners.

When he manager pointed to their table, Heiko turned around and for the first time was aware of Sabrina's presence. Sargon only grinned as he was handed the bill, and nodded assent.

"What's with Joran? You said it loud enough so I would hear it?" Chantar asked curiously.

"Oh nothing. I just wanted you to know that I am here." Sabrina told her.

But Chantar was unconvinced. "You have something in mind?"

"Well, if you insist," Sabrina played as if she was reluctantly conceding. "I have a job for him."

"Is it dangerous?"

"It could be, but he mostly would consider it a challenge."

"Sabrina, you are a little too much like my Great-aunt Lahoma. What are you cooking up?"

"Me?" Sabrina asked, "How can you accuse me of being like Lahoma."

"You're not paying her back, are you?"

"Now Chantar, that's hitting below the belt," Sabrina protested. "You wounded me to the heart. I might just like to borrow some of her money, or just her knowledge about high finances. You know, very high."

"Sargon," she called out, "will you please come here?" When he arrived with Heiko and Okada, she pointed to Sabrina and said, "I don't trust her, she's got some devilment on her mind."

Sabrina rose, totally ignoring Sargon, turned to Heiko. "What a pleasure to meet you again," she told him, holding out her hand.

"The pleasure is mine," he repeated politely.

Until now Miri had been very quiet and amused observed the interchange, then, turned to Lara, "Since we are not invisible, I surmise we are being ignored," she said tartly.

Lara nodded her head in agreement. "I don't take kindly to being ignored. Looking up at Sargon, "Am I invisible?" she asked. "I think only Sabrina and Miri have that ability. How about introducing me to your company?" Although it was said in jest, it had a warning undertone.

Sargon knew the danger Lara could be. He never underestimated her unpredictable temperament. Very sincerely he said, "I'm sorry Lara. It wasn't meant as a snub. I just wanted to see what game Sabrina was playing."

From deep inside her throat came a warning growl and the mane on her back rose. Both, Miri and Sabrina turned and looked alarmed. Lara having voiced her sentiment pointedly inspected her finger nails, her most dangerous weapon. Underneath the nails were tiny openings for razor-thin claws which could be suddenly extended. Then, looking up at him again, "Sabrina isn't the only game player," she said.

Sabrina took Sargon aside. "When are you going to see the boys?"

"They're at the Air Force Academy, and the Dehner's will look in on them."

"You think that was prudent leaving them there, unsupervised? What are they doing?"

"They arrived at mid-term, but I was able to enroll them in the Air Force Academy. They were impressed by the jet-planes and they said they'd like to learn how to fly. Also Martha thought a literature class would be fun for them until the next term starts."

"Oh God, You're not only imprudent, you're nuts. A very strenuous curriculum," Sabrina said bitingly. "What do you think they will do when for the first time they are without supervision, having time on their hands, and no responsibilities? And I bet you gave them money. Do you know what they are going to do with it? They're going to get into trouble. The Dehner's are nice people, but I don't think they are able to handle Jason and Logan. Especially, not Logan."

Sargon looked kind of discomfited. "I think they will behave responsibly. They like Martha and would not cause her any trouble."

"You're more trusting than I am."

"Are you two having a disagreement?" Miri asked.

"Oh just a little difference of opinion," Sargon told her. "You know how mothers are when their little ones are out from under their skirts."

"I would call that condescending," Lara told him. "But you two can settle your spat on your own time. We need to get going."

"You have already formulated a plan?" Okada asked.

"It's coming together," Miri told him. Turning to Sabrina, "Are you coming with us or are you going by yourself?"

"I'd like to go with you if you don't mind stowing Spitfire?"

This time Miri had the Aurora Borealis instead of her Peregrine. The Aurora was the larger ship, its name derived from the colorful light refraction within the atmosphere. Out in space it was totally invisible, mirroring back space.

After the three had left, Okada turned to Sargon. "You allow her an extraordinary amount of latitude," he commented.

"My dear Admiral, there is no such thing as allowing; she is Sabrina." He said it in such a tone that seemed to explain everything.

Chantar amused smile puzzled Okada, and he looked at her questioningly.

"What my husband means is that Sabrina is the heart of the Antares," she stated, enigmatically.

Sargon gave her an inexplicable look, and then a gentle smile. "Yes, I think Chantar explained it most succinctly. Had she failed, I doubt there would have been such a thing as the Antareans. Because of a fourteen-year-old girl, the idea was born. From the beginning she set the tone and pace. The other three girls would never have wrought the cohesive pattern needed to build a world."

Chapter 12

After arriving on the Antares, Sabrina left Lara and Miri in her living room and went to Joran's part of the house.

She found him in the bedroom in his birthday-suit with Marlo inspecting a deep cut he had rather far down, close to his bottom.

"What happen here?" Sabrina suddenly commented, startling both of them.

"Don't you ever knock?" Joran was irritated more because of the pain than Sabrina's indiscretion.

"Why would I want to knock?" Sabrina looked him up and down. "You haven't anything I haven't seen yet."

Marlo started to withdraw, but Sabrina waved her to stay. "Let's see," she examined the cut, then, going into a slight trance she accelerated Joran's own healing process. The cut reddened as the blood rushed to the injured area. Sabrina coming out of the trance, turned to Marlo, "Give me some adhesive tape, I think that's all he needs. It should be completely healed by tomorrow."

Marlo and Sabrina tape the cut together.

"What do you want?" Joran said ungraciously.

"I want you to pack your bags. We're going to Acheron."

"Marlo?" Joran asked.

"If she wants to visit Lahoma, she is welcome to come along."

Lahoma had shown very little patience with Marlo, whom she could not understand. Marlo's submissiveness toward Joran irritated her more than pleased her. Also, she intimidated Marlo.

Marlo silently shook her head at Joran's questioning look. He smiled at her.

Then, lifting her chin, gently gave her a kiss. "You'd rather stay here then."

"I won't be alone. Margali will come by to see me."

Margali was her daughter by Joran.

"Okay, I'll see you after I'm packed," Joran told her. "Where are you going to be?"

"Probably in my kitchen," Sabrina told him, then, left.

In her kitchen, Medea was fixing lunch for Miri, Lara, and Sabrina when Joran entered. He greeted Miri, whom he knew, and gave Lara an astonished look.

Lara was extraordinary to look at with her bluish skin and a mane growing down her back. She was tall and lithe, and almost so thin as to be called emaciated.

"You will be wanting to eat too?" Medea said, interrupting his stare.

"Yes, please," he said absentminded. "Why are we going to Acheron?" he asked Sabrina, his eyes still on Lara.

"If you don't stop staring at me, you might get fixated," Lara said, before Sabrina could answer.

"Sorry, I didn't mean to stare," he excused himself, embarrassed at being caught with his curiosity so open on display. On Acheron, a male did not stare at a female; being on the Antares made him forget sometimes.

"I will tell you when we are on Acheron," Sabrina answered his question. "It depends on whether your mother will become a player, or not."

Knowing Sabrina, he knew it was a waste of time to pursue his curiosity.

*   *   *

Before approaching Acheron, Miri thought it best to conceal the Aurora Borealis on one of the larger moons circling an outer planet. Then they all crammed into Sabrina's Spitfire. Going into orbital approach, Sabrina asked for permission to land on the planet, and for them to send a message notifying the house of Sandor of her arrival, and a request to be met with an air-car.

When they disembarked, Rosana's fifteen year grandson, Elan, came toward her, and without preamble said, "Sabrina, I was told to give you this note."

Mystified, she opened the sealed envelop. It only read, Sabrina, come in through the back door. Lahoma.

The only other ones who knew about the existence of the bolt-hole were Sabrina and Rosana. This meant there was some kind of danger.

"Elan, do you have any cloaks in the car?"

"Yes. Since we didn't know how many were coming, Lahoma gave me several to bring."

"We need four." Sabrina chuckled at Elan's surprised look and patted him on the shoulder. "Child, humor me," she told him.

Elan handed out four cloaks, then watched amused as Joran, instead of wearing a turban, pulled the cloak's hood all the way forward until his face disappeared.

"Now what else did Lahoma tell you to do?"

"She told me to go to Thalia's house until she called for me to come home."

"Good, you do that." When Elan glided off in the car, Sabrina turned to Joran. "You will not say a word, no matter what happens, you'll stay behind me. There's some kind of danger, since she sent a code. We will walk. Keep alert."

Sabrina led off with the others following closely behind, When she didn't go toward the house, Joran pulled on her cloak. Sabrina only held up her hand as she cautiously approached the vicinity of the secret entrance. There was a man suspiciously loitering inside a doorway. She mind-scanned him and her suspicion was confirmed. Someone else knew about the secret entrance and had it watched. If they entered, he would see them. Biting the lining of her bottom lip, she tried to think of a way to distract him. Watching closely, she noticed how fidgety he was. Again she scanned him and grinned. His bladder was full, but he was afraid if he relieved himself he would loose sight of the entrance. Carefully she entered his thoughts and made relieving himself the most urgent thing in his life. Finally he gave in and turned away.

Sabrina motioned to the others to come with her. They followed a long rock hewn passageway until they came to a small door. Sabrina pushed it carefully open. It led into Lahoma's wine cellar, and slowly, trying to be as noiseless as possible, they made their way toward Lahoma's part of the house. They were about to cross the hall that led to her apartment when Lahoma herself came out of her office. Sabrina was shocked, Lahoma looked haggard and she had aged. A gentle mind-touch alerted her to Sabrina's presence.

At first startled, Lahoma quickly put her finger to her lips and motioned for them to follow her. She led them to her bathroom, and sitting on the toilette, she shivered, then looked at Sabrina and told her, "I need your help."

"What's going on?"

"Long story. I got myself in a mess in my younger days and I am still paying for it. I'm being bled dry, and they upped the ante."

"What you are trying to tell me is that you are paying for safety to operate in areas outside the Alliance?"

Lahoma gave her one of her long looks. Then turning to Joran. "I've always knew she was a smart-ass," she told him acidly. Then back to Sabrina, "How long have you known?"

"Since the day your computer broke down, and you asked me to fix it," Sabrina admitted shamelessly.

"I see, you rifled through my documents."

"I always do. I get very interesting things that way."

"I dare say. Now the question is, what can we do to get me out of this?"

"Before we get busy on this, who else knows of the secret entrance?"

"Why you ask?"

"Lahoma, there's guy standing guard."

"Outside of me only you and Rosana."

"I see. All of you, you stay here. I'm going to get more information. Lahoma, if someone comes knocking, no matter whom it is; tell them you have the trots."

"I like your elegant way of putting things," Lahoma responded, giving Sabrina a sour look. To Lahoma's shock, Sabrina just popped out into thin air.

Remaining invisible, she entered Lahoma's office. A man and a woman were in the sitting area. No one was talking. Sabrina rifled through their memories. She was almost shocked when she found out that Dolcie, Lahoma's long time maid, was the informer. Through her the house of Amri had kept track of Lahoma's business transactions. Sabrina also found out that the man was lining his own pockets by asking more, unbeknown to the woman, and his employer.

When she reappeared in the bathroom, she quickly said," Don't say anything. Pointing her finger at Lahoma. "Don't trust Dolcie," she told her. "I'll have to go and hide Spitfire."

She left in her unconventional way. At the space port, she asked for a hangar for Spitfire. At first she was told that there was no hangar available. Then she asked for the manager. When she flashed her special service I.D., she was told that there was a hangar, but it was already occupied by another special agent.

Only after she signed a paper, releasing the manager of all responsibilities, was she given the hangar's location. As soon as she knew she was unobserved, she disappeared to pop inside the hangar.

Inside was a ship of a strange configuration, and it was floating off the floor. She tried to hail it, but received no reply. Having little time, and less patience, she simply raised her vibrations, hoping it to be unoccupied and appeared inside the strange ship.

Bad luck. As she appeared, two beings stared at her. One of them walked toward her and looked her over. "Now how did you do that?" he asked in Galactic.

Sabrina studied him. She had already tried to read both of them and to her consternation found them unreadable. Then she suddenly grinned, and on a hunch said, "Oh, this is something Sabot taught me."

"Oh, Sabot? I wonder if that was wise for him to do."

"It's very helpful. What's your name? "Sabrina asked, trying to look around him to see his companion who seemed to be staying out of sight. Suddenly something familiar touched her. She sidestepped and then just stared. His face looked reptilian. Closer scrutiny revealed that it was cleverly applied makeup. When he snaked a forked tongue at her, she fainted. Only his companion's presence of mind saved Sabrina from hitting the floor.

When she came to, she ground out between her teeth, "Martel, if you ever do this to me again, I'm going."

"What in the hell are you doing here?" he interrupted her threat.

"I was trying to hide Spitfire." Then, looking thoughtfully at them, "I need help. I need something so big to sell they'll be willing to pay any price."

"Whom are you talking about?" Martel went into Galactic so his companion could understand.

"The big merchant houses," she told the stranger. "Do you know of the House of Armedes, Amri, Javan and Hesron?"

"Yes, we know them. They are the merchants of death. By the way my name is Mayar."

"Thank you. I want to sell them a weapon they can't turn down. It has to be something that looks good on paper, but won't work." Turning to Martel, "You think you can work a miracle?"

"If you give me time, I might think up something," Mayar answered instead.

"Time is what I don't have. I need it right now. That's why I asked for a miracle," she told him.

Martel was strangely silent and Sabrina cursed her inability of not being able to read him. She stared at him as if she was willing him to become readable.

Suddenly he scratched his head and to Sabrina's consternation began to chuckle.

"What's so funny?" she exploded at him.

"I have your miracle. Karsten and I had this brilliant idea. It looked good on the drawing board, but when we tried it out, it never worked. We gave it to Thalon to study. He said it should work, but at last we all had to concede it was a dud."

"Where do you have it?'

"Right here, on a disc."

Sabrina's mouth fell open. "Someone must be in my corner," she whispered, awed.

"I picked it up from one of my old haunts. I was going to erase it. Good thing I didn't. I'll run you a copy."

"No Martel, print it out."

Martel went to the back of the ship, while Sabrina paced impatiently back and forth, formulating a plan in her mind. It only took a few minutes and Martel was back.

She asked him to lay it out and to explain it to her.

"Won't it be difficult for you to understand?" Mayar asked.

"Sabrina has an engineering degree," Martel told him.

Martel quickly explained the most salient points, and before Sabrina could get too engrossed, he rolled the plans up. "You said you were in a hurry," he reminded her.

"Oh God, I almost forgot. I left Lahoma in the bathroom sitting on the john." She laughed at Mayar's puzzled expression.

"Don't ask me to explain Sabrina," Martel told Mayar. "She is unfathomable."

"Thanks guys," Sabrina said, clamping the plans under her arm. She gave them a toothy grin and disappeared.

*   *   *

Sabrina reappeared in Lahoma's bathroom, clutching the plans to her chest.

"I'm going to have a heart attack," Lahoma groaned. "Where have you been? Dolcie was here twice, threatened to break the door down if I didn't come out."

"Don't worry. Let's go into your living room, then call Dolcie and tell her to bring tea and sandwiches. Tell her you have company."

"Are you sure?"

"What you got here?" Lara asked, pointing to the paper Sabrina was still clutching to her chest.

"The answer to our problem. Let me handle it."

When Dolcie appeared, she nearly fainted when she saw Sabrina and Joran.

The others, she didn't know.

Sabrina told her that Lahoma was not feeling well, to bring some tea and sandwiches."

It took a while before Dolcie reappeared. In the meantime Sabrina spread out the plans and quickly explained what they were and where she had gotten them. When the door opened, Dolcie's hands were empty. She was followed by the man and woman. Sabrina quickly let the plans roll up.

"You were told to bring tea," Sabrina said curtly.

"I was stopped in the hallway. I told them that Lady Lahoma was not feeling well."

"No, you went to them and told them that Joran and I had arrived. Then explained to them who I was, and that there was more company."

Dolcie paled, and took a step backward. She looked furtively from the man to Lahoma.

"Go bring something to eat, like I told you," Sabrina ordered.

Dolcie gladly took the chance to get out, and with alacrity turned and left.

"Now, what can I do for you?" Sabrina asked sweetly.

"You? Nothing. We came to have a word with that old crone."

When he went toward the table, Sabrina tried to prevent him, and was pushed roughly aside. He unrolled the plans. Sabrina, standing close, watched his face. At first, he kind of leisurely leafed through them. Suddenly his attention was galvanized, and he began studying them more intently.

As Dolcie entered with the tea tray, she was peremptorily waved aside, but Sabrina, reached across him, let the plans roll up. "We will have tea now. You may stay here and join us. If you don't like it, you can leave."

"Lady!" he thundered.

"I think Dolcie has explained to you who I am, and who he is," she said, pointing to Joran. "From now on, you will deal with me. And we will go back to the original agreement, or I will tell Thavis that you have been lining your pocket without his knowledge."

The man, whose name was Linor, paled. He came at Sabrina with his hand raised.

Sabrina grabbed and twisted it until he sank to his knees. Holding him there! "I don't think I will deal with you," she told him. Turning to the woman, "Tara, would you like to handle this? This is a foolish male and has already made too many blunders. You want to go down with him? I can explain everything to Thavis, and I also have something of interest for him." When Tara looked frightened at Linor, Sabrina said sweetly, "There's a lot of money in this, Tara."

Her avarice was clearly written on her face and she looked cunningly at Sabrina. "You will explain to Tharvis that I didn't know anything about this?"

"Of course," Sabrina assured her. "You go to Peres on Acheron and tell him that you found someone with very interesting plans that would be very profitable for him."

"You will hold Linor while I leave?" she asked Sabrina.

"Sure. Go now, and I will give you time to get there." Turning to Joran, "Lock him up; then, come back."

*   *   *

"Now tell me, where have you been? Lara asked after Joran returned.

"I ran into two cute guys who gave me the answer to our prayer." Sabrina remarked.

"Sabrina," Lara growled.

"Really, I did. Does anyone here know some one named Mayar?"

"I don't think so," Miri said.

"He has a funny ship."

"How funny?" Lara asked, being sure her leg was being pulled.

"Well, it just floats in the air."

"Sabrina, if this situation were not that serious, I might smile at your eccentricity," Lahoma said tartly.

"Lahoma, if it were not important to me, I would not ask." Looking at Miri and Lara, "You never heard of a guy named Mayar?"

"Nope. Now, what has he to do with this thing here?" Lara said, pointing to the blueprints.

"A lot, Martel or he, are working on something. He does know Sabot. So maybe he's all right."

"I think Martel can take care of himself," Lara told her.

"Oh. You wouldn't know on what kind of mission Martel is on?" she asked Lara sweetly.

"Ah, that is what you were fishing for." Miri grinned at her. "Not concerned, just nosey. Now, how about telling us what you have been up to."

"Well, I tried to find a hangar to hide Spitfire. I only got the location of one after I flashed my badge. When I got there, there was that funny ship I told you about, floating off the floor. Hoping no one was inside, I popped in. But that was bad luck. There were two guys there. Tried to read them, but couldn't. Got me scared for a moment! Then I got a familiar feeling from the second guy, and I looked at him a bit closer. Looked like a snake. But he wasn't a snake. So I thought Chamealeon. When that damned thing snaked his tongue at me, you know what I did?" Sabrina asked, looking questioning at Lahoma.

"Knowing you, you probably cut his tongue out," Lahoma said.

"No, I fainted."

"You did what?" Joran asked.

Sabrina grimaced at him. "I fainted, I said."

"Okay, go on. I know you're enjoying getting all the attention," Lahoma said bitingly.

"Well, the reason I fainted was because I recognized the snake thing was Martel."

"You're kidding!" Miri exclaimed.

"No, it was Martel. When I asked him about a miracle I was badly in need of he produced it. What you say to that?" Sabrina said, pointing to the blueprints.

"Martel gave you this?' Joran asked.

"Now, ladies and gentleman, the fun is over," Sabrina said," Now, we better get to work."

"Okay, what do you want us to do?" Lahoma asked.

"Lahoma my love, I need to pick your brain. You know more about the big merchant houses than I do. I need to know how to create a market, since we have a product. This thing," Sabrina said, pointing to the plans," is a weapon, but the good thing is, it won't work."

"Is that the thing Karsten and Martel were working on?" Miri suddenly asked.

"Yes. You know something about it?"

"Yes, I know it's a dud." Then suddenly she grinned. "I think I get your drift. That would be a brilliant idea. Joran, can you create a fictitious company and get some junk bonds floating around?"

"Miri, darling, your getting ahead of me," Sabrina complained.

"Ah, you can think faster than that."

"Mother, how bad do you want to get back at the Amris and the other houses?" Joran suddenly asked. It had taken him some time to piece things together from old memories, not quite understood at that time.

"I can't gamble the future of the house of Sandor."

"Yes, Mother, you can. Trust me. I might double your fortune. I have an idea."

Lahoma looked speculatively at her son. She knew his intelligence. That was the reason she worked so hard to get him back into her house when his marriage failed. She had trusted him all these years anyway with her private fortune. "I won't commit the house fortune, but all that I have is yours to use. I'll just write it into my will, and if you lose, you lose your own money."

Joran looked at his mother, then raised his head back and laughed. "True to form; you never disappoint me," he told her, appreciating her.

"You were always sharp, much sharper than Rosana. Rosana is too trusting." Turning to Sabrina, "I hated you when he left to follow you."

"I'm naturally terrible bothered to hear it," Sabrina remarked. "But I didn't take him; he followed me of his own free will. He is free to come and go. On the Antares, he can do his own thing. I don't tell him what to do."

"Later on, I understood."

"Okay, now that we have this out of the way. Will you commit yourself all the way? With your money?"

"How about yours? I know you're pretty well-off yourself."

"Lahoma, I already decided to put my own money into it. I'll take the loss or profit," she said, turning toward Joran. "Who else would like to gamble?"

"We are all in," Lara assured her.

"Okay. Lahoma, you let the other merchant houses know you found a sure thing, and out of the kindness of your heart you're letting them in if they are willing to help finance it. No money, no open door. Then mention that your price of letting them in is letting you off the hook. No more payments for crossing their boundaries. I think they will believe you and come along."

"Yes. I think this is the only plan that will work," Lahoma agreed.

"If you get them to agree, by that time I will have started a Corporation and some phony industries to produce."

Joran looked questioningly at Sabrina. "What are we going to call those babies?"

"What did Karsten call them?" Sabrina asked Miri.

"Plasma disrupter."

"Shouldn't we find a more original sounding name?"

"No, I don't think so," Lahoma said slowly, after giving it some thought. "What are those things suppose to do anyway?"

"According to Martel, this thing can be hand carried, and when calibrated to a certain atomic number, or vibratory rate, that object responding to that number or vibration, will dissolve. Martel and Karsten wanted to use it to do some mining. They thought it would be neat if they could dissolve the rocks, and just pick up the gems."

Sabrina sank into a long and thoughtful silence. Everyone watched expectantly. When the silence went too long Joran asked "What are you cooking?"

"I'll be right back," was Sabrina's enigmatic answer as she popped out again. She reappeared in the hangar, and to her relief, the ship was still there. She tapped on the outer hull, and at the same time raised her vibration and appeared inside.

She smacked a kiss in Martel's direction, and turned to Mayar. "I would like to borrow your ship," she told him.

"Just like that?" Mayar asked her. "When would you be needing it?"

"Oh, sometime after we're set up."

"So it's not right away?"

Turning to Mayar, "She just had a brainstorm," Martel said in the way of explaining Sabrina. "How about elaborating on it?"

"The plasma disrupter is nice, but if we had a ship like this to show, we would get a lot more attention and investors. This ship is real, and can be believed in. The idea of the disrupter is more likely to be taken with skepticism by some."

"I see," Mayar said. "Sounds reasonable. Would you like me to be the one to explain the ship?"

"You could do that?"

"Yes, but you need to give me a tentative time." Mayar told her.

"Mmmm," Sabrina said, scratching her head. "That will be difficult to do. How about if you permit me to experience your personality's vibration, then I can pick you up whenever I need you."

"And rifle through his memories," Martel commented.

"I don't do such things unless it's necessary," Sabrina retorted, a little miffed.

"Sorry, just thought to warn Mayar of your abilities."

Mayar looked reflectively at Sabrina. "I think I will trust you," he said slowly. "All right, do your thing."

"You need to relax and let your mind go blank." She easily picked up his identifying vibration and a little of who he was. He was extra-Galactic and had only come out of curiosity to explore this Galaxy.

"How long ago did you meet Mayar? God, I didn't know you where that old?" Sabrina's rising voice conveyed her total astonishment to Martel.

Martel chuckled at Mayar's questioning look. "She can't rifle through my mind," he informed him. "I'm still an enigma to her. I think that's why she's still enthralled by my personality."

"Martel is an enigma to himself, too," Mayar told her, giving Martel an amused glance. "He was given to me when he was just born. My trade is being a magician and one day I was on a curious planet where things appeared and disappeared; very intriguing to a magician. There was a mountain, and on top stood a temple. Naturally, I was curious and hiked up there. On my way up, on a narrow ledge, I met a woman who was very apparently pregnant. Suddenly her belly moved and slowly an infant materialized. She cuddled it for a moment then handed it to me, looking at me with imploring eyes. Then she just faded away. I mean she became transparent, blending into the rock. Somewhat shocked, I touched the rock but, there was nothing there. That is how I acquired Martel."

"Are then the Chameleon's a magical race?" Sabrina asked.

"No, not really, they have the ability to change their appearance somewhat, but nothing on the scale this woman did. But then I did not find Martel on Chameleon. It was a planet that appeared and then disappeared. Don't asked me where and how," Mayar injected quickly when Sabrina was about to interrupt him. "I even tried to check on his genetic makeup, but he didn't match up with anything I could discover." Then more to himself, "I'm not even sure if he could produce viable offsprings." When he looked at Sabrina and Martel he found himself stared at. "I'm sorry. I didn't mean it as it sounded. It would be interesting to see a child from him."

"Well, I can produce offsprings. He can do it with me since I'm also a mutant."

"But I thought you were from the planet Earth," Mayar asked totally confounded. He thought he had accurately picked her origin.

"She is," Martel explained, "but through contact absorbed the body fluid of the Mir and this altered her chromosome patterns."

"The Mir?" Mayar asked. "But they come from a different universe.

"Yes, they pushed into this universe some time ago. They met up with the Altruscans who tried to use them in their takeover of Earth. And not too long ago tried to infiltrate the Antares."

"And that's when you, "Mayar let the sentence hang unfinished in the air, looking at her.

"Decided that they weren't welcome," Sabrina finished the sentence. "I enjoyed the chat, but now I need to return to the others. They're probably wondering what happened to me, and I'll get a lot of flack."

That's precisely what occurred when Sabrina returned to Lahoma's living room. She held up both hands. "Hold it, hold it. I got some good news. Mayar will lend us his unusual ship. We can use it as another bait. And he is willing to explain its marvelous properties."

"Okay, now let's get down to business and work out a plan, and no more popping in and out," Miri told Sabrina.

Chapter 13

Within six weeks they had worked out a viable plan. Lara left for Sheitan, and Miri and Joran teamed up for Raglan to implement the first stages of the scheme. Sabrina and Martel went to see if Morrigan would care to play a part in it.

When Sabrina and Martel arrived abruptly at Morrigan's compound, Kamila came hurriedly toward them. Her first question was, "Soraja?" fearing something had happened. Sabrina discerned the guilt Kamila felt for abandoning her oldest daughter on the Antares.

"Soraja is fine as far as I know," Sabrina assured her quickly. "I came to have a talk with Morrigan."

"What are you up to again?" she asked, suspiciously. Ever since they had met, Sabrina had disrupted the tranquil life style she enjoyed. She never shared Sabrina's adventurous spirit.

"I have something I need to talk to Morrigan about, that's all." Sabrina avoided looking at Kamila, instead she let her eyes rove about the place when she spotted Morrigan hurrying toward them.

"I just heard you landed. What's up?"

"Morrigan, I have an idea I would like to present to you." Turning to Kamila, "Would you mind if I borrowed Morrigan for a while? I know you're not interested in what I have to say" Sabrina temporized. "I promise we will be back soon."

"Well, okay," Kamila reluctantly agreed. "But you will come back before you leave," She made Sabrina promise, knowing from past experiences how unpredictable she was, disappearing without a moment's notice.

"We'll be back," Martel assured her, looking at Sabrina to agree.

"All right." Sabrina abruptly turned and so precipitated Morrigan and Martel to follow her without further comment.

Morrigan led them to a meeting room and indicated for the two to sit down.

"You were somewhat abrupt," Morrigan chided Sabrina.

"I know. I try very hard not to, but she has always roused this reaction from me."

"Yes, she said you always were kind of impatient with her."

Sabrina gave a rueful laugh, then, turned fully toward Morrigan. "I won't apologize; I didn't come to explain family problems. What I want to discuss is of a vital issue. It concerns bringing down the Orion Hegemony. Are you interested?"

"As Kamila said, you're abrupt. How do you propose to do it? And what part do you see for me to play in it?"

Martel leaned slightly forward in his chair. "Morrigan," he said, his voice serious, "The Hegemony has also hampered Galatia's trade expansion along with many other planets. They have used the Altruscan warring factions to keep a contrived conflict with the Alliance alive. What we're proposing is to try to eliminate their trade monopoly, and the financial backing to the Altruscans to expand their empire. Miri and Joran already went to Raglan to implement our plan, and Lara has gone to Voltar and Sheitan."

"You do this with the sanction of the Alliance?" Morrigan asked, smiling across Martel to Sabrina.

"Well, put it this way," Sabrina said slowly, and pulled a face. "Lara went to the Alliances Headquarters to present our plan before going to Voltar."

"So, you're proceeding on the assumption that the Alliance will agree?"

"Whether they agree or not is beside the point," Sabrina declared, determined. "It could very much be a private enterprise, since private money is used to finance it."

"I see. Now it takes on a less official tone."

"Morrigan, are you willing to consider it, or just trying to equivocate?" Sabrina asked curtly, but there was also amusement in her voice.

"Are you laughing at me, Sabrina my love?" Morrigan asked tartly.

Martel chuckled, his eyes sweeping from on woman to the other. He thoroughly enjoyed their sparring. "Morrigan, do you think the Matriarchal Council will agree? You know, you could come in privately," he said as a diversionary tactic.

"I will consider the private side of this business, but only after we present this to the Matriarchal Council," she told him, her eyes crinkling in silent laughter.

"When can the Council convene?" Sabrina was serious, pushing for a hurried convening. She ignored the amusement, knowing that she was the cause of it.

"Tomorrow, Sabrina. Now we go and visit Kamila. I think she will be planning a dinner in your honor."

"Ahh hummm," Sabrina grumbled as she rose. "I hate those things."

"For once, be gracious," Martel said quietly.

*　　*　　*

The meeting room could have been anyone's sitting room, except that it was large. Comfortable couches and easy chairs were placed strategically around the room so no one was out of eye contact.

Martel was allowed to come since Sabrina insisted that he was important to her presentation. He looked around, somewhat disconcerted at the informality of the room. With a depreciating smile he sat down at the far end, hoping to remain inconspicuous to better observe the Matriarchal Council in action.

The meeting was intense, the questions astute. The discernment of the Council of Matriarchs put Sabrina's ability of persuasion to the test. Especially Manema, the matriarch of Morrigan's compound, she thought that there was more to it. Manema felt that there was an emotional component to Sabrina's desire to go after the Hegemony, especially after the Altruscans. To commit anyone to Sabrina's scheme, she for one needed to understand the reason behind Sabrina's vehemence.

Sabrina finally capitulated to the probing and admitted that there was more to it. "It's a long story."

Manema clapped her hands. A servant appeared and was asked to bring refreshments. Then, turning to Sabrina, "You see, we have ample time for you to tell your story."

A chuckle from Martel brought everyone's head around to look at him in his corner. He bit his lip, and shrugged.

Opeda, another matriarch, turned to Sabrina. "Is this your male?" she asked in a tone she was confident would raise Martel's hackles.

"I'm neither her male, nor her husband, I only consort with her," Martel said tartly.

His replies brought an amused chortle form the whole assembly, and from Sabrina an apologetic look.

When the refreshments came and everyone was taken care of, Manema, with an expressive spread of her hands, invited Sabrina to tell her story.

Sabrina began with Jonathan and her parent's involvement with the Altruscans, her encounter with Garth, ending with her last confrontation on Earth where the Altruscans had used shape-shifters to infiltrate the Alliance.

"Your association with the Altruscans goes back a long way," Opeda said slowly. "Now tell us again of your plan."

"What we want to achieve is the destruction of the merchant houses. Their greed is keeping the Altruscan conflict alive by first creating dissension among the warring factions, and then supplying the weapons for their expansionistic wars, which in turn opens new markets for their goods. The merchant houses have to be equally threatened, so we will manipulate the stock market. We will invest and then pull out of it by withdrawing the funding as soon as the interest is high. We have also a plan to make loans for a new invention. Something, it will be whispered, that can be turned into a terrifying weapon. Also, I have the loan of a very unconventional looking ship. Much of the plan will be developed as we go along. Only the assets that will be pumped into the endeavor have been set. Joran Sandor and Tinian are heading the financial planning and implementations . . ."

"Tinian? Isn't he Miri's mate?" Adana, one of the matriarchs interrupted Sabrina.

"Yes, the same you made such eyes at," Manema told her, amused.

"Now, don't hold it against me if I have a sense of beauty. He is gorgeous."

Laughter greeted her statement. Sabrina looking around the circle and raised her shoulders, "Now, what else do you want to know?"

"Now we have an adequate idea of the overall plan. What do you want us to do?" Adana asked.

"Invest, and show an inordinate interest for the invention. And you will stress that naturally you only want to use it for commercial purposes. That is why you're sending Morrigan and some of her sisters to investigate."

"I see. I think I'll keep you on my good side," she told Sabrina, eyeing her speculatively.

Sabrina only gave her a negligent shrug, and to be more comfortable, shifted her weight on the soft cushions.

"Okay, Sabrina love, now leave us and we will discuss this mares-nest you gave us to unravel. We will give you our decision before you leave."

*   *   *

Very early next morning there was a knock on the bedroom door. In protest Sabrina snuggled deeper into her pillow, while Martel sat up and said, "Come."

The door opened and Morrigan walked in. She went over to Sabrina's side of the bed. "Are you awake yet?' she asked solicitously, pushing Sabrina's hair out of her face.

Grumbling, Sabrina opened one eye. "I will let you know when I am," she told her ungraciously.

"Do you always sleep with a male in your bed?"

"No, only when she is in strange places. I sleep with her because I don't want her to be afraid of the dark," Martel answered, trying to be witty.

"Martel, don't try to be humorous. It's too early," Sabrina complained.

"I see my efforts are not appreciated." Throwing the cover off he was about to stalk from the room when he was stopped by a gasp and Morrigan's astonished look. In a shocked voice she asked, "You do have some, don't you?"

Martel hurried from the room, but before slamming the door to the bathroom he looked back and could see Sabrina's whole body shaking with laughter.

After the door closed, Sabrina and Morrigan exchanged amused looks. "He has a convenient fold to tuck it away," Sabrina told her."

"No matter how old you get, there are always new surprises," Morrigan quipped.

"What surprise?" Kamila asked, coming through the door. She was carrying a tight fitting body suit and sandals for Sabrina.

"What are you doing with those?' Sabrina asked, pointing to the load Kamila carried.

"Morrigan hasn't told you yet? You're invited to the arena."

"I am?" she asked, frowning at Morrigan.

"Well, I haven't had time to consult you yet about your morning routine. But if you want to, you could accompany me to the arena. And if you like, we'll let you play."

"You're full of it this morning,' Sabrina grumbled at Morrigan.

Suddenly there was another knock and a man Sabrina had not yet met came slowly into the room.

"You're not ready yet?" he asked.

Morrigan smiled at him. "We're getting there," she told him. "Sabrina, meet Lars." She introduced him only by name, but unbeknown to her, Sabrina had read her surface thoughts, and knew that he was her mate. It astonished her since she called Kamila sister love.

At this moment Martel deigned to come back from the bathroom, fully dressed, and greeted Lars with familiarity.

"Do I dress before an audience, or do I have privacy?" Sabrina said tartly.

"It hasn't prevented you from doing so before," Kamila said, amused.

"Kamila, my love, we don't give out family secrets," Sabrina told her pointedly, throwing a pillow at her.

"You're not in a very good mood this morning," Morrigan remarked.

"Oh, don't mistake this, she enjoys being contrary." Kamila was still intending on giving out family secrets. She relished getting back at Sabrina.

"Out everyone," Sabrina commanded. Turning to Kamila, "Kamila, love," she asked sweetly, "would you braid my hair."

*   *   *

They met again at the arena. Sabrina walked up to Morrigan to ask what was going on, when suddenly she noticed girls forming a wide circle, surrounding both of them At first, she didn't pay much attention to what was happening. Out of the corner of her eyes she saw Martel making a move toward her, but was held back by Lars. Before it dawned on her, one of the girls suddenly jump-kicked her from behind, and knocked her to the ground. Sabrina fell and rolled and came back up on her feet. She went into a defensive stance. This time she was ready for the next attack, which came with four or five girls converging on her. It only seemed to take a blink of an eye for her to defeat them. When the girls stood back to better gauge her, Sabrina launched herself onto Morrigan, and took her down.

Laying on top, she pinned her shoulders to the ground, and grinned down at her. "I don't like sneak attacks."

"Entering the arena, what did you expect? Calisthenics? We wanted to see how good you were. Kamila said you'd like to have fun."

"I see." Looking up at the bleachers, she spotted her on the top most tier. "She is wisely staying out of reach," Sabrina said.

Later, under much teasing and jostling, they walked to a communal dining-room to have breakfast.

It was mid-morning when Sabrina was called into Manema's office. When she was seated, Manema told her, "We discussed your proposal, and decided to join your endeavors. We can give you some government funding, but Morrigan said to invest some of our private means also. Is that agreeable to you?"

"Yes. I'm glad you are coming in with us. The more glamour about this interesting invention, the better. Also as soon as investors come in, especially the merchant houses, your investment will be returned, with dividends of course."

"We know that Tinian is Lara's advisor, and he also has enhanced Miri's and Karsten's wealth. We don't know much about Joran Sandor."

"He is the financial wizard of the Antares and the House of Sandor. You can trust him," Sabrina said, amused.

Manema didn't join in Sabrina's amusement, and earnestly scanned her face. "It's not an easy decision for us to make. If it's found that we are antagonistic, there could be reprisals. Especially from the Orions."

"Risks have to be taken at times, and I understand your reluctance," Sabrina told her earnestly. "The Orion's power lies with the three houses on Raglan and the one on Voran. The house on Voran has been damaged. The Alliance has a wealth of information on their commercial practices. Then Amedes' industrial base on the moon Merca has been destroyed."

"I thought what I heard were just rumors."

Sabrina was not ready to commit herself, so she only acknowledged that the rumor was correct. "I will give you a rough outline of what we are planning. Our first attack is the stock market. We will invest heavily in the stock market, and also introduce stocks from a new industrial enterprise and flood the market with them as fast as it is prudent. What we want you to do is to spread the rumor about the invention, and then buy stocks."

"We will go into action as soon as you give us the word." Manema rose, and Sabrina was dismissed.

Chapter 14

When Spitfire dropped into real space, Martel, looking over Sabrina's shoulders, was surprised to see the Antares looming up in the cockpit's window.

"I thought we were going to Raglan?"

"I like to give Joran more time before we meet up with him," Sabrina evaded. What she had planned was to have some more time with Martel before joining the others. After arriving home, both went to their respective apartments to change. Later on, when Martel went in search of Sabrina, he found her in her study working on the computer. Since Sargon was not on board, and as soon as Yoshi found out she had arrived, most of the business of running the ship was sent down into her computer. Martel knew if she needed him she would call, so he slowly strolled through the garden. When he came to the lake he divested his clothes and dived in.

After a while he saw Sabrina standing on the sandy edge, watching him. She waved, divested herself of her clothes and then dived in. She came up from underneath, and as her face broke the water, he kissed her. She pulled him under and they played like this for some time.

Later, lying on the beach, their bodies entwined, Martel marveled how Sabrina's nearness never aroused feelings of anxiety in him, as did others. His musing was intruded by Sabrina inserting erotic thoughts into his mind. He chuckled under her kisses, not minding the intrusion, and responded eagerly, following her lead. The give and take in their lovemaking came easy.

What he discovered was that Sabrina not only enjoyed his lovemaking but the feel of his whole personality. She transmitted to him how he felt to her and then let him feel her excitement of him just being Martel. She merged her personality with his and he began to understand who Sabrina was. He perceived the spirit that drove her and her sheer joy in life and living.

*　　*　　*

Next morning, as Martel finished his last cup of coffee, Sabrina walked into the kitchen.

"Martel, I want you to come with me."

"I thought to have a day off and enjoy the ministrations of Medea. But I guess if you want me, I shouldn't complain."

Sabrina's eyes glinted in amusement as she surveyed the scene. Medea was busy at the cooking range, and Martel was comfortably sprawled out on a chair.

"Sit down and eat breakfast," Medea commanded. "I bet you haven't eaten anything yet. Turning to Martel, "If I don't remind her, she'll get involved in what she's doing, and forget to eat."

"Okay, I'll eat and you will quit scolding."

Sabrina sat down and Medea commenced to serve her eggs, pancakes, and she had baked muffins Sabrina liked. "You see," Sabrina complained, turning to Martel, "if I eat everything she serves me, I'm going to look as pleasingly plump like her."

"As long as you say pleasingly," Medea commented, with a growling undertone.

When Sabrina at last pushed her plate and cup away, Medea checked the cup to the see if it was empty. "Ah, to the last drop. Good, I hate to waste good coffee."

"Because you know you can get away with it, that's why you're harassing me this morning."

"See, that's the thanks I get for making sure she's taken care of," she told Martel. Medea tried to look aggrieved, but broke up laughing. "Ah you two get out of here so I can get this kitchen cleaned up."

After they left, Martel turned to Sabrina, "Where are we going?" he asked intrigued, since they were walking toward an area he had never been in.

"The Antares has an Auxiliary bridge. We also have an ear out in space that picks up scrambled messages, and after translating, sends them on to us. I want to see if there's already gossip about our special device."

The auxiliary bridge was a much smaller replica of the Antares' main bridge. It was Android One's station to monitor the ships internal and external workings just in case. For Sabrina's arrival he turned on life support.

"Android One, give me everything Minerva sent."

Sabrina sat at the console with Martel looking over her shoulders. Most of what there was, was just space gossip. But as the screen scrolled down, an item caught her eye. It wasn't much, but the house of Javan was contacting another planet in the Orion hegemony with a ciphered message. Minerva had sent the original cipher and then the English translation.

"Aha, someone's gotten interested," Sabrina murmured to herself. Then for a long time she just sat immobile and deep in thought. Martel already knew not to disturb her, but when she didn't stir after a while, he asked, "What are you cooking up?"

Distracted, she looked up, her eyes focusing at him. "I think we are having a change of plans," she told him. "I think I'm going to put a flea into the ear of the Security Council. This message shows that our plan is already working. But first, I will go and see Minerva, and I think the two of us will do some more gossiping."

"What do you want me to do?" Martel asked.

"You follow the original plan and meet up with the others."

When she rose from the chair, she gave Martel a studied look, before she went to the door.

Following behind, Martel murmured audibly, "I heard walking is good for your health."

Sabrina chuckled. He had understood her momentary hesitation. Alone, she would have raised her vibrations and disappeared. With Martel, she had to walk like everyone else.

At the smaller hangar deck, Sabrina and Martel entered Spitfire. She went to a computer screen and keyed Martel's image and voice into the computer, made a scan of his iris.

"I have reactivated the special trigger device," she said. "If someone enters the ship the wrong way, even you, Spitfire will explode. Always take the steps at twos and put your whole weight only on the second step, never the others. The idea is so simple most people forget about it. But it's deadly. On the Antares only Sargon, Yoshi, and I, and now you, know where it is. If someone tampers with it, or steps on it, the whole craft will explode. The special effect is the Antares' secret, the only others who possess it, are Miri, Lara and Karsten. Sargon stumbled on it a long time ago; but then, this is Sargon's story."

"You're very trusting, you know," Martel told Sabrina, as they exited Spitfire.

"No Martel, if you misuse my trust, I would find you wherever you are," Sabrina said, and her face looked forbidding. "But then, Sargon is seldom wrong about people. I'm doing this with his permission. I never do anything that concerns the Antares without consulting him."

Now it was he who gave Sabrina a studied look. "I see," he said. As he turned to look back at Spitfire, he said, "When do you want me to leave?"

A young Ensign with a curious expression on his face came up behind him, "Are you in the habit of talking to yourself?" he asked.

When Martel spun around, Sabrina was gone. "Only in certain peculiar situations," he told the young man, and entered Spitfire.

Chapter 15

"Knock, knock," Sabrina called out as she entered Minerva's cigar-shaped ship. It had been nameless until Sargon came back from Earth, and he named it Havana.

"No one's here," came the answer back.

"Then who's voice am I hearing?"

"The wind, the wind, breathing through the leaves."

"I came to see the wise woman Minerva, and also to do a little gossiping through a star-studded expanse."

"Sabrina, you will never make it as a poet," Minerva told her firmly.

"I know. I'm a dismal failure."

There was a soft chuckle as Minerva came out from behind a tree, limping toward Sabrina. She looked like a misshapen dwarf who had been used by someone as a punching bag. But her spirit was alive, and her personality engaging. No one who met, or spoke to her, would afterward remember her twisted body. She also had a soft and melodic voice.

"I surmise you didn't come to try out the new songs I wrote. I hoped so much to share them with you."

"There's time if we go to work right away. Let's see what we can gather."

The whole ship was laid out as a garden with babbling brooks and willow trees. Flowers were in abundance and in the most riotous colors. There were birds and bees and small furry animals. Many of her fruit trees were in bloom, the air was simply intoxicating.

Sabrina had stopped, her eyes shining with pleasure as she gazed around her.

"I thought you were in a hurry," Minerva chided her.

"Minerva, I have always time to admire something as beautiful as your place."

Minerva smiled happily as she tugged at Sabrina's sleeve. "Let's go and work, and then, we sing?"

She loved Sabrina's contralto when it blended with her soprano. She also loved to sing with Chantar. She had written a song for Chantar and thought to try it first on Sabrina. Just to see if she liked it. She was mostly alone, but she didn't mind her solitude. Ever so often Sabrina or Miri would pop in to keep her company. Also Sargon and Karsten looked in on her. She had her lifeline to the outside world with the listening devices the two men had installed. She was part of a wider world, she had a job, and she felt useful.

Her small house sat in a meadow beside a brook. It was very cozy inside. It was furnished to give maximum comfort and decorated to have style. The first time she met Sabrina, on Sargon's advice, Minerva handed her a catalogue and asked her to go furniture shopping for her. Then, everyone brought her small gifts, and Sabrina had painted several pictures for her. Minerva's most cherished ones were a portrait of Sargon and of Karsten, the men she loved the most, and were the most loving toward her.

Sabrina worked for several hours scanning space for other messages mentioning the device. There was none. She sat a long time sunk deeply in thought. Then composed a message in a code she knew was already broken for the Alliances Security Council, warning them that there was a rumor going around about a deadly device they'd better check on. She signed it S.M. Sandor.

Suddenly she sniffed. A most pleasing aroma wafted into Minerva's work room. It made her smile. Minerva had prepared something for her to eat.

She turned the scanner on automatic and left for the kitchen.

"I thought this would bring you around sooner or later," Minerva said, smiling at her.

"You thought right," Sabrina agreed. Going over to the stove, she lifted the lid. "Soup, hummm, and just the way I like it."

They ate, for a while in companionable silence.

"Now tell me what have you decided on?" Minerva finally asked.

"I sent a message warning the Security Council about a rumor."

"That's good, but, do you still want to listen to the song I composed for Chantar?"

"Of course."

Minerva hurriedly left and quickly came back carrying her lute. She strummed the strings, then, picked the melody. It had a lively rhythm. She sang it first by herself, letting her lovely soprano soar.

"Now, you sing along with me. I wrote it with your contralto and Chantar's soprano in mind."

Sabrina sang it with her, and to make her happy, some more songs. But finally she said, "Minerva, I thoroughly enjoyed singing with you. Thank you for sharing your songs and your time with me. But I have to leave soon. Usually around this time, Daugave time, Melkan is alone in his office working on things he plans to do the next day."

*   *   *

Sabrina appeared on Raglan on a sunny mid-afternoon. Scanning for familiar vibrations, she tuned into Joran. After she ascertained that he was by himself, she just popped into his office.

Joran jumped out of the chair, grabbing for his weapon. It took a second before he realized that it was only Sabrina. He let out a juicy invective, as he slowly dropped back into his chair.

Sabrina smiled, "Don't you like my popping in? It's very convenient, you know. I don't even have to open doors anymore."

"I don't give a hoot how convenient it is for you. I don't care to have a heart attack, so next time, knock."

"Yes, Sir. I only came to see how you were doing, and if there's something I should know," she said sweetly. "Did Martel arrive?"

"Yes. He and Tinian went off together. I haven't heard from them yet."

"Probably won't for a time. We got an interesting blurb from Minerva. Javan has contacted a subsidiary on Daugave to find out about the device. I sent a message to the Security Council, warning them about a rumor that was out, and suggested they'd better check up on it. That should give Javan something to think about. Now, if you would be so kind and fill me in."

"I have set up several phony companies, hiring people from Raglan. We also have a small industrial complex that builds certain weapon components. The owner agreed to help us if we helped him to convert and update his machinery. He would like to have a more lucrative business."

"You agreed?"

"Only in part."

"How much in part?"

"Well, we're helping him to buy the plant as soon as his contract with the house of Javan runs out so he can convert it to a more profitable enterprise. Like making tools; the reward of helping us. Those weapon components are very specialized, and he knows that after we get finished with the houses on Raglan, there will be very little demand for them."

"What about the stock market?"

"With that, we need to proceed more slowly. We don't want to arouse suspicion. Sargon and Karsten have begun to buy stocks, later to dump them back on the market. But that will be much later."

"Is there anything you need me to do?"

"No, everything is proceeding well here."

"If I don't see him first, tell Sargon that I will appear at the Security Council to complain about a rumor that's gotten out. He'll understand."

"Where are you off to?"

"First stop will be Daugave, and the Security Council, and then I will see about my boys.

Chapter 16

Sabrina came unannounced to the home of General Dehner. To her surprise the door was standing open. From inside came Logan's and Jason's voices.

"I'm telling you, I'm going to handle it my way." Logan's voice sounded strident.

"I wouldn't if I were you," Jason replied, more even-toned.

Following the two voices she arrived in Martha's living room. Sabrina's eyes widened as she saw her two sons. Logan, now nineteen, was wearing a leather outfit with a tightly fitting vest and pants, and his hair was long, bunched into a pony tail at the back. He was straddling a chair. Jason, eighteen, wore blue jeans and a shirt, and his legs dangled over the back of the couch. His hair was cut so short it stood straight up on his head. She smiled inwardly. They were a good looking pair.

"Are you having some kind of problem?" She smiled slightly and asked softly.

Jason spun his legs around coming up on his feet; and Logan froze on his chair. Both looked shocked, and turning pale, stared at their mother as if she was an apparition.

"What did I walk into me sweet boyos?" she asked, still with her deceptively soft voice. "What's with the pony tail?" pointing to Logan, her voice dropped an octave.

"Something I grew."

"I can see that."

Jason exchanged a warning look with his older brother.

"Did your tailor run out of material when he fashioned your vest?" she crooned, touching it and rubbing the material between her fingers. Logan's vest, made of synthetic leather showed off his well-developed biceps and muscular chest to advantage. Sabrina stalked around his chair as she inspected him. That's how girls like it, came a leak from Jason's unguarded mind.

Logan sat motionless, not knowing what to expect next. Jason almost stood at attention. Sabrina was an imposing figure.

Suddenly Sargon's presence infused itself into the room. He was standing at the door, holding himself very still.

"You gave us a hell of a scare walking in like that," Jason said.

"Jason, you'll either be silent, or you're leaving." Sabrina's voice held a warning note. Her mind had already tried to probe Logan's, but had come up against a dense shield.

"Logan!" Sabrina warned.

"Sabrina! I thought I heard your voice." Martha had come from the back of the house. "My God, I thought we would never see you again. And there you are in the flesh. You know you have two lovely boys. We really felt honored having met them. Captain Thalon and his beautiful wife brought them by. We really had some good times." All this tumbled from Martha, until Logan interrupted her.

"Martha, you can't fool Sabrina. Thanks for trying." He gave her a wan smile.

"Okay me boyo, let's have it. Give it to me."

Reluctantly, Logan lowered his shield.

"Of all the callous and stupid things you could have done," Sabrina exploded.

"Now Mom, it just happened," Jason tried to defend his brother.

"You stay out of it, unless you're somehow culpable, too. Enraged, she turned back to Logan. "Why didn't you use bio-control? How did this slip by you?"

"Mom, she said she was pregnant. I never thought to check her. It just happened, Mom. I didn't plan it that way."

"Where is she?"

"She's still in the hospital. Dad and her parents hired a lawyer. I'm going to adopt the baby."

Turning to Sargon, "Did you explain to her why she can't keep the child?"

"Yes."

"Sabrina, lets go to the kitchen and have a cup of tea, please." Martha looked pleadingly up at her.

Sabrina's face softened, "I guess you're right. It's too late to worry after the horses; they are out of the barn." She followed Martha, who had walked ahead, but at the door Sabrina turned and looked back at Logan, "You're out of uniform, Mister," she told him.

Looking at Logan tight-fitting outfit, "At least wear blue jeans," Sargon told him.

Sitting at Martha's kitchen table with her hands around the cup, her anger began to dissipate. "Do you know what happened, and who the girl is?" Sabrina asked, looking at Martha.

"She's the daughter of a friend of ours. I really feel responsible because I introduced them. She's a nice girl. She had broken up with her boyfriend and she was torn up about it. I guess she clung to Logan. And what happened, just happened. The boyfriend is back now, and they have made up. But there's the baby with Logan's eyes."

"I surmise when she met Logan he was wearing contact lenses."

"Yes, that's why it was such a shock when the baby was born. She didn't know about those tiger eyes, as Logan calls them. The parents contacted me to see if I could locate Logan's parents. I got in touch with Captain Thalon and we arranged for adoption papers to be drawn up. Are you coming to the hospital?"

"Yes, be assured I will be there."

*   *   *

When Sabrina walked into the hospital room, she was wearing a dress. The first thing she saw was the empty bassinet, then, a young, dark haired girl, her face stark against the white pillow, laying on the bed.

"You're Caroline?" she asked.

"Yes Ma'am."

"I'm Sabrina, Logan's mother. How are you feeling?"

Caroline let out a deep sigh.

"You were worried about meeting me?" Sabrina asked, gently.

"Yes Ma'am, I was," Caroline shyly admitted. "The way Logan and Jason talked about you, I was really scared."

"Well, I haven't eaten anyone, yet. I came early to have a chance to meet with you, and get to know you a little. I'm sorry it happened. You didn't know about Logan's eyes."

No Ma'am. I didn't."

"I bet it was a shock," she said with an amused smile. "And don't call me Ma'am, my name is Sabrina."

"I really like him. He's nice and sweet. But Robert came back, and we made up. He knows about the baby. He agreed to raise it, but when we saw her eyes, we knew she wouldn't have a chance growing up normal. It's not that I don't love her, but it wouldn't be fair to her." Tears gathered in her eyes, and began spilling over, making a damp spot on the pillow.

Sabrina reached for tissue paper and gave it to her. "I brought a film I was going to show Martha about my world. Now I think it's a good idea for you to see the home your little girl will grow up in."

Sabrina reached into her purse she carried over her shoulder and inserted the tape into the VCR.

"This is the Antares as you would see it from space," she explained, after the Worldship came into view. "And this is my home, the House of Hennesee, as it is called. What you see now is the entrance," as she was talking, she watched the girls face as Pegasus rose out of the floor toward her.

Caroline gasped, then, rose up from her pillow. "That's awesome!"

"It startles everyone the first time they see it and I love to watch the reactions. This film will only show the rooms on the bottom floor. And here are some old pictures I wanted Martha to see. They are taken of Logan and Jason as little boys. The two were always playing near the water and got soaking wet, so most of the time they just shucked their clothes."

Sabrina watched Caroline's eyes crinkle in amusement as she watched Logan and Jason, then four and three years old, splashing in the pool. "Then there's my garden, and the waterfall at its end."

"There's Meghan," Caroline suddenly said, pointing to the screen. Meghan was leaning over the bridge which led across the fall up to her domicile.

"Ah, so you met my little sister."

"She's your sister?"

"She's called my little sister, because I was designated her big sister. I raised her. She was eighteen months old when she joined my group. What you see now," Sabrina continued, "is the baby daycare. Your little girl will spend some time there, too."

The film showed infants and toddlers playing with toys. Then the scene moved on to the classrooms, and Sabrina explained that the kids were going to school there until they were fourteen, and after that would move over to the Academy. As the film progressed it showed the cafeteria, the playgrounds, and parks.

Caroline's eyes widened when the film showed areas were people lived. "They all look different," she remarked.

"Humans come in many shapes and forms. I had the same reaction as you. You can't imagine the shock Captain Thalon's eyes were when I saw them for the first time."

"They are kind of interesting," Caroline acknowledged with a smile.

Suddenly Sargon's presence insinuated itself into Sabrina's consciousness. He had entered the hospital, and was coming up the elevator. When he appeared at the door, "I thought you had Logan with you," Sabrina remarked.

"I think he likes Martha's company better," Sargon replied. "I see you had a tour of the Antares," he said to Caroline. The bridge of the Antares came in view, and at Caroline's gasp he smiled, "Kind of intimidating, isn't it," he said, while he walked to the window. "There's

Logan and Martha," he commented, and turning to Caroline, "and your parents with the lawyer, and also Robert."

"Yes, Bob said that he would be here, too."

"I'm glad he's coming," Sabrina said, as she rose to retrieve the cassette. Turning back to the girl, "At least he's supportive of you."

The others entered the room as a group. When Logan came in he gave Sabrina a look that said, see I made concessions to your ordering me. He did wear blue jeans, but he also wore a leather jacket, and his long hair was hanging loose down his back.

Sabrina, after his challenging look, ignored him. She went and shamelessly rifled everyone's mind.

The lawyer immediately came to the point, having only a short time before he needed to be somewhere else. "I have the papers drawn up with Logan Thalon Hennesee as the sole custodial parent. All that needs to be done is to sign, and enter the baby's name."

At that moment Caroline's physician came in, turning to Logan, "I don't think we can let the baby go home with you. She is refusing to take nourishment, and is weakening. I want to start intravenous feeding and put her into an incubator."

"I would not do that," Sargon interjected, moving toward the physician.

"Mr. Thalon is a physician, and he knows more about how to treat this infant," Sabrina said quickly to stall the Earth doctor's objection.

"Have a nurse bring the baby in here," Sargon said.

Unsure, the doctor looked at him, but again Sabrina quickly injected. "Please do as he says."

The doctor himself brought the baby. Sargon pointed to Logan. "Give her to him."

After removing his leather-jacket, he eased himself into a chair, then, held out his arms for the baby.

"Bond with her," Sargon told him, his voice gently breaking the silence in the room.

Logan only gave him a quick look, then, his face became blank as his mind merged with his little daughter. After a while a gentle smile appeared on his face, and he looked up. "Her name is Amanda. One worthy of love. I think that name is befitting. She will be all right," Logan announced.

"Did she name herself, or did you name her thus," Sabrina asked quickly, because Logan named himself when she first bonded with him.

"I named her. Now she will eat. Give me that bottle," Logan told his father. After some coaxing Amanda took the nipple into her mouth. "She doesn't like the feel of the nipple she says," Logan remarked, "but I told her that's the best I can do." He looked down at his little daughter, and then at his mother, "I think we might have another Sabrina here. She has a mind of her own."

"And she told you all this?" Caroline's father said as he drew his brows together, and shook his head. "Aliens," he thought to Sabrina's amusement, still aware of his thoughts.

Sabrina gave him a long look, and then a reassuring smile.

When the lawyer spread the papers out on a small table, Sabrina and Sargon put their signatures under Logan's.

Logan gave her a questioning look and Sabrina nodded. Since all the formalities were taken care, it was be best for Logan to leave without making the parting more agonizing. He reached for his leather jacket and shrugged into it, while switching Amanda from one arm to the other. Then, he winked at Caroline. "She'll be all right. I will take good care of her," he told her, and walked out of the room.

During all this time Caroline's mother had stood silently beside her husband. Now she sat down at the edge of the bed, and cradling her daughters hand's in hers, "Honey," she said softly, "there's nothing I can say to make you feel better. I know it's hard, but Logan is a nice boy. He'll make a good daddy.

Robert put his arm around Caroline's shoulder and pulled her toward him. He looked up at her mother and said. "Caroline is going to my wife and I love her. And we both are going to make it through this."

Her father's eyes were moist as he awkwardly bent over this daughter, kissing her on the brow. "We all will be there for you," he said hoarsely, then took his wife's hand and both left together. Stopping at the door, he looked back, "If you need something, just let us know."

All during the encounter, Caroline had been crying. Now she broke down, her sobs were heart-rending. Sabrina slid quickly off her chair and went to the girl. Caroline's arms came up and around Sabrina's neck, her face buried into her shoulder. Sabrina gently rocked her, like a child.

Robert, looking at Sargon and Sabrina, said, "I'm glad Caroline met you. It will make it a little easier having to let go. You're nice people. I will take care of her. Caroline and I have always been good friends. We grew up together. I left because I thought I was in love with someone else, but she turned out to be a dingaling. Looking at Caroline, "I'm really very sorry to have caused such a mess."

"It's all right, you came back." Turning to Sargon, she said, "I thought I was pregnant with Bob's baby. But it turned out to be wishful thinking. I tried to get pregnant on purpose, so Bob wouldn't leave me. But he was already gone before I could tell him. And then it turned out that I wasn't pregnant. Then I was pregnant with Logan's baby. I got myself into such a muddle. Turning to Sabrina, "Thanks for showing me where she's going to live. It really helped."

Sargon went to her, and taking her hand in his, he stroked the side of her face, and said softly, "She will be well taken care of. She has a big family." Then Sabrina and he left, leaving Caroline comfortable in Bob's arms.

Chapter 17

Sabrina walked into Chantar's hotel room, dressed in her Antarean uniform. All she meant to do was to drop in quickly to say goodbye, then leave to go back to Joran on Raglan.

Chantar sat before her mirror having her hair done up. She looked up surprised as Sabrina walked in. "And where do you think you're going, dressed like that?"

"I only came to say hello and goodbye. So it doesn't matter how I'm dressed."

"Don't you get sassy with me! There's a reception, and you are going to be there."

"Is that an order from the Captain's wife?"

"No, it's a request from your best friend."

"I'm glad you amended it. I would have to have a talk with Sargon."

"I haven't done anything," Sargon said from the door, "So why would you have to have a talk with me?"

"I'm told that I can't leave."

"Of course not! There's going to be a reception."

"I don't have anything to wear."

"Oh, Chantar has taken care of that. Have you dear?"

"We anticipated a cop-out, so I brought that dress you designed for the last fashion show. You never had a chance to wear it." When Sabrina tried to protest, Chantar raised her hand, "I also brought your jewels and make up, you name it, I brought it. So you see you can't back out."

Sabrina raised her shoulders in a helpless shrug and with a deep sigh and a sheepish grin, said, "Well, if you put it that way."

"Now that's settled, now let's do something with your hair."

Sabrina's hair was still short. She looked into the mirror, and shrugged her shoulders. "Not much you can do with this," she said.

Chantar turned to her hairdresser," You have any ideas?"

"I think if the lady would be dressed, I could see better what kind of hairdo would look good on her."

"Get dressed, Sabrina," Chantar commanded.

"Yes Sir." Sabrina saluted and sharply turned toward the closet. "Well, where is my dress?"

"Open the closet door, dear, and quit playing silly games."

Sabrina chuckled as she opened the closet door. The dress was hanging right in front. "You did expect me," she said, with a little sniff.

"Well of course. We had your boys."

"Now, if you will be so kind and clear out so I can change." She gave Sargon a pointed look, as she started to undue her trousers belt.

"What ever for," Sargon said, taken by surprise. She had undressed in front of him without thinking a thing of it.

"Now, let's get you dressed," Chantar said, after Sargon slammed out of the room.

Sabrina went to the mirror and sat down. She inspected her face critically and then her hair. "I think if I just sweep it up, it should be all right." Sabrina asked the hairdresser.

"That should do it," she agreed, and gathered up her paraphernalia.

Sabrina slipped the dress over her head and began arranging its folds. "Chan, you ought to join Sargon. I'll be down in a minute."

"Okay, but don't be too long."

After Chantar left, she picked a strand of pearls, and only applied minimal makeup to enhance her feature. Giving herself a last glance, she left the room and closed the door softly behind her.

Sargon, standing by Chantar and Heiko, was the first to notice Sabrina's presence and turned to look. Sabrina was standing on top of the stairs surveying the guests. Soon her presence insinuated itself into the very room. Everybody turned to look. She was coming slowly down the steps, wearing a simple chiton made of white silk. It fell in soft swaying folds. On her left shoulder she wore a clasp in the form of Pegasus. She looked like a Greek goddess come out of the pages of mythology.

When she moved to stand next to Chantar, Heiko said, "Thalon, you have the propensity to attract the most beautiful women. How do you do it?

"You haven't met the rest of the Original Four yet, Heiko," Chantar told him.

"No one could be more beautiful than you, Lady Chantar," Heiko said, and he meant it.

When the music started up, Heiko asked Sabrina if she would dance with him. Later on Sargon asked her to dance. As she moved to the music there was a pause in his movements. "You're pregnant," he said surprised.

"Yes, I know."

"Oh, this time you're aware of it. Does Martel know?"

"I haven't seen him since."

The evening was pleasant and after Sabrina danced several dances, she decided to cool off a little. Walking toward an open patio door, she sensed a presence watching her from behind the curtains, but no hostility. As she came closer, suddenly the hackles on the back of her neck rose. With a sudden movement she swept the curtain aside. It revealed a man dressed in dark clothing.

"Are you Sabrina?" he asked, his voice was husky, the accent Altruscan.

"Who are you?"

"I'm Shah Rah T'Sen. I wish you no harm; I only want to talk to you undisturbed. I only want you to hear me out."

"Follow me."

She led him outside toward a table and chairs. She sat down and indicated with her hand for him to follow suit.

"You are Sabrina?"

"I am."

"You are supposed to be dead," he said with a small grimace. "Do you remember me?"

"Yes."

"And you still followed me."

"State what you have to say."

"There's a rumor about a new weapon. When I followed the rumor, it led to nowhere. It led to a wheel within a wheel within a wheel. This made me suspect a very able woman, the only one who could create such an elusion. Garth thinks that you are dead, and he revels in the surety of his belief. I have come to put all this enmity aside. I have come because you are the only one I can conceive to trust. I want the Orion Hegemony destroyed before it destroys my world. They have been using us long enough, stirring up old hatreds while they are growing big and fat on the tears and blood of my people. The only one I know who can bring this off, is you. Your hatred for my people goes a long way back, back to Za-or. The name Hennesee kept popping up, and it finally caught my attention. I looked through old records Za-or had left behind. They led me to you. You were a child at that time. I know you lost your parents. My sympathy, I lost mine, too. Will you help me?"

While the Altruscan was talking, Sabrina riffled his files and found that he was sincere in his offer.

"You are planning to break down the old coalitions among your people. Divide and conquer. That's an old ploy. It might work. Many of your people became rich of the Orions, and gained power. You think it easy to persuade them to let go. But you're right, if their power-base, the Hegemony, is broken, you could have a chance."

"You agree that easily?"

"All I want is the useless, senseless, stupid wars to stop."

"Wars are always stupid, and lead only to destruction." It was Sargon's voice breaking into their conversation. He had noticed Sabrina's absence and through telepathy informed her of his approach.

When Shah Rah T'Sen quickly rose from his chair, Sabrina held up her hand, "There's no need for you to go," she said quickly. "Captain Thalon will support you as well."

Sargon grabbed a chair from another table, and swinging it between his lanky legs, sat down. "I have been aware of you for some time. I'm only surprised you came here. How did you know Sabrina was still alive?"

"What gave me the idea was how easy Merca's defenses were penetrated. That could only have come from the inside. Kasa, the commander of the complex, did not agree with how Garth handled the situation with Sabrina. Eyeing Sabrina, "Kasa suspected that you were beamed up as soon as the door closed behind you."

When Sabrina ignored his remark, Sargon asked him, "How far will you go in supporting us?"

"Half measures never suffice. I will go with you all the way. Maybe even prepare the way for us to join the Alliance at a future date; if you help to set up a viable economy after all this is over."

"This, you will have to take that up with the Alliance at the proper time. Do you have a plan on how you will go about bringing down the Altruscan power structure?"

"Yes. There are many who are weary of losing sons and daughters to a war that brings nothing but misery. Many have begun to see how we were used by the Orion Hegemony, and have joined me."

"Your name denotes that you are of an old royal house, is your goal to set up a monarchy?"

"No, Captain Thalon. I would like to go back to an older time when we were governed by the rule of Elders, elected by the people. It worked well for many ages. We have already written a Constitution which will never place power in the hands of one man."

"Power corrupts. It has always been that way." Sargon became pensive. He sat motionless, thinking back to his home-world, and the decadent power structure that ruined it. Suddenly he became aware of being stared at. "Sorry, got lost in my own thoughts," he apologized. "I will convey what you said to the Alliance Council. That's something I can do for you."

"It will be sufficient," Shah Rah T'sen said, as he rose. He bowed briefly to Sabrina, then turned and melted into the night.

* * *

This time, before entering Joran's office, Sabrina sensed Tinian and Morrigan within, so knocked on the door.

When she entered, Morrigan grinned at her. "When do you ever knock?" she asked.

"Since last time I nearly gave Joran a heart attack," Sabrina replied, and grinned back at Morrigan. "Where have you been?"

"We were on Daugave and met Sargon and Chantar there. He told us you had an interesting conversation with an Altruscan."

"Yes, it was an eye opener."

"I need you to sign this voucher," Joran interrupted, pushing the ledger toward Sabrina.

"How much of my money do you want?"

"All of it, naturally."

"You don't come cheap, Joran," Sabrina said, looking aggrieved.

Watching the interplay of their facial expressions, Morrigan whooped with laughter and Tinian chuckled. "Why do you allow her to treat you like that?" Morrigan asked Joran.

"I don't. She's just trying to show off."

A series of amused expressions chased over Sabrina face. "Don't be insolent, Joran," she said with mock sarcasm. Turning to Morrigan, "Your being here means Manema has agreed to fund this project."

"Yes. She has collected from several of the houses after Tinian has assured them that Joran is as reliable broker."

"Ah, she didn't trust me," Sabrina said, amused.

"She's a cautious one where money is concerned," Tinian told her.

"Now, how far have we progressed, and what other help do you need?" Sabrina asked.

"The only thing I need from you is your money. Since I have that, there's not much for you to do. Tinian and Karsten have done most of the ground work. We had a showing of Mayar's ship. You never saw so many impressed people. Also, the demonstration of the new device

215

went off without a hitch. We have more orders for the ship and device coming in from the three houses than we can handle. But that's what we had hoped for, so we can explain delays in delivering the goods."

"You sound like you're enjoying yourself," Sabrina stated accusingly.

"The most fun I've had in a long time," Joran admitted. "With the Galatian money and yours to pour into the market, we should be done here within three months. We're buying stocks, slowly so as not to arouse suspicions. And in about two months, when the interest rates are high, we're going to start selling. Karsten is doing the same thing on Voltar. He has opened offices there to handle the orders for the ship and for the device. He has started buying stocks."

"We're going to break for lunch, would you like to go out to eat with us?" Tinian asked.

"I would like to, but I better not show my face. As far as the Altruscans are concerned, I'm still dead."

"What's on your agenda then?"

"Tinian, me darling," Sabrina crooned, "if you don't mind, I'm going home."

*   *   *

As Joran had forecasted, in two months the stock market crashed throughout Raglan and Voran. As the houses collapsed, most of their countries sank into a deep depression. Also Shah Rah T'sen had done his bit. The Altruscan Empire was in chaos. The power of the warring clans was broken. There were still pockets of resistance. Many of the warriors resorted to piracy, threatening shipping lanes. The Alliance was hard-pressed to protect and to keep order.

Chapter 18

When Sabrina returned home to the Antares, she was tired and feeling not too well. Although this pregnancy being the least difficult, she still felt squeamish at times. She was surprised when she was met by Logan in the entrance hall with Amanda in his arms. She tried to suppress the nausea she felt, and at least be civil. "How's the baby?" was the first thing she asked.

Amanda was nestling against his chest, curiously surveying her grandmother.

"Amanda is fine. That's not what I want to see you about."

"You're upset about something?"

"You're damned right." was Logan's curt reply.

"It must be serious since you have lost all vestiges of manner." This time it was Sabrina whose voice was cutting.

Logan ignored her remark. "You started this thing called house rights."

Sabrina's eyebrow went up, and she took a closer look at Logan, but his mind shield was clamped down. "As you know it was Kamila who started it. So, why the ire toward me?"

"Margali claimed house rights. I just wanted to let you know."

"She did what?" Sabrina was dumbfounded. "Who put her up to this?"

"Probably Joran. She said she wanted her baby to have all the blood lines, whatever that means, so she chose me."

"I hope it was not too arduous for you?" Sabrina said far more waspishly than she had intended. She knew she was being unfair.

Logan could feel his temper boil up inside. "Mother that was a stab in the back. That's not fair!"

Sabrina gritted her teeth. She knew that was the last thing he had expected. She had been peevish. She eased her face into a smile, "Sorry, you're right. Remarks like that are unhelpful. What did your father say?"

"He said since you women started it, there was little he could do. He told me to enjoy it."

She stared at him, and then began to laugh. "Sorry, but at least you knew Margali. You grew up together."

"That's just it. She's like a sister. Can you imagine going to bed with someone you think of as a sister?" Logan voice had risen, and he was almost shouting. Amanda, disturbed at the emotions she was picking up, began to cry. "Ah darn. Now I've done it. Now she's crying."

"Well, just calm down. It's not the end of the world. Did Margali conceive?" "Yes, she's about three months pregnant." And the damned thing took three tries, Sabrina gleamed from Logan's unguarded mind.

Then of a sudden he became aware of his mother's figure. "You're pregnant," he said, pointing an accusing finger at her abdomen.

"Yes. So I am. Any comments?"

"No, I guess not." Then for the first time he tuned into her. "You're not feeling well. I'm sorry, that was thoughtless of me to have you standing her in the entrance hall. But I guess I was too mad to notice."

"It's all right. I'm going upstairs and shower. Have Medea bring me a cup of tea, will you?"

"After you're rested, I'll bring Amanda up to visit."

"That will be nice."

"Then I'll see you later. She's wet anyway. Sorry Mom."

Logan left, and she went to her apartment. After a while Medea came up with the cup of tea. She must have had some warning from Logan since she only set it down, then, quietly left.

*   *   *

That evening Sargon was giving a homecoming party for Joran. He also invited Tinian and Karsten, and had asked them to be sure to bring Miri along.

When Sabrina entered Sargon's house, the merriment was already in progress. She moved somewhat ponderously, and being eight months pregnant, she sought a chair to sit down.

Miri espied her, and looking at her gloomy face, pulled Sabrina's hair. "What's the matter with you?" she asked, irritable, "If you want to be a sourpuss, you could have stayed home. Don't you spoil my fun by being a party pooper. And I don't see what you have to complain about. You came out filthy rich from that project."

"Miri, Sargon almost ordered me to come, otherwise I would have stayed home. So go and pester Tinian and leave me in peace."

"Well, if you want to feel sorry for yourself, you can do it all by lonesome."

Miri left before Sabrina could apologize. She was depressed because she hadn't heard from Martel, and no one knew where he was. For a while, when he was captain of the Minoan, it was easy for her to pop in and spend time with him. But now, he was undercover. Martel was now totally immersed in the character he played. He wasn't accessible to her anymore; he was only like an echo on her mind. Being pregnant, she wished very much for him to be with her. It didn't help telling herself that she went through it twice before. *All by myself. Later, Marlo,* her face radiant with happiness, brought her a tray with food. Sabrina only picked at it, and after a while decided that she had fulfilled the gist of Sargon's order, and started to leave when Sargon came up from behind.

He placed a heavy hand on her shoulder, "And what are you up to, my dear?"

She turned around, and was just going to tell him to enjoy his party, when her eyes fell on Martel.

Martel stared at her. Pointing his finger at her belly, "You're pregnant!" Rounding on Sargon, "Why didn't anybody tell me!"

"I wanted it to be a surprise for both of you," Sargon told him

Sabrina laughed as her arms came around Martel's neck. He drew her close, kissing her.

"I didn't know this was a smooching party," Miri commented, breaking into a wide grin. "Surprised both of you, didn't we?" she said. "It was the hardest thing to keep this from him. Martel tried several times to call you, but we told him that you weren't home. I hate to lie, but this was for a good cause, don't you think?"

"Some day I will get back at you for that, Miri."

"Oh, but it wasn't my idea, it was Sargon's."

*　　*　　*

A month later Caphira, Sabrina and Martel's daughter was born.

This time, being cautious, Sabrina at the first sign of labor went to sick bay. Sarah examined her, and was just about to send her back home, when on a hunch, she called Sargon. When Jason was born, there was very little warning. And Jason was born without Sabrina hardly going into labor.

When Sargon walked in, he brought Karsten along.

Sabrina looked up from the examining table. "I thought you were gone," she said to Karsten.

"And miss all the fun? How are you going to have your baby this time?"

"The natural way, I hope."

"With you, there's no telling. Since you're curious, Sargon and I are working on a project. That's the reason I'm here."

"I know it wasn't to succor me in my hour of need. Where's Martel?"

"He'll be paged as soon as you show signs of getting serious."

When Sabrina started to get up, Sarah pushed her back down. "Just you lie here for a while. I still like to keep an eye on you."

"Aw, as you know, I like to be fussed over," Sabrina groused when the door opened. A tall, well-built man Sabrina had never seen before came in.

When the door opened Sarah turned and then her face went radiant.

Sabrina taking one look at her face exclaimed, "Oh, for the love of Mike!"

"Who's Mike?" the stranger who elicit such a radiant glow from Sarah asked. Sarah laughed. "Tobari, meet Sabrina, the biggest troublemaker on the Antares."

"A nice way to introduce me," Sabrina scowled at her. "But since he seems to produce so much happiness in you, I'm going to like him."

Sabrina had already scanned them both. She knew Tobari was her husband and also a physician, and that they were working together.

"I'm glad you like my husband," Sarah said.

After a few minutes of amiable chatter, Sargon and Karsten excused themselves went into the next room.

For a while Sabrina listened detached to Sarah and Tobari. Then she had a funny feeling, and telepathically began monitoring her baby. Suddenly she knew it was time. She told Sarah to get Martel.

"You're sure?" Sarah asked astonished, "you haven't dilated an inch."

"I don't understand it either, but I feel like it's time."

"As you say." Sarah called Sargon and then went to page Martel.

Karsten came to examine her. "Sargon, come monitor this. I don't understand. Like Sabrina, I think this kid is trying to be born."

"I know, I'm picking up the same activities, but she hasn't dilated" Sargon said, his hands gently manipulating Sabrina's belly.

Martel came in with his long easy strides. "I don't see how you need me with the whole Antares in attendance," he said, looking from Sargon to Karsten. "But I'm glad you waited on me. When is this thing to commence?"

"I think it's going to be about now. I think she waited for you to come," Sabrina told him.

Suddenly there was a lot of activity within Sabrina's abdomen. It heaved and moved. It was quite visible. Then of a sudden her water burst and the baby was lying between her legs. Caphira had bypassed the arduous journey through the birth canal. The afterbirth came the natural way.

Sargon collapsed into a chair. He was laughing so hard he was crying. Sarah only looked shocked.

"I surmise that's not the way babies are normally born," Martel said in his best Mendes imitation.

"No," Karsten said, cleaning the baby's face, then laying it on top of Sabrina belly as he cut the umbilical cord. When he was finished, he took the baby from Sabrina to examine her.

Suddenly Sargon exploded. "I think I'll give up on you. And you better not have anymore babies, I can't stand the shock."

To Martel astonished look, Sargon explained. "Logan was born by C section, and needed a blood transfusion. Jason just popped out while she was coming down the elevator. And your daughter, well, she did her own thing, and just materialized."

"Oh, I see, what you are trying to tell me is that she never does anything the expected way."

"You got it," Karsten told him, laughing. "You'll never be bored with this one," he said, pointing with his chin to Sabrina, while cleaning Caphira. Suddenly there was a sharp intake of breath, "She's disappeared!" Karsten exclaimed. As he turned, Caphira had reappeared, and was suckling on Sabrina's breast.

"I'm with you," Karsten told Sargon, "I give up. Walking up to Sabrina, "Are you all right?"

"I am. Thank you both. Isn't she gorgeous?" she asked, looking up at Martel.

"Well," Martel said slowly, "she's little, I give you that. And she's my daughter, that's a plus."

"Oh, you don't think she's beautiful," Sabrina said aggrieved.

"Martel, to a mother all her children are gorgeous. So don't stick your foot in it. If you have to lie, do so."

"Sargon, I will take your advice since you've know Sabrina a lot longer than I have."

Chapter 19

Because of Amanda, Logan had to quit the Academy and because of this special situation, was instructed privately, mostly by Ian's adopted son, Charles. Also, for the first time, he and Jason were separated. Logan had moved back into Sabrina's villa, into the wing across from his mother. It was next to Margali's apartment to be close to Noel, his daughter by Margali, who had been born two months ago. There were now three babies in Sabrina's house.

Sabrina had lost touch with Ian McPherson and Elisheba since their marriage, and then, she and Elisheba had grown apart. Since they lived in the village, Sabrina very seldom saw her. From Charles she knew that she was very happy, and that her two girls had entered the Academy and were doing well.

When Charles came to see her with a long face, Sabrina's first worry was Elisheba, since she had never completely recovered her health. When Sabrina asked him, he said, "I didn't know I was that transparent. No, it isn't Elisheba, its Ian. He's been kind of slow lately, he is growing forgetful. He won't see Sargon, and since Sarah's gone, I can't convince him to have a physical."

"You think he'd mind if I look in on him?"

"As long as you don't mention his health or try to talk him into seeing a doctor. Your visiting him, I think is better than any medicine."

"I have some new engineer journals I could take to him. Then, I do like to see Elisheba. I'm bad about not keeping in touch. You go and see Logan, and I will pick up Caphira."

When Sabrina arrived in the village, for a moment she had to think were Ian's house was. When she rang the doorbell, with Caphira in her sling resting on her hip, it was hard to keep the journals from slipping out of her hand.

When Elisheba opened the door, her eyes grew wide, "Sabrina, please do come in," she said overjoyed, leading her into her living room. "I haven't seen you in ages. Charles tells me that you are doing fine, and you have a new baby."

"Elisheba, may I introduce Caphira?"

"Oh, she's gorgeous," Elisheba crooned, taking the baby out of Sabrina's arms.

Sabrina was somewhat apprehensive, hoping Caphira would behave. Of late, if she didn't like someone, she just disappeared, and Sabrina had to track her down. She didn't think Elisheba would appreciate such a surprise. But apparently, Caphira liked her, and stayed comfortably snuggled in her arms.

Unobtrusively she took a closer look at Elisheba. She had aged; her fiery red hair was streaked with grey. But she had lost all that weight, and her figure was slim again. She dressed Antarean style, in the loose trousers and tops every one adopted after Sabrina brought the fashion home from Acheron.

They talked of this and that, reminiscing about the old days when they had been young. Sabrina, going through Elisheba's surface thoughts read, we all have aged except you, you still look young. There was a little envy coloring her thoughts.

"I'm remiss as a hostess. Would you like to have some tea?"

"I would love to, but let's go to your kitchen. This is a little too formal for me."

The kitchen was more informal. Also Ian would more likely come in here, then into the living room. Ian came in moments later and looked surprised when he saw Sabrina. She was shocked at what she saw. It was not only that he had aged, but he looked haggard. His skin was grey and his face sunk in, with his cheeks all hollow. He was in great pain.

"Hello," he said listlessly, "we haven't seen you around lately."

"Duty calls sometimes, as you know. Ian meet Caphira," she introduced him to her three-months-old daughter.

"At your age, you shouldn't have anymore babies," he said grouchy.

"Are you trying to be the bright spot in my day?"

"You must forgive him, he hasn't been feeling well lately," Elisheba tried to smooth over Ian's bad behavior.

"No need to excuse me," he said defensively. Eyeing Sabrina suspiciously, "Why have you come around now? You haven't had time for us before."

"Ian me darlin," Sabrina said softly, imitating his Scottish burr, "Ye shudna ha' said that. I ha' no patient wee stupid people. Ye know me weel eneugh."

"Ay, imph'm . . ." of a sudden he broke into laughter. "Ay lass, been good seeing you. Your burr's a little thin, I would na try it too much." He left, shutting the door softly behind him.

"You've got him laughing. He hasn't done that for a while."

"He is in pain," she told Elisheba. "Love, be quiet for a moment," she told her, holding up her hand. She went into what she called going down levels and telepathically contacted Sargon. When she knew she had his attention, she sent, "Sargon, I'm at Ian's. Come. Now!"

Within a very short time Sargon entered Ian's house. As he came into the kitchen, Elisheba's eyebrows rose, and she gave Sabrina a suspicious look.

"Sargon, find Ian. He's a stubborn old fool, and he needs you," Sabrina told him.

The silence in the kitchen became palpable. Elisheba sat hunched over, her hands gripping her cup. Then came Sargon's telepathic message, "Tell Elisheba to come."

"Elisheba go to Ian's room. I'll be in here waiting for you."

After Elisheba left, Sabrina phoned Margali at the daycare.

Margali answered the phone with, "Sabrina, what can I do for you?"

"Margali, I'm in the village. Do you know the house with the round gables?"

"Yes."

"Come and get Caphira."

When Caphira was gone, she sat back, and tuning into Sargon, she felt his command to Ian to let go. Then she perceived Elisheba's weeping, and her clinging to Sargon. She slowly rose and went into Ian's bedroom.

When she saw Ian, his face was peaceful, his hands folded across his chest. She went to Elisheba, still clinging to Sargon and put her arms around her. They stood silent, both embracing Elisheba. Then Sargon went to the phone and called sickbay telling them where to go, and to bring a gurney, Sabrina led Elisheba back into the kitchen, and gave her a fresh cup of tea.

She sat down opposite of Elisheba, and patiently waited until she was able to speak.

"He is dead!" Elisheba's distress was thick in her voice. "Sargon said he would have lived only a little while longer. He said there was no sense in suffering all that pain. Ohhhh, Sabrina, Ian is gone," she wailed.

Sabrina went to her, kneeling down on the floor, "Elisheba love, I know it hurts badly. I know you're missing him already. Come, let's go, Sargon will call an assembly. We will mourn Ian together."

Soon a slow rhythmic clapping of the hands started by Sargon was heard throughout the ship, and was then picked up by others. Everyone who could put down what they were doing, joined in. When Sabrina and Elisheba left the house, there was already a somber procession heading for the Queen's Chamber. Soon they were overtaken by Elisheba's three daughters. Sabrina took Danella's and one of the twins by their hands and silently walked on.

When the women entered the Queen's Chamber, a large picture of Ian was propped up against a stand draped in black, with a black ribbon across its frame. There were flowers arranged around it. When every one was present, Sargon took the podium.

"I have called you to give our farewell to Ian McPherson. He was my friend, and the friend of many of you. He has passed. Let's bow our heads, and observe a moment of silence."

Then one by one all of Ian's friends stepped forward, giving testimony.

Of a sudden Charles voice sounded throughout the ship. "Ian McPherson was a great chief. At the passing of a Chief, there should be the sounding of a drum."

Suddenly the sound of a great drum reverberated throughout the ship.

Chapter 20

Sabrina sat in her study working on a new lesson plan she wanted to introduce. It seemed the new crop of young Antareans were getting brighter, and the level of teaching material needed to be up graded. Both patio doors to Caphira's room, and the one in her study were wide open, so she could hear when she awakened. When Sabrina last looked in on her, she had been sound asleep on the floor, surrounded by her toys.

Caphira now was an energetic three year-old, full of curiosity and impishness. If she had not been bonded to Sabrina's PSI awareness, she would have been even more troublesome. Like her older brother Jason, she practicing wish-craft, and could disappear at will.

Sabrina, rubbing the back of her neck was for some reason becoming tense and her concentration slacked. She could see no reason to feel that way. She was not tired, and she found the theory exhilarating, so her energy level should have been high. Also, her mind wasn't working properly. It became an effort to think. These thoughts went slowly through her sluggish brain. Suddenly she realized a mind-silence. Usually, she had to screen out the people's surface thoughts, what she called the ships mind-babble. Her greatest shock came when she probed and found no feed-back. It was as if everyone had gone to sleep.

She touched Martel's, and then Jason's mind. They were as yet unaware that anything was amiss, but responded immediately to the alarm given by her mind-call.

Suddenly she felt the life support system on the ship went out. Sabrina's first action was to run toward the exit, but then she stopped. Because of the Antares ecosystem, the living areas would not lose oxygen like the bridge and other vital areas.

At every major exit throughout the ship was a room containing spacesuits. She slipped into one before sealing off the living area against intruders. Then the elevator doors would not open; she received the same information from Jason and Martel.

"Use the crawl spaces," she sent. "Get to the bridge. Get life support working."

She had years to explore the Antares. There weren't many nooks or crannies she hadn't poked her nose into. Toward the center of the auxiliary bridge, was a nucleus of energy where the crystals were housed. Toward this area, through a labyrinth of narrow crawls spaces, she inched her way laboriously upward. Sargon had maintained an auxiliary bridge just in case something like this happened, and the Antares was invaded.

She was perspiring inside her spacesuit. That's an impossibility she thought. What am I laboring against? Then it dawned on her, an energy field. Whoever invaded the ship had put up a force field. The thought chilled Sabrina. It would hinder Jason and Martel. It would even hinder her in reaching her destination. She fought the inertia pervading her very bones. This field also deadened her mind, and she couldn't use her PSI abilities. She tried to breath against the weight constricting her chest. Breathing was becoming more and more difficult. The effort to scale the crawl-ways made her legs and arms shake from the exertion.

It had almost taken all her endurance, but she made it. Leaning against the wall outside the auxiliary bridge, she took a painful and quivering breath.

The auxiliary bridge worked on its own energy source. When she entered, the environmental control and the consoles came on. Also, miraculously, her energy came back. She made a mental note to herself about this phenomenon.

In the early days, when the girls had been young, and Sargon needed to keep tabs on them, he had used an extensive surveillance network. It was in an adjacent room. As soon as she entered the room, the monitors came on line. She concentrated on the ones showing the bridge. Apart from the crew lying crumbled on the floor, there was nothing to see. Going through the light spectrum, she tried the wavelength at both ends. Suddenly she spotted a movement, and she turned the recorder on.

There where wraith like figures, like ghosts, moving purposefully around on the bridge. They were not human. A small head sat on top a long elongated body with wings attached to it. They reminded her of flies. Huge flies with mandibles and antennas on top of their heads. The biggest shock came when one turned around and seemed to looked directly at her. She had expected insect eyes, but the eyes were like those of humans.

She shook herself, trying to get free of this nightmare. She made a sensor sweep of the outside of the Antares and discovered the ship they had come in. The ship was not as insubstantial as the crew. It was quite tangible, and looked real. Also, there was a strange shuttle parked in the smaller hangar deck, next to her Spitfire.

Sabrina went to a storage room where a few items from the previous inhabitants of the Antares had been stored. Sargon had surmised that the original populace had been more insect-like than human. Sabrina reasoned that maybe some of the weapons left would work on these invaders.

A long time ago, when she had found this store room, her inquisitiveness, and using her engineering talents, she had manipulated some of the more interesting items there. One had been a weapon, and Sargon, against her protest, had taken it away from her. Now she was looking for it.

She knew she was working against time, but she had to proceed slowly and she had not idea to what wavelength or intensity to calibrate the weapon. In her desperation she sent out a call for help, her mind picturing Sabot as she remembered him.

A thought pattern formed itself in her mind, giving her the degree of intensity and wavelength. She silently thanked him as she calibrated the weapon. It was like a disrupter which sent out vibrations on the lowest tonal scale.

She set the transporter for intra ship beaming, and when she materialized on the main bridge, she immediately aimed and fired at the intruders. Then, to reach the engineering station, she literally hurled her body across the intervening space, switching Antares' polarity to positive. The polarity of the Antares was normally neutral, balanced between positive and negative. Switching its polarity to positive, the other ship was repelled and thrown out of orbit. She was just calling Acheron, and any ships in the vicinity, alerting them to the intruders, when the elevator doors open, and Jason and Martel came spilling onto the bridge.

"She's done it again, all by herself," Jason quipped. "Couldn't you at least wait for our help?"

"Well, you can turn the life support back on," Sabrina placated him.

A quick look passed between mother and son, and Martel could feel Jason's admiration, and the love Sabrina was sending him. He had long ago learned to ignore their bantering. Jason went to where Sabrina was standing, and turned the life support back on.

"You let everyone breathe stale air? Just to be a hero?" Jason accused her.

"Child of mine, sometimes you are a trial. First things, first. Isn't' that what Sargon taught you?"

"Please Mother, don't quote Sargon, please."

There was a stirring from the crew, and a sigh from all of them. The fresh air had revived them, and they rose slowly, like drunken revelers, from the floor.

"Sabrina, what happened," Chen asked, looking perplexed at her wearing a spacesuit, and then around him.

"You remember anything?"

"Remember what?"

"It's okay. There will be a briefing later. Chen, call all the stations. Martel, Jason, after you get out of the spacesuits, check on the schools. See if everyone is all right. I'm going to see about Sargon."

After shrugging out of the suit and before she disappeared through the wall, there was a tiny smile on her lips. It was good to be able to use her abilities. She had missed them sorely when she had to work her way through the crawl spaces.

She appeared again in Sargon's living area. He was lying in a garden chair by the pool, stretching as if he had just awakened from a nap. When he saw Sabrina, his face clouded, charily showing his annoyance.

"What in the hell are you doing here?" He thought it was one of Sabrina's intrusions, just to aggravate him

Sabrina looked at him in disgust. "You're stupid," she told him, to his surprise. "Meet me in the briefing room, now." She turned sharply, and walked away. Five minutes later Chen, Martel, and Sargon were assembled in the briefing room. Jason had gone back to check on the other members of the family, especially on the little ones. Sabrina was already waiting for them, the communication console showing the control room of Acheron's space station.

"We have scrambled fighter craft's to intercept," the commander of the station just said, as Sargon slowly sat down.

"Keep me informed," Sabrina said, terminating the conversation.

Turning to Sargon. "We have been invaded," she said, and let it hang in the air.

"I apologize," Sargon said, "my behavior was atrocious."

"Well, that's very gracious of you," Sabrina said slowly, scratching the side of her neck. "Especially when I just saved you're live, and the whole damned ship."

Before Sargon could reply, the communication console came on again. "Captain Hennesee, we just blew them out of space. They are destroyed. Now, tell us, what have we been shooting at?"

Sabrina without a word inserted the disk, sending the pictures to Acheron's station, while at the same time showing it on the screen in the briefing room.

"Oh my stars," Chen said.

Sargon watched without comment.

"Captain Hennesee, our thanks," the Commander said, looking ashen. "We will send you a communiqué. Acheron out."

"I guess Jason, Sabrina and I haven't been affected because of our genetic make up," Martel said.

"Who noticed it first?"

"It was Sabrina who alerted us," Martel said.

"How did you notice?"

"I became irritated."

"I thought that was a natural state for you."

"Levity will get you nowhere," Sabrina told him with mock severity, shaking her finger at him. "Seriously, at first I wondered why I felt so drained, and my brain was getting so sluggish. Then I noticed that there was no mind-babble from the ship. It was like everyone had gone to sleep at the same time. When I sent a mind-probe, only Martel and Jason answered. The elevator doors wouldn't open, and the life-support was out. I closed off the living areas and then went through the crawl spaces up to the auxiliary bridge. There I recorded the disk and then, well, I found the weapon you took away from me. You remember? A long time ago? I received a thought pattern from Sabot how to calibrate the weapon. I beamed to the main bridge and shot them. I guess that's all," Sabrina said, pulling on one earlobe.

Sargon turned to Martel, "Is there anything you can add?"

"No, that's about it. After, I received the mind-call from Sabrina. Jason and I tried to reach the bridge. We got there a little after Sabrina. By that time she had taken care of most of it."

"You're amazing. You've done it again," Sargon said with a shake of his head. The last time Sabrina had saved the ship was from an invasion of a Mir, and she and her unborn child nearly died. It had resulted in chromosome damage which had genetically altered her baby, and wrought some amazing changes even within her genetic make up.

"What are friends for," Sabrina said, depreciatingly.

Sargon rose slowly from his chair and went to Sabrina. He gently raised her face toward him, then looking at Martel. "With your permission," he said, then kissed Sabrina.

Sabrina was enveloped in so much love, the tears came spilling down her cheeks. Her arms went around his neck and he pulled her up, holding her tightly against him.

Martel, bonding with Sabrina, had freed them both, and it made it possible for him to show Sabrina how much he loved her.

Chapter 21

Caphira had turned twelve, and Sabrina, for the first time left the Antares. She was in an advisory capacity on the Earth-ship Intrepid. The Captain, Ned Taylor, was not too sure of Sabrina's intent toward his command. Too often she would take command away from him to show different maneuvers.

They were seated in the cafeteria when the alarm sounded. Both rose in an instant, and were at a run toward the lift. On the Bridge, the forward screen showed a vessel in attack mode.

"Lieutenant, report." Taylor shouted, rousing the young man out of his stupor.

"Sir, we opened hailing frequencies, but got no reply."

"This is an Altruscan war ship and in all probability a pirate. In a few seconds you will be under attack," Sabrina informed them.

"Are you sure?' Taylor asked.

"Yes. I know my Altruscans. Taylor, I'm taking command."

"The hell you will!" was Taylor's automatic response.

"Be reasonable, Dear," Sabrina said. I supersede any rank on any Alliance ship. This situation is very serious. Your crew is yet untried in combat, and so are you. I have fought the Altruscans many times. And, I always win. Magnify screen." Sabrina commanded.

"Are you making your takeover an order?" Taylor asked.

"Yes. Comply. In five seconds we will be under attack. By the way, in all appearances, you're still in command. I don't want them to see me, or hear my voice. As far as they are concerned, I'm dead."

The Altruscan vessel approached cautiously, feeling out the Earth-ship, and gauging its reactions.

"Navigator, at my order, turn sharply starboard, and veer off at Warp three. Gunner, have your photons ready, spray them as we leave. Then I want the ship to turn around on my order. Have the phasers bombard their hull from starboard. I want the bridge hit." Sabrina watched the Altruscan ship firing up their engines for a run toward them. "Now navigator," Sabrina's commanded.

The Intrepid veered off. As she did, the Gunner emptied all the photon tubes at the Altruscan vessel.

"Navigator, turn about."

"Yes Ma'am."

There was a startled look on Sabrina's face. She hadn't been called Ma'am in a long time. When they turned toward the enemy ship again, they came upon her from starboard. The Intrepid phasers sheared off the Altruscan's bridge. Sabrina knew that they had an auxiliary bridge within the belly of the ship, and was not surprised as the ship veered off and sped away.

Sabrina went to communications, and on a tight band sent a signal toward the Antares.

Within minutes an image appeared on the Intrepid' screen.

"Chandi, who is on board to fly Spitfire?"

"The only one I know of is Martel, but he's got orders from the Alliance to join Karsten and Zoe."

"Tell Martel to disregard Alliance orders, and key Spitfire to these co-ordinates."

"Will do. Antares out."

Sabrina sent a scrambled signal toward the planet Daugave, the Alliance's seat. "Priority one, priority one, this is Captain Hennesee. Need widest measure of leeway. Canceled Captain Alemain's orders to join Commander Karsten."

She swiveled the chair toward Taylor. "The ship is yours," she told him as she rose, and before entering the lift, she turned back. "A fighter plane's coming toward us. When you see it, just tell the pilot that I'll be with him in a second. His name's Martel."

Martel appeared above the Intrepid and then dropped to starboard.

The Intrepid opened hailing frequencies. "I'm Captain Taylor, if you're Martel, I'm supposed to tell you to wait. She'll be with you in a second."

A chuckle came over the intercom. "Yes, I'm Martel, and she's just arrived on board."

As Spitfire veered off, and after stuffing her duffle bag into a wall locker, Sabrina dropped into the co-pilot's seat behind Martel.

"Now what's your all fired-up hurry about?" he asked.

"The Intrepid was just attacked by an Altruscan war ship. Guess who its Captain was?"

"Garth."

"Yes, and I want him."

"Figures," Martel said, and headed for the Orion.

*   *   *

Martel kept Spitfire just far enough behind the Altruscan ship as not to be picked up by their sensors. Sabrina, her arms around Martel's neck, watched the readout on the screens. When she nibbled at his ear, he half turned, "You want to make love? Or you want Garth?" he asked, with a deep chuckle in his throat.

"For right now, I want Garth," she told him.

To their surprise the Altruscan ship headed away from Betelgeuse and used Bellatrix as a navigational lock-on. Their destination seemed to be a dot in space, a small yellow dwarf between the belt and the outstretched arm of the Orion.

"You know, seen from earth, this part of the sky forms a constellation called Orion, the Hunter. As a child I had no idea of the distances between the stars that seemed so close together to me. From Sheitan, it's just part of the Milky way."

"You're quite pensive. What brought on this serious mood?"

"I don't know. Maybe I'm closing a chapter in my life."

Martel, leaning his head back, brushed Sabrina's cheek with the side of his face. "We could go home. It is not in your job description to pursue Garth."

"No, but the piracy has to stop. I think Garth is the main character in this. Maybe after we eliminate him, there will be peace in this sector."

"That's not all of your intention."

"No. I like to get even."

"That's more like it."

Sabrina chuckled. "You think you know me that well?"

"No, but I'm getting a slight inkling."

Speeding through space they monitored the conversation on the Altruscan ship. Half ways through Martel's second sleep period the Altruscans approached a small planet, third from the sun.

"Martel," she called, "wake up!"

"What's going on? Where are we?"

"The Altruscans just established orbit around a small planet. I'm not familiar with the language. Can you understand?" Sabrina asked, after he entered the bridge.

"Yes, you're lucky, I do."

"You do? That's the first time you've said it," Sabrina teased him, sticking her tongue out at him." Martel had refused going through the marriage ceremony Sargon had planned for them, declined to accept Sabrina as his wife. And Sabrina was ever so thrilled at squelching Sargon's effort in trying to give her away. "What are they saying? What's the planet's name?"

"The planet's name is Selsa, and they're asking permission to land. What did you expect?"

"Well just that much. I want to go down there to stalk Garth for a while. I like to get a feel for the lay-out before confronting him."

"I'm going with you."

"You're going to walk?"

"Sabrina!" he said sharply. "Fun and games aside, I'm not letting you go there by yourself."

"Well, do you think they'll let us land?"

"No, but if you beam me down first, their sensors won't pick up the beam-down. They're somewhat more primitive, although don't tell them that. Several decades back, the Hegemony swallowed them up, and the Altruscans had, or still have, a base there."

"The Altruscans could hit on the beam-in."

"No, I don't think so. The base is somewhat out of date. The planet was just a convenient bolt hole."

"Okay, if you insist. Let's find a safe place to put you down, and I guess we will use your Mendes persona," Sabrina said. She was glad she didn't have to confront Garth all by herself.

For a while they monitored Garth's activities through their sensors; also, the news media. Martel was translating all the pertinent points. There was no mentioning of an Altruscan ship landing.

Planet time, it was late afternoon when Sabrina beamed Martel down inside a hangar. Then she went and parked Spitfire on the biggest asteroid circling the planet before joining Martel.

"There are two airplanes in here, and I bet one belongs to Garth," Martel told her. "You want to find out first where his headquarters is?"

"Yes, I want to see the base he operates from."

Just then, Garth and another man were coming from a building toward the hanger. Sabrina and Martel eased back inside to hide behind some crates.

"No matter what you think, I'm sure there was a ship following us," they heard Garth saying, his voice acrid. "I have been out there longer than you. I don't believe in echoes. So go to the tower and monitor any incoming crafts. The Earth ship should not have been able to inflict that much damage. I would like to know who commanded that ship."

As the Altruscan sped away, Garth made his way into the hanger. As he came closer, Sabrina and Martel could see the scowl on his face, and that he was biting his nails. He pulled himself up to one of the planes, and went through the starting sequences. Soon the plane's noise and exhaust filled the hanger, giving Martel and Sabrina a difficult time breathing. As he taxied out, a troupe of Altruscans arrived, ready to board Garth's plane.

Sabrina grabbed Martel's arm. "That's Shah Rah T'Sen," she said astonished.

"Wonder what he's doing here?" As she wondered, she rifled his files and found that his objective was the same as hers; taking out Garth.

"Well, what is he doing here?" Martel whispered impatiently, not able to gather information the way Sabrina did.

"Same as we. He discovered this hidey hole. By the way Garth doesn't know who he is. He thinks he's someone interested in a little piracy to fill his coffers."

"Okay, plan of action?"

"Before Shah Rah T'sen climbs into that other plane, walk up to him, and whisper "Sabrina" into his ear."

Martel barely suppressed a chuckle as he looked at his mate. "You're something else," he told her.

Sabrina grinned at him, brushing his cheek with her lips. "Be a good boy and go ahead." She gave him a gentle shove, and then watched as he approached Shah Rah T'Sen.

After Martel walked up to the Altruscan, he crooked his fingers for him to lean forward, then, whispered into his ear. An astonished look passed quickly over his face as he looked at Martel. Then he nodded his head without scanning the hanger.

"I'm glad you could make it, Mendes," Shah Rah T'Sen greeted Martel.

"Wouldn't miss it," was Martel's rejoinder and climbed up into the plane, then followed Shah Rah T'Sen to the cockpit.

They took off after Garth, and after several hours landed far in the interior of the landmass. There was a small airstrip, not far from several barracks. When Shah Rah T'Sen exited the plane, he told Martel to remain behind.

Martel taxied the plane into a hangar, and was in the process of shutting the engine down, when Sabrina popped in behind him.

"You did that real good," she told him.

"I'm glad I was a good boy," he teased, alluding to her earlier remark.

"I think we have company," Sabrina told him, and ducked down between seats.

Shah Rah T'Sen cautiously entered the plane again and looked around. "You mentioned a certain lady," he said.

"Hello, Shah Rah T'Sen," Sabrina greeted him, coming out from behind the seat.

"Where did you come from?"

"Sometimes someone does not ask leading questions. I surmise you know Garth attacked a Federation ship."

"Yes, he bragged about it. But it also had him worried. He said that the Earth ship's Captain was too experienced to be a novice in space battles. Was it you he confronted?"

"Yes. I was on the ship in an advisory capacity."

"That would make sense. What's your intent?"

"Revenge on Garth."

"Yes that also makes sense to me. I remember what he did to you."

"You were there?" Martel almost turned on him.

Sabrina held up her hand, "Mendes, he did what he could. He couldn't appear too obvious. If it looked like I had a champion, it would have prolonged my ordeal. Garth would have enjoyed baiting him."

Martel stepped down from his offensive posture, and relaxed. "What's Garth's plan?"

"He needs to get his spaceship fixed. Otherwise he's stranded."

"How did he get in possession of a warship?"

"He stole it. That's why my government sent me, and if it's possible to retrieve it. Or, blow it up."

"If Garth is taken out, how will your government deal with the rest of his Altruscans?"

"Their existence is not acknowledged. I have contacted the government here, and they have talked to the Alliance. There is already a ship en route to remove the Altruscans from here."

"And you?"

"I'll go with the Alliance ship."

"I see," Martel said.

"And what is on your agenda?" Shah Rah T'Sen asked Sabrina.

"Garth."

"What will happen to your aircraft?" Martel asked him.

"I think I will leave it here as a present."

"Garth is mine, right. So you two commence walking over to the barracks and pretend that you have nothing more on your mind then to spend a pleasant day."

"And you?" Shah Rah T'Sen asked.

"You don't worry about me."

* * *

Garth restlessly paced the floor. His crew watched apprehensively. Most of them began slinking away, leaving the room as unobtrusively as possible. He was known to be vicious, and his behavior unpredictable. He could lash out at the slightest provocation. His mind was not on his deserting crew, but the battle with the Earth-ship. His instincts were on alert. Trusting his gut feelings had made him a survivor. The counter attack of the Earth-ship had been brilliant. He could not have done better himself. That was what stuck in his craw. But she was dead. His nemesis was dead. He had to believe it. He had battled Sabrina before

245

and knew her tactics. They had always been unusual and surprising. When the door opened and Shah Rah T'Sen stepped in followed by Martel, his emotion exploded at the sight of a stranger, and he turned on Shah Rah T'Sen.

"Who is this? Are you consorting with Alliance spies now?"

"I don't think Carr would take it too kindly you doubting his intelligence," Martel said, his voice oily smooth.

Garth let out a curse on all the generations of Carr's.

When Martel contemptuously turned his back on him, it incensed Garth. He was just in the process of launching at him, when.

"I wouldn't do that, if I were you?" Sabrina's voice suddenly sounded in the room.

Garth spun around and staggered backward. His finger stretched accusingly toward her, "You're dead," he croaked, saying it again and again. Ashen faced, he was gasping for breath, clutching at his chest. His eyes were nearly bulging from their sockets.

"No, I'm not," Sabrina stated in her most reasonable tone. She was standing at ease, her arms hanging loosely at her side. There was a derisively amused look on her face.

When he reached for his weapon, Shah Rah T'Sen knocked it out of his hand.

In his fury he turned on Shah Rah T'Sen. Sabrina, kicking him in the back made him stagger; his fist fell short of the intended face.

Garth lunged himself at Sabrina. But she easily side stepped him, and his face met the floor.

With a deep animal growl he began circling her, looking for an opening. She tricked him to precipitate a rash attack. It landed her foot right in his groin.

He doubled over for a second, then again made an unfortunate lunge. His anger blinded him. As he gathered himself again off the floor, he began circling, observing her movements more cautiously.

"Oh, finally got smart," she said in his language. "Come on baby, I'm waiting on you. But this time you better watch out; this time I'm not trussed up, and I wont pee on you." This was the one thing Sabrina had never forgiven him for. She hadn't minded him kicking her and parading her in the nude around the compound. But when he shoved her to the ground and relieved himself down her back, he had signed his death warrant.

As she taunted him, she had never seen so much hatred on anyone's face as he stared at her. He let off a string of vicious invectives.

"Tut, tut," Sabrina said, wagging her finger at him. "Nasty boy; bad language. I think this is getting sort of ludicrous," she said, and waded in on him. He was vicious, and got a few kicks off on her. But when she was finished with him, he had two broken collar bones, his left arm was broken, and on one side, his ribs were caved in, piercing his lung. As he looked up at her, his breath was labored, and blood was spurting from his mouth and nose. "I guess I ought to finish this, it's getting tiresome." She loosened one of her asterics from her belt and let it fly. It embedded itself deeply in Garth's neck, cutting the artery. She watched as he died, finding not much gratification. Then she turned to Shah Rah T'Sen, "Who'll take care of this?" she asked. Her voice was listless, and her demeanor bleak. He only shrugged his shoulder. Sabrina gave him a long look then turning to Martel, "I guess the job Jonathan started so long ago, now is really finished." And to Shah Rah T'Sen, "There will be no more Altruscans menacing space?" When Shah Rah T'Sen shook his head, no, she said, "Now that the Orion hegemony is broken, you can chart your own course. I hope you choose wisely."

She left, walking out through the door. When she found there was no one watching, she disappeared instantly, to reappear on Spitfire. After getting the craft into orbit, she locked on to Martel and beamed him on board.

*   *   *

Martel's brows were drawn as he watched Sabrina entering their destination into the computer. "Hey, that's not the Antares," he finally said.

"I've been feeling antsy about Sarah for some time. Running into Garth drove it out of my mind, but now it's back. We'll stop by Rhiansu, just to see how she's coming along."

"That's close to Khitan?"

"Yes. But it's on our way home."

"I'm just thinking about Caphira." Martel said. "You know I suddenly disappeared on her."

"She's a big girl, she will understand . . . I hope."

When Spitfire dropped into real space, approaching the relay station above Rhiansu, they were warned to stay away. The man on screen told them that Rhiansu was quarantined.

"Rhiansu, this is Spitfire, explain the nature of your quarantine?" Sabrina asked.

"We have a planet wide epidemic. It is a virus that has been brought in by outsiders. There's no vaccine, so there is no cure. As I said, my advice is to stay away."

"Can you tell me the status of a Doctor Sarah Thalon?"

"I will ask around, then, call you back."

"All right, Spitfire establishing orbit."

Turning to Martel, "I know there was something nagging at me, and I'm terribly worried about her."

"Let's wait till we have confirmation on her status before you worry too much, or until you're able to talk to Sarah."

To stay stationary above the relay station, Sabrina matched Spitfire to its rotation. Waiting seemed forever, but suddenly her screen came alive and they were contacted from the planet.

"Spitfire, this is Rhiansu, are you still there?"

"Yes, I'm still above you."

"I thought the blip on our screen was you. I will patch you through to the hospital."

"Thank you, Rhiansu."

The screen went blank again. When it came alive again, the tired face of an old man was looking near-sighted at her.

"I was told that you are enquiring about Doctor Thalon. I'm Doctor Samon. Whom am I speaking to?"

"I'm Sabrina Hennesee. I'm her friend."

"Ah, Sabrina, she talked much about you. I'm sorry Sabrina, I don't have good news. She worked so hard, and thanks to her, we have an idea on how to combat this problem. But when she caught the virus, she was too weak. She didn't make it. We cremated her body according to our custom. My condolences." When Sabrina didn't answer, "Are you still there?" he asked.

"Yes, I am. How about Doctor Tobari?"

"Her husband died before she did."

"Thank you Doctor Samon, Sabrina out." Her face was somber and her voice sounded calm. All her emotions were kept in abeyance. Spitfire veered off. Out in inter stellar space, she keyed in the Antares' position, then, let the special effect take over.

Before disembarking onto Antares' hangar, Martel laid his hand on Sabrina's shoulder. When she turned to look at him, his face was grave with his concern for her. But she had shut him out. Usually, there was a tie between them, they shared emotions. Now, this tie was broken; there was a void. She covered his hand with hers and gave it a gentle squeeze. "I will go to see Sargon," she told him. "Will you see about Caphira?"

"Okay, she'll just have finished school and be on her way home," he said, glancing at his time piece.

But Caphira, sensing her mother's presence on the ship, used her homing capabilities to intercept her parents.

"There you are," Sabrina heard an indignant and strident voice. When she turned, Caphira was running toward them. When she stopped, she had one hand braced against her hip, shaking her finger at Martel. "Who do you think you are disappearing on me like that," she berated her father. "Am I just a package to be deposited with whoever is around? But thank god it was Kara."

Martel had a hard time to keep a straight face. To him this incensed twelve year old daughter looked absolutely adorable, but then, she had a right to be mad.

"That was my fault, Caphira," Sabrina told her.

"I'm not talking to you," Caphira told her, her eyes angrily raking her mother up and down. "You left me too, and then you snatched Dad away. They told me that you called and ordered Dad to join you. I hope you two had fun, or whatever you did."

While Caphira thus vented her feelings, Noel and Amanda had come up on them and were listening to the last part of Caphira's diatribe.

Noel was staring penetratingly at Sabrina, and then began walking slowly around her. "Grandy, why are you as tight as a clam?" she suddenly asked.

"Granddaughter, what makes you think you have the right to scan me?"

"You're our grandmother, and that gives us the right," Amanda told her.

"Especially, when something doesn't feel right. So, what are you trying to hide from us?"

She smiled down at her daughter and two granddaughters. "I love you too," she told them, "and we will talk later. But now I'm going to see Sargon. Go home with Martel."

"Well, you're in luck. Sargon just came home too with Ayhlean and Soraja," Caphira told her. "Well, almost everyone was gone. Why do you think I am mad? There was only Kara left, even Margali was gone. She and Joran, and Chantar, and Chiara," she counted off on her fingers. "All of them had gone to Acheron because Rosana thought she was going to die again, so she called everyone home. I think she does that on purpose to keep everyone hopping. And if you think you're tight, you should see Sargon. He nearly snapped my head off when I demanded to know what was going on. He told me not to be impertinent. Do you believe that," she asked, her voice breaking as it rose to its highest pitch. "I'm worried, and all he could tell me was not to be impertinent!"

"I'm sorry you had such a hard time, Caphira. Like I said, I'm going to see Sargon and then we talk. Okay?"

"If that's the best you can do, I guess I'll have to be satisfied," Caphira grumbled.

"Don't be so ungracious, daughter."

"Come along," Martel said, herding all three in front of him.

*　　*　　*

She found Sargon, Soraja and Morrigan on the patio. As she walked in, Morrigan rose slowly, almost reluctantly, from a wicker chair.

Sabrina quickly scanned Sargon. For once he was open for her to read. A groan escaped from her. "Kamila?" she asked.

Morrigan strode toward Sabrina, then taking her hands in hers, "Sorry Sabrina, she is dead."

Sabrina fainted into Morrigan's arms. When she came to, she was lying on a couch. Caphira, Noel, and Amanda were peering down at her, while Karsten took her pulse.

With a bang the sliding doors flew opened, and Martel came bursting through, muttering, "Damned kids." Then seeing Sabrina lying prone on the couch, "I knew something was up when Caphira popped out . . ."

"Well, suddenly Mom wasn't there anymore," Caphira defended her action.

"Then the others made a turn about face, and disappeared on me, too."

"I know, through the crawl ways," Sargon enlightened him. Since Chen and Logan had been kids, the crawlways have become a short cut through the confusing maze of the Antares.

When Sabrina tried to get up, Karsten pushed her back down into the cushions. Then looking at Martel, "Can you tell us why this woman fainted? What has she been up to? She was supposed to be on the Earth-ship Intrepid, and you were the designated babysitter."

"Long story," Martel said.

"It's okay, we're all ears." Karsten said, and a sweeping glance included the kids.

Martel smiled at Karsten, then, eased himself into a chair close to Sabrina. "The Intrepid was attacked by Altruscan pirates, commanded by Garth. She led the attack and crippled his ship. Before they could get away, she called the Antares and asked who was there that could fly Spitfire. That's how I got roped in. We followed Garth to a small planet named Selsa. She confronted him there and she killed him. Then on a hunch we went to Rhiansu. Did she tell you yet?" Martel suddenly asked.

"About, Sarah?" We already knew. We had a communiqué from Rhiansu."

"But what . . . ?"

"Made her faint? I guess it was what she gleaned from Morrigan. I surmise the cumulative stress, and then the shock, made her faint."

Martel looked questioningly at the warrior woman as she rose and sat down beside Sabrina on the couch, taking her hand between hers.

"Sabrina, in the last years, Kamila of a sudden seemed to be getting old and feeble. Her mind began to wander. Sometimes she was on Galatia, sometimes on the Antares. She confused the two. She felt deserted. When she didn't get her way, she accused everyone of not loving her anymore, then, threatened to kill herself. She attempted to commit suicide several times. But we noticed that she never took enough pills, or cut her wrist when no one was around. Last time she used the threat, we didn't intervene. I hope you understand and forgive us."

Sabrina laid her head back against the cushions, her face was drawn. Tears started to seep from between her long lashes. She cried softly.

Caphira, not able to endure her mother's grief, lay down beside her, embracing her with her long, skinny arms.

Sabrina hugged her daughter close, knowing not to shut her out. She let her feel the grief she felt, and why she was crying. After she quieted down, Karsten reached into his back pocket and handed Sabrina a handkerchief.

"Karsten, Sabrina never gives handkerchiefs back," Sargon warned him.

Sabrina smiled wanly at Sargon, but held her peace. "Are you going to set up the memorial service?" she asked him, instead.

"Are you up to it?"

"Soraja?" Sabrina asked Kamila's daughter.

Soraja, her face drawn, and her eyes still puffy with dark shadows below them, sat close to her father with her head leaning against his shoulder. She looked up. "It's all set up. If you want, I'll call Davida."

Sabrina nodded. Soraja went to the phone. When Davida came, she looked drained. She said nothing, but came and sat on the couch. Sabrina slipped her arms around her. She let Davida weep, holding her close, rocking a little back and forth, murmuring words of comfort.

"Let's start the drum," Davida said, again composed, but tightening her arms around Sabrina. Looked at her father, "Call assembly."

As the drum began to reverberate throughout the ship, Sargon took his two daughters, and linking his arms with theirs, slowly started the journey to the Queen's chamber.

*   *   *

Alone in her garden, Sabrina let her grief have free reign. When Ayhlean walked up to her, she reached out and pulled her down beside her.

"Now it's the two of us," Sabrina said sadly. "I never considered any of us dying. I thought we were immortals."

"We are immortals, but not our bodies. Age will get us. You're a mutant, maybe slower. Look at me," she said, pulling Sabrina's face around.

As she looked at Ayhlean, she could see the faint traces of aging, also her hair was beginning to grey.

"Oh girl, don't you sign out on me," Sabrina said gruffly, trying to keep the tears in check as she pulled Ayhlean into her arms.

Chapter 22

One evening, Sabrina sat by her fountain, enjoying the bright holographic moonlight, when Sabot popped in unannounced.

"Sabrina," he said softly.

"A social call?" Sabrina asked, unruffled by his sudden appearance.

He looked at her with affection. "No child; as always, its business. I have finally located all the enmeshed Mir. The only ones left are Doeros and Triscaro. I like for you to accompany me to Daugave, and introduce me to Okada."

"I wish you would sit and enjoy this beautiful evening with me."

"Yes, your moonlit night is beautiful and peaceful. But this is the last of the Mir, and it's time for them to go back to where they came from. The rift is closing."

Sabrina sighed and rose. She went into the house to change into her Alliance Uniform. After she was dressed, Sabot joined her in her bedroom.

"Now give me your hand so you won't sidetrack or get lost," Sabot told her. A flash of mirth crossed his face at Sabrina's astounded look.

She gave him her hand with a gentle smile.

"This is the last time I will need your help. The Altruscans are very effectively taken care of since their money base, the wealth of the Orion

Merchant Houses, is broken. Now the only thing left to do is get the Mir back into their own universe."

He gave Sabrina's hand a squeeze and both dematerialized.

On Daugave, the sun was just coming up over the horizon and Headquarters was empty and silent, except for the duty personnel on night watch.

Still invisible, Sabrina stirred Sabot toward Okada's office. They materialized inside the empty room.

Sabrina took a deep breath. "The older I get, the harder it is for me to come back to this dimension. If it weren't for Martel and Caphira, I think I would stay," she told Sabot.

"Love has a strong pull," he agreed, understanding her.

The door to the anteroom opened and they could hear Okada's adjutant and secretary getting ready for the day's work. Some of their comments Sabrina and Sabot heard were revealing. Sabrina had a hard time suppressing her chortles.

When the door suddenly opened, Sabot and Sabrina quickly became invisible again. The secretary laid the mail and newspaper on Okada's desk, and turned his computer on.

"Is this all the mail?" the adjutant asked. "Yesterday, he had a fit because someone mislaid a dispatch he was expecting."

"I heard that," Okada said. He had the ability to walk silently and often seemed to appear out of nowhere.

"Sorry, Sir," his adjutant said. "Just wanted to make sure we had everything ready before you came in."

Okada harrumphed, and walked into his office. When he came through the door, Sabrina and Sabot materialized in front of him. Okada gave a surprised grunt and slammed the door.

"Sabrina, someday you will go too far. What are you trying to do? Give me a heart-attack!" he bellowed at her. He had just snapped his mouth shut when the door flew open and his adjutant came in with his weapon drawn.

Sabrina held up both hands and said, "Noguro, it's just me. It's okay."

"How did you get in here?" Noguro asked astonished. "Kiko," turning red he amended, "Lieutenant Sudara was just in here."

Don't ask question you don't want answers to," Sabrina told him.

Noguro swallowed and looked at Okada.

"Go on, it's all right. As you can see it's only Captain Hennesee," he said mildly, but his face belied his tone.

Noguro was loath to leave and the door closed very slowly. He heard Okada say, "Now, if you would be so kind as to introduce your companion."

"Oh, how remiss of me," Sabrina said, imitating his mild tone of voice. "Admiral Okada, may I introduce Sabot."

Okada walked toward the window and looked out to gain time, then swung around and came back again. He ignored Sabrina and looked at Sabot, waiting for an explanation from him.

"Admiral Okada," Sabot said with considerable humor in his eyes, "Dealing with Sabrina, I have learned that this is not always a straight-forward affair. She will have her jest, and I have learned to humor her. Because of her abilities, I have asked her again to help me, and also to introduce me to you. I have located the last of the shapeshifters. The only thing left is to deal with Triscaro, whom I have as Sabrina would call it, on ice. Now we need to devise a strategy to get Doeros. I have also located the Mir's Queen. She is loath to leave this universe after finding the experiences she's gaining here fascinating."

Turning to Sabrina, "When she discovered the Antares, she considered it the perfect nest to colonize. She was very angry when you discovered the infiltrator . . ."

"Yes, and she looked so harmless, just an insignificant slip of a girl."

"And now we have to find a way to get Commodore Doeros and Triscaro in the same place," Sabot continued.

"By the way," Sabrina said, looking at Sabot, "does Doeros know about you?"

"I'm not so sure. He might have his suspicions."

"Admiral, we need a good cover-story."

"Don't look at me. You're the one with the devious mind," he told her. "You have five minutes to cook up something." Checking his watch, "I have to be in a briefing in ten minutes."

Scratching the top of her head, she gazed out of the window. "You know," she said turning around, "we could use Triscaro as bait."

"I knew you would come up with something," Okada said, snapping his fingers. Pursing his lips, he looked at his fingers, and then across at Sabot.

"I know, she rubs off," Sabot told him dead-pan,'

* * *

Admiral Okada looked out through a well curtained window onto a shaded courtyard. The single tree was already bright with autumn colors, the small lawn manicured to perfection. This room, it was his personal sanctum very few dared to invade. This was the place he retreated to when he had a need for solitude and privacy.

He had just left his dining room, feeling satiated and mellow. He was preparing himself for a nice quiet evening. In his mind, going over the day's agenda, he felt that everything had been taken care of. Sitting down in his chair, he picked up the news releases his wife had arranged for him on a side table. His last thoughts before beginning his perusal lingered on Sabrina when off a sudden she popped in.

His mien turned icy when he realized what had happened.

"Must you always do the unexpected?"

Irritated, Sabrina said, "You gave me an impossible assignment. Anything coming from me would be suspect to Doeros. You are his superior, you think of something."

The vein on Okada's forehead began to throb when she, without being invited, sat down in the chair opposite his. The audacity of it, he thought. Then, he smiled inwardly. He liked her very much. She had courage, but also a lot of arrogance.

Sabrina, discerning his mood, only smiled. She eased herself more comfortably back into the chair and elegantly crossed her long legs.

His wife, Midori, hearing voices, cautiously opened the door and looked surprised at the woman reclining serenely in the chair across from her husband.

"Come in," Okada said. "Midori, this is Sabrina Hennesee," he introduced her.

"Sabrina Hennesee, I'm glad to meet you," she said politely. As she bowed, her mind raced through all the defenses of the house. All were set, but none had given warning of an intruder. Even if she had beamed in, an alarm would have sounded. She gave her husband an inquiring look, but his face remained bland. "Would you like for me to bring some refreshments?"

"You might as well," he said, resignedly.

After the door closed behind Midori, Sabrina said, "You know, if you would bring up Doeros' file, we might get an idea."

Okada looked at her. "I had envisioned a quiet evening," he told her, aggrieved.

"I understand. Yesterday I was yanked out of a quiet moonlit night, sitting beside my fountain." Her face was full of accusation.

As he rose from his chair, Okada, shaking his head, started to laugh as he went over to his computer. After he typed in a password, Doeros' file came up.

The door opened, and Midori came in with a tray. Okada, took it from her, put it on low table.

When he turned toward the computer, Sabrina had taken the chair he vacated, and was scanning through the file. "Sabrina," he said quietly. When she didn't react, somewhat louder, "Sabrina!"

Distracted she looked up. "He sure has a lot of leave accumulated," she mumbled.

"Would you join us for sake?"

Sabrina only gave him a distracted look.

"Lady Sabrina," Midori asked politely, "the sake is just at the right temperature now. Would you be so kind and join us?"

"I'm sorry. I'm remiss," she said, her eyes still glued to the screen. "Meritorious service?" she mumbled as she came toward the low table and sat down on the couch.

"My order is to forget Doeros for the moment and enjoy the sake," Okada said.

"Yes, Sir," and bowed to his wife, she said, "Lady Midori, my apology if I appeared rude. But Admiral Okada has given me a difficult problem to solve." She gave Okada a pointed look. Then she scanned

Lady Midori's surface mind and being on safe ground asked, "How are your children?"

"Oh, they are grown," she said with a sigh. "Now they have their own life and that keeps them very busy. Do you have children?"

"Oh, yes. My two sons are grown too. And my daughter will soon turn fourteen and be joining the cadets. It is very gratifying when your children have gown up to be worthy members of their society, but sad when the nest is getting empty."

For a while politics and shop-talk were forgotten and they talked like parents about their children. When Sabrina deemed it polite to leave, she said her good-byes and walked out the door the normal way. But as soon as she knew Midori had retired, she popped back into Okada's retreat.

He was gone, but the computer was still on.

"Sure that I would be coming back," Sabrina mumbled.

Commodore Shadam Doeros was the second son of a landholder. The first son inherited the land and title, the second son, at an early age, had left home to be enrolled in a military academy.

All his records, his efficiency reports were outstanding. There were many recommendations from highly placed individuals. He had risen rather quickly in rank.

"An unblemished record," Sabrina mumbled, "and what am I to do with that?"

Very dissatisfied, she dematerialized from Okada's house, and returned to the Antares.

*   *   *

Two days later Doeros himself gave them an opening.

Very early in the day he presented himself in Okada's office and placed a letter of resignation on his desk.

Astonished, Okada looked up after reading it.

"Sir," Doeros said, "my brother suddenly became very ill. If he should die, I'm the only male heir left of my generation. His children are still too young to take charge of the land. If there is a default, because of a lack of someone to manage it, the land will go back to the overlord, and so be lost to my family. I would greatly appreciate if I'm informed when a ship will leave here for the sector my home-world is in."

"I'm sure we could arrange somehow for you to go back home. As soon as I have any information I will contact you immediately."

After the door closed behind Doeros, Okada rubbed his temples, "Where is Sabrina when I need her?" he groaned, when all of a sudden Sabot popped in.

"Sabrina should be here in a second," Sabot assured Okada, correctly reading his distraught look.

True to his word, Sabrina was there not an instant later.

"I was ordered here," Sabrina said quickly before Okada could voice any displeasure.

"Doeros needs transportation to go home . . ."

"I know, I know. But what you don't know is, is that he plans to assume his brother's identity. The confederation between the Altruscans and the Orion Hegemony is dissolving. Also, since he knows that most of the shapeshifters have been rounded up, he thinks it is time to disappear. He has no desire to rejoin the Mir. He has learned to like his individuality, and his autonomy."

Okada looked at Sabrina and nodded while chewing on his bottom lip. Turning to Sabot. "Where is Triscaro?"

"He is on Coronis. Serenity and I lured him into the sector close to Coronis. Triscaro tried to pirate Serenity's ship. Serenity beamed him aboard her ship and immobilized him with her venom before wrapping him up in her web. Now, I need a ship to pick up Triscaro and Serenity."

Okada went to his computer and brought up a roster of names.

At every name he mumbled, "Too far away," until he came to Alemain. When he brought up his file, after going through it, surprised, he suddenly said "Who is Caphira Alemain ra Hennesee?" he asked.

"My daughter."

"I know she's your daughter."

"Well, her father is Captain Martel Alemain."

"But he doesn't list a wife."

When Sabrina only shrugged, his face tightened a little, but he only said, "He is closest to Coronis. And since you are familiar to him, I guess he won't be disconcerted by anything you might do."

Chapter 23

Captain Martel Alemain just received information that a team was to replace his bridge crew, and that orders were on the way for his new destination. Also he was to relinquish the bridge. When the Minoan was hailed, Spitfire was on his screen and Sabrina asked for permission to dock on the Minoan.

When the door opened, Sabrina, and Serenity the Arachnid in her human form, stepped on to the bridge. Martel rose with, "Captain Hennesee, you have the bridge."

Sabrina gave him a curt nod, then, ordered everyone to clear the bridge, except for Captain Alemain. "You have Doeros on the Minoan?"

"Yes, and he is asleep right now."

"Good. We have Triscaro on Spitfire."

"Who got Triscaro?"

"Serenity did. Martel, please man the science center."

Serenity took the helm, and Sabrina keyed the new destination into the computer.

"Where are we going?"

"We're having a rendezvous with the Mir. We need to convince her to leave this Universe. Sabot will join us when it becomes necessary.

Serenity will set up a dampening field so she will be restricted to the bridge alone. Before she comes on board, you will need to leave the bridge too," Sabrina told Martel.

It was two hours ship time when they arrived at their new destination. Sabrina nodded for Martel to leave the bridge. As Martel rose to leave, Sabot appeared.

Sabot and Serenity went to set up the dampening field around the bridge. Suddenly the alarm went off. Sabrina immediately shut it off. Having the sensor on forward, they watched as a ship dropped out of hyperspace. It looked like a rectangular box.

The communication center lit up, and a rustling sound came over the radio frequency. A large, scintillating, and convoluted ovoid form suddenly beamed in on the Minoan bridge.

"We, I am Mir." The statement came in a burbling kind of voice. Directing her attention toward Sabot, "You have two of my selves?" she asked, telepathically.

"I will return them to you, but you must leave this Universe," Sabot mind-sent to her.

We, I do not brook any interference in Our, My functions."

"I am Sabot, we are asking you to leave. This is a different Universe. You have no place here."

"We, I do not brook any interference with Our, My functions," came the reply again.

"You present a danger to the inhabitants of this Universe."

"This is not Our, My concern. We, I receive form from assimilating life here."

"I understand, but life forms here are singularities, they do not desire absorption."

"Absorption is Our, My way. This sustains Our, My life."

Sabrina turned to the entity. "You have established contact with the Altruscans. They have used you for their purpose."

"This is none of your concern."

"But it is our concern." Sabrina turned to Sabot and Serenity and shrugged. "We are not getting anywhere. She will do what serves her interests," she said, after putting her shields up and shutting the telepathic communication down. Turning to Sabot, "Is there any way to mend this time/space rent?"

"It is already closing. This is why it has become imperative for the Mir to leave."

Suddenly Triscaro, wrapped in a cocoon, Serenity's web, appeared, and was floating in mid-air. When he realized where he was, and what was going on, he fought to free himself. It only made the cocoon tighter. He protested, making inarticulate sounds. When the Mir moved in to absorb him, he screamed.

Somewhat shaken, Sabrina watched Triscaro's struggle and then his dissolution.

"Now Doeros," Serenity said.

"He is already on his way," Sabot told her.

The lift doors hissed open, and Doeros, disoriented, staggered onto the bridge.

"What's going on? Who called me?" he asked, his voice thick and throaty.

When he saw the Mir, he held up both hands as if to ward her off. "I'm not like her," he croaked. "I'm human, I'm human. Just look at me," he begged, holding his hands out. "Please, please don't have her absorb me."

"What happens when the Doeros body wears out?" Serenity asked him. "You will have to insert yourself into another body. You are energy, you will neither dissipate nor die, and you know that. You also know it's a short time before the rift is closing. It is your intention to kill Shadam Doeros's brother, and assume his identity. You know as well as I do why you cannot be left here."

Doeros looked at Serenity, his eyes as devoid of human emotions as hers. Then they raked Sabrina. He only said "You," but there was so much hatred in that one word, it made her shudder. When the Mir approached to absorb him, he put up no resistance.

Suddenly the Mir turned toward Sabrina, "She is one of us?"

"No," Serenity told her. "She has only absorbed some of the Mir's essence."

"We, I am interested, she is one of us." This came as a statement, and she moved toward Sabrina. Nothing was going to deter her.

When she came too close, Sabrina simply vanished.

"Well," Serenity said, taken aback, "This is an interesting development I didn't know about. Sabot?"

As an answer, one of Sabot's bottles popped in, and giving off a sucking noise, the Mir disappeared, and Sabrina popped in again.

"Does this take care of all the Mir now?" she asked Sabot.

"Yes."

"You will leave now?"

"My job is done."

"Will I ever see you again?"

"Yes, Sabrina-child, someday. I don't think I will be able to get rid of you all the way."

When he said it, he gave her a gentle, but amused smile. Even before he had made himself known to her, he had clairvoyantly perceived that some day she would seek him out to make an unusual request of him.

She returned his smile with warmth. In some ways she liked it when he called her Sabrina-child.

"What will happen to the Mir?" Serenity asked.

"The Mir had an interesting experience here. When she first came here, she was incorporeal. She maintained life by absorbing others like herself. But here, she sent particles of herself out to insinuated themselves into solid life forms, dissolving their protoplasm, thereby gaining some solidity. Now, her form is of energy plus matter. Doeros and Triscaro acquired the density of human flesh. Also, the experience of individuality. To watch the results should be fascinating."

He bowed to Serenity and gave Sabrina a wink, then, he and his bottle disappeared.

While Sabrina still stared at the spot Sabot had vanished from, Serenity called Martel to come to the bridge. When he stepped of the elevator, and when he saw Sabrina's pensive face, he asked, "Well?"

"The Mir is gone and so is Sabot."

"You'll miss Sabot?"

"He was an interesting fellow."

"He was that. What are you going to do now?"

"I'll take Serenity on Spitfire to Coronis and then I'm going home. When will I see you again?"

"In about a year. So pop in any time you like."

"Be assured that I will do that."

*   *   *

It was a year later and when Sabrina, coming home from the village, walked into her house and found Sargon, Karsten, and Martel lounging in her living room. As soon as they saw her, all conversation stopped.

"What's up?" Sabrina asked suspiciously

"Oh we're just discussing an idea we had," Karsten said in his easy-going manner.

"I see," was Sabrina's disinterested reply as she put down the data recorder she carried under her arm.

"Well, it's like this," Martel began, "Sargon and Karsten are interested in investigating a once-in-a life time occurrence, and they asked me if I would care to come along."

"It would be a two-year project," Sargon informed her.

"What would you say if I'd go along?"

"Martel, I think you need to discuss that more with your daughter than me."

The door opened again and Caphira and Amanda came spilling through.

"What's going on?" Amanda asked.

"Not much," Sabrina told her

"Aha. Then why do I always go on alert when you say, 'not much'," Caphira quipped. "Sargon?"

"Captain Thalon," Sargon corrected her.

"You can play captain on the bridge, but now you're in my house, and here you're Sargon." Caphira stated firmly.

"Gramps, are you letting her get away with this?" Amanda asked her Grandfather.

"Technically your aunt is correct," Sargon told her, secretly amused by Caphira's audacity.

"You hear, I'm your aunt and don't you forget it," Caphira teased Amanda.

"Yea, but I'm still older than you. I think that counts for something."

"Oh well, but then I always try to be kind to older women."

"Amanda, how would you like to have your nose rearranged?"

"Caphira, you know there's no contest here." Looking at Sabrina, "Grandy, don't you think it's about time you told us what's going on instead of enjoying Caphira and me arguing."

"I think that question should be asked of Martel."

"Okay, what's up?" Amanda asked.

"Your grandmother thought before I make a decision to go on an expedition, I should first discuss it with Caphira. Do you agree?" he asked of Amanda.

"You're gonna do what?" Caphira exploded. "You're gonna leave?"

"Yes, for about two years. You think you're old enough to take care of yourself until I come back?"

Caphira grimaced at her father, and harrumphed. "That's a leading question, and you know it. What about Mom?"

"She's going to stay here."

"Like last time when I had one parent here, and all off a sudden I had none, and no one talked to me."

"That was different, Caphira. Your mother ordered me to come right away." Martel was pursing his lips to hide a grin.

"Yeah, sure. That was your excuse then, and it's wearing thin." Caphira's remark was laced with acidity.

"I didn't know you were that troubled by both of us being gone."

"Pop, I'm just a kid, and I like to have both of my parents around. When you leave, at least talk to me first," Caphira said, sounding more conciliatory.

Giving Sabrina a quick look, "That's what we are both doing right now. I'm going go leave with Sargon and Karsten, but I promise to be back. Okay?"

"If you don't, I'll hunt you down throughout this Galaxy, and you can bet on that." Turning to Amanda, "Let's go, we still have some play time before study hall." Giving her father a long, last look, she stalked off with Amanda in tow. Before quitting the room, she half turned, looking back at her father. "Will you say goodbye before you leave?" she asked.

"Of course."

Since the Altruscan threat had subsided, and the Shapeshifters were gone, there was no more need to maintain a Special Force. Sabrina and Miri had resigned their commissions, and Karsten and Sargon were staying on in an advisory capacity. So when the Chirons asked if Sargon, Karsten and Martel would like to join a scientific exploration, all three eagerly accepted.

*   *   *

Two years later, when Martel arrived back on the Antares, Caphira was waiting for him in the hangar deck. As soon as she spotted him, she let out a whoop, and at a full run, jumped up on him.

"Oh Pop, You did come back. I've been counting the days."

Martel looked at his brown, curly-haired daughter, with her soulful black eyes and smiled. "You missed me that much?"

"Yes. I missed you very much. There's no one to take my side if Mom gets too mean."

"I see. You want me as an ally?"

"What I want is for you to love me."

"That's better," Martel told her. He kissed her gently on the forehead before setting her down.

Sabrina had kept to the background to let her daughter, who had been so impatiently waiting, meet Martel first. When she slowly approached, his eyes lit up and his steps quickened. He embraced her fiercely, but their passionate kiss was interrupted by a very happy sigh from Caphira. She had her parents together again.

Martel stayed with his family until Caphira left for Acheron to enroll at the Academy there. These were the happiest years of his life, being together with Sabrina and Caphira. The house was always full of life with family going in and out, and his greatest joy was being there while Caphira, Amanda, and Noel were growing up. He was delighted when the three girls shared their discoveries, and very often their secrets with him; he had fun participating in their horseplay. But the last year, before they left, he changed; he became more and more restless. Often he would go off by himself. He became silent and taciturn. Then one day he disappeared. No one knew where or why.

Chapter 24

Sitting at the conference table Sabrina noticed that the young had replaced the old. Soraja and Jason were now the captains of the Antares. Davida had taken Sarah's place as Chief Medical Officer. Chen had grown into Ayhlean's job and was the Chief Administrator. Logan had replaced her. Sabrina and Sargon were the only old ones left. Some time ago Ayhlean had died in her sleep. Also Marlo was gone, as was Joran. This was the last year for Caphira to attend Acheron's Space Academy, she would be assigned to a ship after graduation.

First Martel had left and then Caphira. The usually lively house had become unbearably large and empty. Most of her grandchildren were either assigned to other ships or had become cadets and moved away. She gave the keeping of her Roman Villa over to Margali, her husband, and their children. She had moved into the village and taken an apartment there. She began to stay away.

When an offer came to take command of the Trefayne, she took it with alacrity. She had worked with the Chirons before, and they found her acceptable. The Trefayne's assignment was a scientific mission and the tour was for five years.

After returning to the Antares, the first thing she did was to go to her apartment to take a shower and change clothes. Then she took a walk through the village and later went to the beergarden for lunch. It was early afternoon, and not many people about: she saw no one she knew.

When she finally went to her Villa, as she expected, it was empty. Margali and her husband Tiras were at their jobs and the kids at school.

She slowly meandered through the garden toward the waterfall, pausing here and there, getting more melancholic. There was a sadness, it was autumn in the garden, the leaves in their last splendor. Soon it would be winter to give the trees rest. As she came to the waterfall and walked toward the cluster of pines, someone was sitting on her bench. She mind-scanned, but couldn't read the individual. Her interest perked, and her strides grew longer. As she approached, she realized the being was something she had never encountered. The skin looked leathery and dark green. The eyes were black on black, and a shock like lightning ran up her spine.

"Martel," she breathed.

"Hello, Sabrina," Martel said tonelessly. "I'm surprised you recognized me."

"Martel, you're an ass, you know." Then it dawned on her, "You left because you felt you were changing?"

"Yes, and I had no inkling into what. I wanted to spare you. Karsten said that I was an idiot. So, I finally agreed to come back and see for myself how you would react."

"Well, did I make the grade?"

"You did."

"Now what? Are you going to run off again?"

"No, I think I'll stick around for a while."

*   *   *

Chantar canceled an engagement to return to the Antares for the birth of her first grandchild. It was a girl, and Sirtis named her Na'ira.

Sirtis and Jason, while still being children, had bonded with each other. They had always been together, playing or fighting, there was no way of separating the two. So no one was surprised when Sirtis entered Jason as the father of her child.

Chantar's stay lasted for several months. When another theatrical engagement came up, she was loath to cancel it. "It will be only for two months, and then I'll be back," she assured Sirtis. Turning to Sabrina, "Will you look in on them occasionally while I'm gone?" After Sabrina's assurance, Chantar felt less guilty about leaving.

The engagement had been a huge success. She came back to the Antares looking happy and energetic. She was full of plans for a musical. She wanted to work on it over the winter, and then present it for the next season on Acheron. Since Sargon was called to Daugave, she decided to return to Acheron and Martel volunteered to take her.

Two days later Martel called. He was staying at Chantar's chateau, and asked Sabrina if she would mind if he stayed for a few days longer. She wasn't too happy about it, there was a feeling of unease troubling her. For some reason she wanted Martel back. When she told him, he just grinned at her.

"I'll be back in two days, Sabrina. It's beautiful here, and the cold makes the pain go away."

Martel was still changing in appearance. His skin was becoming more leathery and the change brought pain. Reluctantly she agreed. All day she tried to put the uneasy feeling from her mind. She kept busy with working in engineering. She was just checking the calibration on a data recorder a young ensign had handed her, when suddenly she perceived a groan. Her first though was one of the engines. Her heart skipped a beat and she froze to listen, but then she realized the sound had been in her head. Then there was Sirtis' scream, 'Mother!' and then a void in her mind. "Sargon?" her mind quested. She disappeared in front of the eyes of a shocked ensign who slowly bent down to retrieve the data recorder from the floor.

Sabrina materialized in Sargon's study. He was leaning over his desk, his knuckles white from gripping its edges. She quickly went to him. "Chantar?" she asked. When he didn't answer, she scanned his mind. The place Chantar's personality had filled, there was an emptiness. She was gone.

Suddenly the door flew open and Davida and Chen came running in.

Davida immediately went to her father. "Dad?"

He pulled Davida into his arms and held on to her. "Where is Sirtis?"

"'Jason and Logan are with her."

"I must go to her." He looked to Sabrina. "You know?" he asked.

"Yes, I felt it through Sirtis. Chantar is gone," she said, her voice controlled. Before she could say more, her face went blank.

There was an immense void. The warm spark, the link between herself and Martel, was gone. It had suddenly snapped. She screamed. Her scream was echoed by Caphira who appeared with a frantic look, and vanished along with Sabrina.

Sabrina and Caphira appeared above Chantar's ancestral home. It was gone. The snow and half the mountain had avalanched down, burying everything in its path. What was still standing looked like a jagged spine piercing the sky. Caphira was beside her; their minds touched. Both were chilled, feeling the horror and death.

Suddenly there was a big jolt, and the mountain began to rumble and shake. It brought Sabrina out of her stupor, "Earthquake, Caphira," she yelled as she reached for her daughter.

"Oh, God! Mom, Chiara and her kids are on Acheron!"

She and Sabrina dematerialized to reappear in the House of Sandor.

Some of the masonry had cracked and the furniture lay strewn on the floor. The horses were screaming in the stables. This more then anything galvanized, Sabrina into action. She grabbed for Caphira, and both ran for the stables. The grooms were there, and Kendra was trying to let the screaming horses loose, while keeping from being trampled.

After the horses were calmed down, Sabrina and Caphira went looking for Kendra. They found her outside by the back buildings, digging at the rubble. Some of the hidden ones had been inside. When they were found, they were all dead. Kendra rose, tears streaming down her face, as she stared with empty eyes at Sabrina.

"Where's Chiara and the children?" Melora, Machir Aram's daughter asked.

"Chiara?" Kendra asked, turning to Melora.

"Chiara is with Chantar."

"Oh God!" Sabrina groaned and crumpled to the ground.

"What's going on?" Melora asked, suddenly shaking with apprehension.

Caphira's face looked like a woman walking in a nightmare. "Oh Melora. The mountain. The snow came down. They are gone."

"How do you know?" Kendra screamed, grabbing and shaking her shoulders.

"We were there." she answered, her voice only a whisper.

"How do you know," she repeated, then, slowly sank to the ground beside Sabrina, pulling her into her arms. "Martel?" she asked.

When Sabrina started to moan, Melora, knowing about the bonding, wound her arms around and held her tight.

Kendra and Melora's children were huddled in terror underneath an archway. When the aftershocks began, with the help of Kendra, Melora led Caphira and Sabrina for safety underneath the arch.

Suddenly a woman, coming from the street, apparently in shock, with her head bleeding, appeared in front of them. She was carrying an injured child and begged, "Please, help! Please, help me!"

Sabrina looked at the woman, then, held out her arms for the child. It was a small boy, not badly hurt. She sent Melora after bandages.

When he was taken care of and given back to his mother, Sabrina, as if coming out of a daze, looked around her. This was not the time to grieve. That could come later. There were things to be done. There was a need. Abruptly she turned and dashed into the house. The communication equipment was housed in the vaulted part of the basement and Sabrina hoped that it was still functioning.

The equipment had its own energy source, and when Sabrina tried it, it was still operational. She contacted the Antares.

Nira, Nesrim and Chandi's daughter, was on the bridge.

"Nira, pipe me into Sargon's apartment."

"Sabrina, the order is not to disturb Sargon."

"Nira, the order is rescinded: disturb him."

"It's on your head then." She transmitted Sabrina to Sargon's apartment.

The first thing Sabrina saw was a broad back turned toward her. She gently called his name, but with no response. Pensively she watched him for second. She understood. Losing Chantar that abruptly and unexpectedly, he was in shock.

Suddenly she knew what to do to rouse him from his stupor. She let a string of vile invectives loose in his language. There was a hunching of the shoulders, and a slow turn toward her. He looked at her incredulous, and then a very angry. "What do you want?"

"Sargon, I'm on Acheron. There was an avalanche. It wiped out everything."

There was a groan and he almost turned away from her when he stopped in mid turn. "Martel?" he asked, but Sabrina's face told him. "Sabrina, I'm so sorry. I'll be on Acheron. I have already ordered one of the Scouts readied . . ."

"Sargon, There was also a very strong earthquake. Tell Davida to set up a field hospital. Assemble a team to assess the damage, and to determine how far this earthquake affected Chambray and the outlying areas. Set up a communications network. Lahoma's house only sustained minor damage. Sabrina out."

She cut communications. She didn't want to answer any questions. She needed to be busy. She would do what she could here, immersing herself in work and other people's needs. That Chiara and her children were gone too, that would hold for later.

When she reached the top floor again, Melora had assembled the household. "Let's organize the neighborhood, and see what we can do," she said. "No sense in standing around here."

*   *   *

It was a week later when Sargon finally discovered where Sabrina was. He found her inside Spitfire, hugging Martel's jacket tightly to herself, engulfed in emptiness and grief which seemed past her control.

Martel . . . Martel, she repeated his name with intensity, like a litany; like it could bring him back. Emotionally, she had still to face that he was gone.

Sargon stood very still inside the door. When he heard her dry, racking sobs, he slowly walked over and encircled her in his arms.

"I'm sorry. It hit so hard. I couldn't think beyond myself, and my pain."

Sabrina nodded her head, then dug deeper into Sargon's arms for comfort.

Merging his mind with hers, he gave her all the solace he could. A long time passed, both taking comfort from each other.

Sabrina slowly raised her head. "What are you contemplating?" she asked astonished.

"You're not supposed to read my mind," he rebuked her gently.

"Well, that goes with the territory. Now what is that you are ruminating on?"

"I want to go back to the Galaxy I came from."

"You think that's wise breaking all your connections here?" she asked, regarding him steadily. "You have friends here. There, everything might have changed, and you will find nothing you would be familiar with. Have you thought about that?"

"I have."

"And is there nothing to change your mind?"

"The Antares will go. Whoever wants to stay here can. Lara Ensor has agreed to share her planet with the ones who will stay behind."

Sabrina gave him a searching look. "You sound bitter."

"No, not really. Only, very tired."

"And so you want to go home?"

"Is it not enough reading my mind, now you're psychoanalyzing me too?"

Sabrina gave a short laugh. "Don't be so touchy," she told him curtly, but she forbore to comment further.

*   *   *

Later that evening, Sargon called assembly. His pronouncement was met with a deep and shocked silence. Slowly a rustling of voices was heard within the deep chamber. From the back came the sound of a strident voice, "Have you thought what this would mean to the rest of us?"

Sargon turned toward the voice, a deep scowl furring his face. Sabrina quickly cut in with, "He has. If you don't like it, you can stay. You can enlist with the Alliance, or choose any planet you like to live on," she told him. "This decision does not have to be made today or tomorrow. There will be ample time and you will be given any assistance you might need."

"Since you seemed to be the sole authority without it being further discussed I'm superfluous here." The words had come in a deep angry growl. Sabrina held her peace and let him stalk off.

Chapter 25

It took more than two years for everything to sort itself out. Most of the Antares born stayed. All of Sargon's children stayed. Even Logan. Cassy, Miri's and Karsten's daughter decided to stay with the Antares while her parents settled with many of the Antareans on Lara's planet.

It was almost close to the end of that second year when the situation between Sabrina and Sargon was beginning to change. After Chantar's death, he had avoided her most of the time. All their interaction had been on a business basis. But lately he began to seek out her company. He was finally able to talk about Chantar, and Sabrina about Martel.

One day shortly before leaving the Milky-Way Galaxy, Sargon was jolted out of his reverie. It was like a scream echoing through his being. The silent scream had come from Sabrina. Before her children could react, he sent that he would take care of her. He found her in the gym, sweating and short of breath, finally giving up hitting the punching bag. She was angry at being alone and that her pain and her needs had not gone away. There was a great void. She had found no peace. Martel was gone.

Tired, she stopped, and only then noticed Sargon standing behind her with his hands on his hips grinning at her.

"If you need someone to hold you, why don't you ask me?" he told her.

"You're not available, remember?" she shot back at him.

"That was then."

"You mean you're not afraid of bonding with me," she asked him incredulous.

"It's because you have no need to bond."

"No, you're right, not anymore. Not after Martel."

*   *   *

The trip back to Sargon's galaxy took three stages. It was done at night, when the Antareans slept. The first two, traversing the intergalactic void, went without incidence. During the third and last stage, Sabrina woke up screaming. When Caphira and Cassy rushed in, Sabina, sitting up in bed had sweat beading up on her forehead. Shaking, she clutched her pillow to herself.

"What happened? Did you have a nightmare?" Caphira asked, sitting down at the edge of the bed.

"What you mean?"

"Mom, you were screaming the house down," Caphira told her.

"Sabrina, you look frightened, do you remember anything?"

Sabrina looked up at Cassy with glassy eyes, trying to piece it together in her mind. "Something broke. Something was tearing asunder. But I don't know what. I only know it frightened me."

Even Sargon had picked up on Sabrina's nightmare and came walking into her bedroom.

"Oh goodness, did I waken you too," Sabrina said. "I'm sorry, it was only a nightmare. But I have this feeling of doom. That's the only way I can describe it," and reaching for his hand, "check the crystals," she entreated him earnestly. "Please, check the crystals."

"I will, tomorrow."

"Well, since you seemed to be all right, I guess we can go back to bed and tell our lazy husbands that you had a nightmare, and assure them that you are all right," Cassy said, gently pulling at Sabrina's hair.

"I'm sorry." Sabrina stroked Cassy's arm, and then she hugged Caphira, and gave her a kiss on the cheek. "Thanks for coming."

After the two left, Sabrina lifted her cover, "Why not sleep the rest of the night with me, since we seem to have made the jump already."

Sargon smiled at her. "Afraid of nightmares now?"

"A good excuse not to sleep alone."

*   *   *

Even before she awoke, she knew Sargon had left on Scout I, and that the Antares was parked somewhere in interstellar space.

She showered. After dressing in uniform she had a leisurely breakfast before going up to the bridge.

When the lift's doors opened, she was met by Soraja's smiling face.

"Dad went scouting with Scout I, and he took Chen and Jason with him."

"Yes. I already know. What's on your itinerary?"

"Nothing. He only told me to mind the store."

"Okay. I'm going to see what he's doing."

Sabrina visualized the interior of the Scout and keying into Sargon's personality, disappeared.

When she popped in on the bridge, he was busy matching the old star maps he had brought with him in the Explorer with the existing space outside.

They were nearing the solar system of his world.

"I'm picking up a large object coming toward us," Chen informed his father.

"Magnify."

Chen turned back to his monitor, with Sabrina looking over his shoulders. "Still out of range. I will tell you as soon as I can get it on screen."

"Okay. Go to impulse power, and let's meet what's out there," Sargon told Jason.

"Going to impulse," Jason replied.

Two hours later they had the object on screen.

"Take evasive action," Sargon told Jason as he stared blankly at the mountain size asteroid coming toward them.

"We don't have asteroids," Sargon mumbled to himself.

"What you mean?" Chen asked.

He gave his son a distracted look. "We mined and then destroyed them. So there should be none in our solar system. Soraja," he said after contacting the Antares, "there's an asteroid coming your way. Mine it and then break it down."

There was a moment's silence, then, Soraja turned to her crew and gave orders to ready a small ore freighter. "Deploying asteroid muncher," she told Sargon.

"Soraja!" came a somewhat sharp retort.

"Yes, Dad?" she said sweetly.

"Oh, never mind."

"Did you check the crystals this morning?" Sabrina asked him.

"Not yet, I'll do it when we get back to the Antares"

"What's that out there?" Sabrina asked, pointing to the view screen which showed a huge planet.

"We're coming up on my solar system. This is one of the outer planets. Its name is Aion. Mostly gaseous, but we believe there's a hard core in its center. The next two planets are probably on the other side of the sun."

"What's your sun's name?"

"It's a yellow giant and we call it Incal. Incal is also the symbol of our God. My world is called Istranavu, the jewel of Incal. The next planet should be Numinos, it's mountainous and has a little atmosphere. Then comes my planet Istranavu. Amatos is like your Mars. Then Izmal, which is inhabited, and then there's Acanatha and like your Venus shrouded in clouds and too hot. Then comes Incal."

"You still want to go in on impulse?" Jason reminded Sargon.

"No, you can speed it up a little," Sargon told him.

"How will you contact your people?" Sabrina asked

"We'll take the Scout in and see what we're going to run into."

"Of course! I don't know why I asked?"

"Dad," Chen called, "we have impact on our shields. They're lighting up like an Aurora Borealis."

Sargon bumped Chen off the science station and began sifting though the incoming sensor data.

Leaning on his shoulders, "Space debris?" Chen asked.

"Looks like it," Sargon said astonished. "We're coming up on Numinos." "Dad, there's a hell of a dust storm on that planet," Chen told him as he checked the incoming data. "But, that doesn't explain where all that space debris is coming from."

Sargon was silent, his brow greased. He went over to Jason and took control of the Scout. He veered away from Numinos, and boosting speed, flew back out into space toward where he computed earlier Istranavu should be.

Suddenly there was a loud gasp, and Sargon, halfway out of his chair, was staring at the monitor.

"Put it on screen," he commanded.

Ahead of them was a belt of debris, including rock fragments, some planetoids size, irregular chunks, crashing into each other. There was sand, gravel, intermixed with earth. It was so dense, no light shone through.

They were still plowing into the dust.

"Dad, sensor overload. We'll burn up the shields," Chen warned him.

"Change course," Sargon told him, "and head toward the boundary of the belt.

"What's going on?" Sabrina asked.

"I don't know. Sabrina would you take a spacewalk?"

"Okeydoke." There was a barely noticeable hesitation before Sabrina dematerialized. She went with a feeling of foreboding.

Chen laughed at his father's exasperated look.

After a while Sargon began pacing the bridge. Being in tune with Sabrina, he had caught her slight hesitation. Then, by his reckoning, she should have been back.

When Sabrina popped in her face was somber.

"What did you find?"

"Sargon, there's no planet," she told him bluntly, but her voice was very soft and level. "I think all that mess out there is what's left of Istranavu."

Sargon blanched. "That can't be, Sabrina," he protested. "Istranavu is a large planet, it's about half the size of your Jupiter. There were people on it . . ."

"Sargon! There's nothing there. The planet you call Amatos, it has no atmosphere, or its atmosphere has been ripped away. Izmal has sustained catastrophic bombardment, but it still has an atmosphere. And I think it can sustain life."

Sargon sat down in shock, overwhelmed by the destruction of his world, and the unimaginable loss of so many lives.

*   *   *

After returning to the Antares it took some time for Sargon to overcome his shock. For a while he retreated within himself and left Sabrina to run the ship.

In the beginning, Sabrina only made short forays toward other solar systems. The surprising thing was that everywhere she went she found life. If it was absent, it was an anomaly. Soon she made experimental contact with other worlds. If she was well received she established diplomatic relations.

One day, still trying to measure the extend of the asteroid belt, Sabrina and Logan, skirting the outer fringe on the other side, picked up a faint signal.

"Are we going to investigate?" Logan asked.

"Might as well," his mother told him.

"Okay, going to impulse." After a while, "Mom, it's a space station," Logan said, surprised.

It hung in space, motionless, looking like a pinwheel.

"Check for life readings."

"There are none."

"Let's explore."

Donning spacesuits, and taking a portable generator along, they beamed over to the station's control room. It became immediately apparent that it had been abandoned for some time. The symbols on the computer key board were in the universal language of that Galaxy. Before leaving the Milky-way, Sargon had insisted they learn it.

"Well, we can read. That simplifies it. Let's see if we can raise the computer," Logan said to his mother.

When she turned the computer on and, after a period of warming up, the screen came on. At first static blurred the image. When it cleared, it showed a woman. Bringing it in focus, Sabrina stared as her mouth dropped open. The woman's eyes, her pupils were contracting the same way as Sargon's.

"Cat eyes," Sabrina said, astonished.

"Mom, tiger eyes," Logan corrected.

Smiling up at him, she waved him off. "Never mind. Let's see what else we can glean from this. She turned on audio.

"I am Cis. When you find this station, it will have been abandoned. We are too few to operate it. We have waited a long time, but the supply ships quit coming and no one contacted us. There is a planetary map showing the star system we have evacuated to."

All other records were erased, except for the star map, pinpointing the planet.

"I guess that's where they went after abandoning the station," Sabrina mumbled as she turned her head to look up at Logan.

"We could go and see."

"Don't you want to contact your father first?"

"No. I don't want to disappoint him if it doesn't pan out."

Back on Scout I, Logan calibrated the distance. "It would take three days. How about the special effect?"

Raising an eyebrow she asked, "Are you that impatient?"

"Well, yes. Let's get going."

After they decelerated and approached the planet, they were immediately hailed.

"At least, they're space faring," Logan said. "This is Scout I of the Worldship Antares; we are asking permission to land."

"This is Samgar-Anath, we have never heard of a Worldship called Antares," was the answer they received.

Logan gave a short laugh. "I am aware of that. We are contacting Planets interested in establishing diplomatic relationships with us."

"How many people are on board your craft?"

"We are only two."

There was a slight pause. "Establish orbit and we will advise you."

They orbited the planet, scanning it from space. There were several continents, most of them densely populated; also huge tracks of empty land and several mountain ranges. The Scout was in orbit close to an hour when finally permission to land was granted. They were given the coordinates, and when they broke through the clouds, their destination was an airfield outside a metropolis.

After shutting down the engines, Sabrina reached for sunglasses, giving them to Logan. "For now, wear them," she told him.

Both stepped up to the open hatch and looked down. There was a small group of beings meeting them. She had seen similar-looking aliens before, so she wasn't too surprised. Their heads were small, sitting on top of rotund bodies, which were supported by long and spindly legs. Their eyes were round, the noses flat, and they had a thin-lipped mouth.

"They would never win a beauty contest," Logan whispered to his mother.

"Beauty is in the eye of the beholder, my son," Sabrina whispered back.

Both cleared the hatch and slowly came down the ramp. Turning to the delegation, she held out her hands, palms up. "We are grateful to you for receiving us. The Worldship Antares hopes to established peaceful relations. We are newly come to this Galaxy, and we are reaching out to all sentient life."

"We have received information of a planet-shaped craft. I surmise this ship is your home-world?" Samgar Anath said.

"Yes. We are explorers and scientist. If there is anything we can assist you with, we are willing to work with you."

"Why did you come here?"

"To explore."

With her peripheral vision, Sabrina suddenly noticed a disturbance. A woman, humanoid, and towering over the smaller people, came striding toward them. Sabrina tried to mind-scan, but met with a tight barrier. In turn, Sabrina felt being scanned and looked back at Logan who nodded. When she came closer, Sabrina felt a shock and a reverberation from Logan. It was the woman from the station.

There was a short communication between the leader of the group and the woman. When she turned toward Sabrina, her look was searching. "I am Cis. I am Incala of the Astari. You are the first of my kind I have seen for a long time. Where did you come from?"

"Cis, we are not from this Galaxy. We are explorers. We have only recently come here. We are interested in contact."

"Then your ship has the capability to travel between galaxies?"

Logan stepped up beside his mother. "Yes. We found your space station and thought to see if we could meet you."

Sabrina gave him a rebuking look when he interrupted her. She was not ready to reveal her primary objective yet. But she guessed Logan had become impatient with her careful probing.

Cis' eyes traveled from on to the other. "You have never told us your names. I have a feeling that there is another reason that you came here."

"I am called Sabrina and this is Logan." Then, turning to Logan, "Take your glasses off."

A gasp escaped from Cis, as she watched the pupils of Logan's eyes contracting. "He is Incala," Cis said astonished, pointing at him. When she stepped up to Sabrina and looked at her eyes, "You're not of the same race," she stated. Turning to Logan, she completely ignored Sabrina as if she didn't matter. The amused look that passed between mother and son was not lost on Cis.

"We are not a race or races, we are a people," Logan explained to her. "In the beginning we came from many different backgrounds. The designation race has no meaning on the Antares, we are all Antareans."

"That may be so," Cis replied, "but your sire must have the same ocular peculiarity as you have."

"He has."

As Cis talked with Logan, her excitement caused her mental barrier to become a little leaky and Sabrina gleaned several interesting items from it. Suddenly she turned to Cis. "You are not Incala, you are from the warrior caste. You only adopted the designation of the high cast."

Astonished, Cis looked at her. "How did you know?"

"Don't ever underestimate Sabrina," Logan told her, alluding to the snub.

Sabrina's attention was suddenly diverted. She felt an energy impinge on her senses which were not as tight because of her scanning of Cis. An old man, supported on the arms of two younger individuals, came toward them. He nodded at Cis, but stepped up close to Sabrina. His hand reached out toward her forehead, and then came the mental command to lower her barriers.

Sabrina scrutinized him. She was amazed at the laughter scintillating in the eyes of this old man. She realized that he was amused by her.

"Come you green-eyed beauty, let's communicate," he sent her.

Suddenly Sabrina laughed. "You're a cool dude," she sent back, and there was a startled look.

"Strange image," he sent. "Obscure language?" he inquired

"See, don't be too hasty. Now what can we talk about?"

"I'd like to read your mind."

There was a chuckle from Sabrina, and she sent a mind probe. What she received was a humorous and gentle aura. She gave Logan a quick look, and he sent a go-ahead with a shrug.

When Sabrina lowered her barrier, there was a general probe, and then a chuckle from the old man. "I see, Sabot," he suddenly said orally.

"Oh, so you can talk too," Sabrina said.

"Cis's people have been searching for their own kind. They have been welcomed here, but I think, your coming will give them an opportunity to join up with you."

"That will not be my decision to make," Sabrina told him, and turning to Cis, "This venerable Old One is too hasty, I think. We have to talk, and then I will make a decision. Is there anywhere we can sit down and have a conversation? Maybe get something to eat?"

"There is no such place. We cannot eat what they eat. Their metabolism is entirely different from ours."

"Then I will invite you into Scout I, and we will share what we have." Sabrina bowed to the Old One, and sent him a feeling of affection which he returned. She walked back to the Scout and went to the small galley.

Logan and Cis came slower. "Are you in command?" Cis asked him.

"No. Sabrina is in command."

"Your father, is he of the warrior caste?"

"What is the distinction between castes?"

"The warrior cast, the skin is reddish in color, like mine. I am part of the warrior cast, and Incala. The farmers have brown skin. The merchants are white, like this woman," meaning Sabrina. "The Incala, they are golden skinned. They are the sun-born, the children of the gods, the rulers. Your skin is . . ."

"Tanned. That means I have skin pigments and my skin darkens."

"So, this is not your natural color?"

"No."

"Then what is it?"

"You mean where the sun doesn't shine on?" Sabrina interrupted the conversation.

Cis looked at her with a peculiar expression on her face. "He said that you were in command, but you are taking curious liberties with each other. Are you of the same family?"

Logan looked a question at her, but Sabrina shook her head.

"We are one people, Cis," she said instead.

"But who is his father?"

"He is one of your golden-skinned Incalas," Sabrina told her.

"But of them, no one survived," Cis said, incredulous. "Our last ruler was insane. He killed off everyone because they opposed him. There were never many of the golden ones. What's the name of your father?"

"We don't know. He goes by the name of Sargon, which is an acronym of his name. He says his name is unpronounceable in our language, and that it is too involved. Whatever that means," Logan told her.

Cis laughed. "They did have involved names, given to them by the soothsayers. But usually they have a family name, or a pet name."

Sabrina put the food on the table and said, "Help yourself, Cis, now, your message on the station said that the supply ships failed to come, and that you left with your people."

"We didn't know, but later learned that our planet must have exploded. There is an asteroid belt where Istranavu used to be."

"Do you have any idea how it happened?"

"No, Sabrina. There were warring factions because of the emperor's instability. This is why my parents acted as many did, by sending their children off planet. Mine sent me to live on the Space Station."

"How many people do you have with you?"

"We are about two-hundred. Most of us are of the warrior caste. But we also have scientist. The station was an outpost."

"Sargon has thought to come home, but what he found was the asteroid belt. If you want to know Sargon, why don't you come with us, and meet him?" Sabrina said.

"You are not willing to answer my questions," Cis stated.

"I will answer some. It is not my place to answer questions about Sargon. If you meet him, he will tell what he wants you to know. He has been searching for his own kind too."

"Is he bonded?"

"He has lost his mate."

When Cis looked at Logan, he shook his head, "Not my parent," he told her.

"Then he is free to bond?"

"Yes, Cis," Sabrina told her. "Are you curious enough to come with us?"

"Will you wait so I can talk to my people, and if they agree, I need to get some of my things together," she said, looking at Sabrina.

"We will wait."

When Cis left, Logan turned to his Mother with a searching and disquieting look. "What's on your mind?"

"Why do you ask?"

"You're being evasive."

"I want for Sargon to meet his people."

"And Cis?"

"If they like each other, it might mean a chance for Sargon. He has been far too despondent lately."

"You would give him up?"

"As you know very well he is not mine to give up. We are friends. I cannot give him what he needs, but maybe she can."

"I hope that's all you are hatching."

*   *   *

Before docking on the Antares, Sabrina had asked that Sargon come to the hangar deck to meet her. She didn't tell him the reason why she requested his presence. After she opened the hatch, she held Cis back until she was sure Sargon was on the hangar deck. He was just coming toward Scout One. When Cis came through the opening, the first person she saw was Sargon.

Sargon almost stopped in mid-stride, and his eyes widened as he beheld her. He immediately recognized her as one of his own race. She was tall and well built. Her hair was black, and her eyes dark brown. She approached him cautiously, and full of curiosity.

"Welcome on board the Antares," he greeted her in his native language.

"Thank you. You are the one they call Sargon?" Then looking closely at him, she immediately recognized what and who he was. He had all the physical and facial signs of being of the highest caste of the Astari, the Incala. "You are of the house of the descending Falcon, the house of the last Emperor," she said, astonished.

"Yes."

"I have seen pictures of you. Your name is Thalon. They accused you of killing the Emperor. They searched Istranavu, Amatos, and Izmal, but they couldn't find you. You were tried in absentia. My family watched your trial. My mother was incensed. She said it was all a sham. Almost following the trial, there were riots. Soon war broke out, engulfing all three planets. After that there was complete chaos. My Mother sent me off planet with the rest of the family. That is why I survived. Many of the warrior cast did the same. Nobody knew of your fate. We thought you dead. Most of the people suspected that you were removed because the ruling powers were afraid that you would become a rallying point for the dissidents."

"I suspected that much. What happened to my parents?"

"Your mother committed sepuko, she killed herself in protest, and your father died very shortly after."

Unbeknown to Sargon and Cis, Sabrina was still standing inside the hatch mind reading their conversation. Now she slowly came into Cis' view.

Cis turned toward her. To Sargon's astonishment, Cis assumed a crouching stance. When Sabrina didn't react, standing at ease, Cis looked back at him.

"She said that she was not your mate."

"This is Sabrina. She is not my mate. Why do you ask?"

"I am sensing a bond. I came because I was told that you were without a mate, and what I heard interested me. But . . ." There was a probing look, a sensing. "I do not understand. If she is not your mate, who is she then?"

Sargon shrugged. "She is Sabrina. She has always been a part of my life, and my heart."

Sabrina, mind-reading, looked amazed as she perceived this last statement.

"Are you eavesdropping?" he suddenly asked her in English.

"I didn't know there were eaves on the Antares," she said, using their old joke. "Since I don't speak the language, what do you want me to do? I have certain talents, don't ask me not to use them."

"How foolish of me." He said it acidly, ignoring the joke.

Cis looked surprised. The behavior didn't match the feelings she read, and confused, she looked from Sargon to Sabrina.

"Don't mind him," Sabrina mind sent.

"She is a telepath?" Cis asked Sargon.

"Among other things," he told her.

"I thought if it was possible, I would consider bonding with you. But, sensing how it is with the two of you, I don't think it can be possible. I don't share, and I don't think she will either. Since I don't want to fight her for you, her death would make any relationship between us impossible. As you can see, my position here is an untenable one."

Sargon was completely caught off guard, and he let an unguarded expression of dismay escape.

Sabrina, more aware of his feelings than he cared, read him all the way. He was excited. No, he was elated. After all this time, after all the many years of loneliness, for the first time there was the possibility of mating with a woman of his own people. The love for Chantar had been a deep, abiding one. Only the bonding, an experience he could have with this woman, had not been possible because Chantar's race had not developed the intricate bonding centers. Then, by the reckoning of his race, he was still young.

Sargon suddenly felt the pain of an inexplicable loss. He was sure Cis would walk out of this life. He also felt raw and exposed under Sabrina's scrutinizing probe. He turned abruptly and walked away.

Cis also started to walk away heading toward the exit, but before the door opened, Sabrina's mind call stopped her. She slowly turned.

"Wait, Cis. Stay. Don't leave," Sabrina sent.

As Cis stood, contemplating Sabrina, the door opened from the other side and Jason walked in.

"What's going on?" he asked his mother. Amazed he looked at Cis. He had just come back from an expedition and the news about finding survivors of Sargon's planet hadn't reached him yet.

Using the universal language of this galaxy, Sabrina told him, "This is Cis, Jason. Use the galactic language. Logan and I found a small colony stranded on a planet. She heard of Sargon, and came to see him."

"Fascinating," he said. "Sargon must be very pleased. Is she going to stay with us?"

"I don't know."

"Why not? What's going on?" He couldn't read his mother as easy as Caphira, or Logan, who had many of Sabrina's talents, but he noticed certain reluctance.

"I will talk to you about it later. Why don't you take her to the cafeteria and see if she would like to have something to eat. Cis, why don't you go with Jason?"

When the two left, Sabrina turned toward her Roman Villa. She knew that for a while she had the house to herself before Caphira and her two children came home. In a pensive mood, she entered the house she had built so long ago. Her Roman Villa. Deep in thought she wandered from room to room, remembering. When she came to the painting she had done of Martel, she paused. There was still this emptiness inside no one could fill.

Slowly she moved on, running her hands caressingly over her furniture, especially the china cabinet Yoshi had made for her. Wonder whatever happened to him, she thought. After he married Lady Kiritsubo, Heiko's daughter, he had left the Antares and settled on Daugave. There was a similarity to Japanese culture and he felt more at home there.

When she came to the stairs she stopped, but only looked up. It had been Martel's part of the house. Now Kyrion, Logan's son, lived there.

Going into her bedroom she stopped before the mirror and examined her face. She was beginning to show age. There were fine lines around her eyes and mouth. From her bedroom she walked through the patio doors, and crossing over the grass, entered her rose garden. She gave a deep sigh. Most of the blooms had fallen off and the leaves were turning. It was simulated fall to give the trees and bushes rest. Soon it would be winter in her garden.

When she came to where Medea's apartment had been, she paused in front of it, remembering her and Tomar, Lantos and Asa. They were gone a long time ago. Slowly she walked on until she came to the bench under the stand of firs she had enjoyed so long ago with Martel. Sitting down she listened to the waterfall and went into meditation.

For a long time there had been this pull, this feeling of someone waiting for her. Martel, she thought, I'm coming. Her life had been rich, filled with love, with adventure, also sadness and loss. Now it was time for her to go. Cis made it possible. Not wanting to abandon Sargon, she had stayed on longer than she cared. In the later years they had become just friends. They had shared so much together. Now Sargon had a chance to again find companionship and love, and this time with a woman of his own race.

What she had gleaned from the old man was that he was of the same people as Mayar, Martel's mentor. He held Cis in high esteem. She maintained discipline among her people and a high ethical standard. Cis reminded her of Morrigan.

Coming partway out of her meditation, she felt Na'ira standing silently in front of her, trying hard not to disturb her grandmother. As her eyes slowly opened, she smiled. She loved Na'ira, her youngest granddaughter.

"Are you coming for me?"

"Yes, Grandmother. Mom says it's time to come in. She has set the timer for rain in about ten minutes."

"Okay, child." Sabrina rose and taking Na'ira's hand, walked in companionable silence toward the house.

"You are too silent," Na'ira suddenly said. "What have you been thinking about?"

"Something I had to decide on."

"And have you made a decision?" Na'ira asked, eagerly.

"I will soon tell everyone, but for now we better hurry or we will get wet."

After they entered the house, Caphira came toward them. As was her habit, she scanned Sabrina's emotional emanation and came up against a tight mind shield.

"Mother, what are you up to?" was her instant remark.

"Why do I have to be up to something," Sabrina parried, keeping her tone light.

"Come on Mother, you don't fool me."

"I know daughter; I never could."

"Then quit stalling."

"Run along Na'ira," Sabrina told her, "and find your brother." When Na'ira balked, she gave her a stern look. "Now child!"

Reluctantly Na'ira left.

"Now, let's have it, Mother."

"Let's go into the living room." Sabrina led the way, and with foreboding, Caphira followed.

Sabrina began with, "Have you met Cis?" When Caphira nodded, she continued, "She is Sargon's equal in almost all things. Her grandfather and father have been of the Incala. They could bond, but she sensed the bonding between Sargon and me. She says she will not share. Chantar never understood the sharing between Sargon and me. It did not intrude into their relationship. But with Cis, it is different. I want Sargon to have a life. I understand how lonely he is. He deserves to have a chance at loving someone completely. You know what is involved. You have it with Aldon."

"What will you do?" Caphira's voice broke.

"Daughter, I am old. I have lived almost twice my life span. I am 144 years old. It is time for the last of the Original Four to leave." When Caphira started to protest, Sabrina held up her hand. "Caphira, all the people I know are gone. This is a new generation needing a chance to make their mistakes. Your father is gone. I will not marry again. You are old enough to take over the house of Hennesee."

"But how? What will you do?"

"I will call an assembly in the Queens chamber. But first I will talk with the others. Now go and find them."

Caphira first went in search of Aldon, then the rest of the family. Logan and Cassiopeia, Miri and Karsten's daughter, were first to come. A disconcerted look passed between them, as they sat on the couch.

Sabrina in her easy-chair, turned away, was looking out the window. She didn't turn when Jason and Sirtis entered. Silently, Jason pointed to the seat next to his.

"What's up?' Margali asked, poking her head through the opposite window.

"Come on in," Cassy told her. "Where's Caphira?"

"She said she's going to get Aldon and the kinds," Margali informed her, as she climbed in through the window.

"Why's everyone so gloomy?" Amanda asked, as she came in with her daughter Kami.

Logan only shook his head at her and patted the space beside him for both to sit close to him.

When Caphira came back, crowding behind her came Noel, Lisa and Kyron.

A little later, Aldon brought the rest of the kids. Dayan sat close to Caphira, his mother, and Raza, Logan and Cassie's daughter, plumped herself down next to him. Last to come in was Na'ira who's usually bouncy steps seemed to be dragging.

"Now, since we are all here," Logan began, "don't you think it's time to end the mystery?" He had been apprehensive ever since he entered the room. The atmosphere felt depressing. Then, Sabrina's detached behavior was so alien to her usually gregarious nature. Also, her mind shield was clamped down tight.

When she finally turned toward her family, her face was somber. Silently she looked at everyone in turn. Then she nodded her head. "Thank you for coming," she said. "I want you to hear me out. What I have to tell you is primarily a family matter. I have been in meditation and have very carefully thought everything through. I tell you this so you understand that it is not a rash decision. It has been long in the making. I have decided that this is the time to bring my life to a close . . ."

A groan, coming as one sound, went through the room. Sabrina held up her hand. "Give me the dignity to say when. I have lived twice my life-span, and I am the last of the Original Four. Will you honor my decision?"

For a long time no one spoke. Everyone's face was pale, the shock clearly visible.

Slowly Logan rose. "I know you well. I also know that there is no way anyone here will change your mind. You are doing this for Sargon."

"Yes. Primarily for him; but also for me. Since Martel's death, there has been a nagging feeling that it's time for me also. I have stayed because of Sargon's loneliness, something we shared. But now he has found life. For the first time he has found a mate to bond with. Cis is life for Sargon and I long to give it to him. Will you call assembly?"

There was a long, searching look from Logan before he went to open intra-ship communication. Everyone rose and began the rhythmic clapping of hands. It was some time before it was picked up throughout the ship. After Logan was sure the message was passed along to assemble in the Queen's chamber, he left.

When Sabrina, mind-scanning the Queen's chamber, was certain that most of the people had assembled, she asked her family to follow her. She left feeling a deep sorrow; she knew this was the last time she was leaving her home, her palace, as Ayhlean had called it.

Suddenly the sound of the big drum reverberated through the ship. It was an Indian drum, calling a powwow. It should only sound when a big chief dies, McPherson adopted son, who had been a Seneca, had told them. The first time it was heard on the Antares was after McPherson's death. Then again it sounded when Ayhlean and Sarah had died. The drum had sounded for three days after Chantar and Martel had been killed by the avalanche.

Now her oldest son paid her the honor of sounding the drum.

The chamber was in dead silence when Sabrina, surrounded by her family, entered. They marched toward the center, then, dividing the formation, formed a semi-circle.

Sabrina's steps were slow and measured as she walked toward the center. Sargon was already waiting for her. Her honey-colored hair, now long, was hanging past her shoulders and she was dressed in a long, flowing gown. As she came toward Sargon, a tiny smile played around her lips.

His face had been ashen ever since the sound of the drum. The feeling of dread heightened as he watched Sabrina's slow progress toward him.

She stood next to him as she faced the assembly." I had to talk with my children first, and they have agreed. Now I have called this assembly. Jason," she called.

Jason came down the aisle with Cis.

Turning to Sargon, and then to Cis. "I will say this in Sargon's language first, of which I have a smattering of words. Cis, this male, he is yours," she told the astonished woman.

Sargon spluttered, "How dare you," he shouted at her, but not so much in anger but from a growing feeling of dread.

"Sargon," she said in English," will you for once shut up. You will hear what I have to say." Then she repeated the formal of surrender in English. A sound of disbelief went through the assembly. "I thought you would feel that way," she told the Antareans.

"Let's have this for everyone to understand," Logan suddenly said, coming into the chamber. The drumbeat, recorded on a tape, was still sounding. "Sargon has given me a translator which will translate English into Saldi, his language."

Cis gave Sargon a look of astonishment when Sabrina gave her the words of acceptance.

Cis repeated them. Then she turned to Sargon, "I have accepted you, and I will be your mate. I also have the right to name you. I will call you Jesuri, star gift." She turned to Sabrina. "I still don't intend to share him with you. Will you do battle? For him?"

"No, Cis. What I give, I give freely. It is not the man which is my gift. He was never mine to give. Someday he will explain it to you", turning back to the assembly, "The drum beats for me. I will make this short. I came to tell you that I have decided that this is the end my existence. It is my right. My life has been a long one. Also, I am the last of the Original Four. I have outlived the others by many years. Now it is my time to go. I have called you here, to tell you farewell."

There was a profound silence of disbelief as the Antareans watched Sabrina raise her vibrations and spread her arms wide. Although there was no wind, a wind seemed to envelope her, blowing through her hair and billowed the dress behind her. Soon she became less tangible and more ethereal until she faded away as the solemn sound of the drum reverberated through the ship.